# M*A*S*H
# GOES TO LONDON

"Where's the boy who was hit in the head?" Hawkeye and Trapper demanded of the bobby outside the Emergency Treatment Room.

"In there, sir," the bobby said. "But you are not permitted to go in."

A phrase Hawkeye had recently heard came suddenly to his mind. "I come on the Queen's Business," he announced, grandly.

"God Save the Queen!" Trapper said.

"God Save the Queen!" the bobby parroted. He came to attention and Hawkeye and Trapper marched past him into the Emergency Room.

The doctor attending Woody turned to look at them.

"Are you gentlemen physicians?"

"Finest kind," Hawkeye said.

"Sir," Trapper said, "you are addressing the senior physician, surgeon and social-disease consultant of the Finest Kind Fish Market and Medical Clinic!"

"Oh," replied the doctor, "you're a couple of Yankee cutters, huh?"

**M*A*S*H GOES TO LONDON**
is an original POCKET BOOK edition.

**Published by POCKET BOOKS**

# M★A★S★H
## Goes to London

### Richard Hooker
### and
### William E. Butterworth

A POCKET BOOK EDITION published by
Simon & Schuster of Canada, Ltd. • Markham, Ontario, Canada
Registered User of the Trademark

MASH GOES TO LONDON

POCKET BOOK edition published June, 1975

2nd printing ........... April, 1975

This original POCKET BOOK edition is printed from brand-new plates made from newly set, clear, easy-to-read type. POCKET BOOK editions are published by POCKET BOOKS, a division of Simon & Schuster of Canada, Ltd., 330 Steelcase Road, Markham, Ontario L3R 2M1. Trademarks registered in Canada and other countries.

---

Standard Book Number: 671-78941-4.

Front cover illustration by Sandy Kossin.

Printed in Canada.

# M★A★S★H
## Goes to London

# Chapter One

At 1100 hours Zulu (or Greenwich) time, which is to say four in the afternoon Maine time, Her Majesty's Ship *Insubmergible* was making her way through heavy seas off the rock-bound coast of Maine, U.S.A., out of Boston for Saint John's, Newfoundland, Comdr. Sir Basil Vyvian Percy Smythe, Royal Navy, Commanding.

Sir Basil, who was known to his friends as "Dinker" (not of course to his crew, who behind his back called him "Rabbit Teeth"), was on the bridge. Sir Basil was not in a very good mood, although being at sea, even in a storm, was immeasurably better than where he had been for the past two weeks. Before the installation of one small naval cannon aft, and another, smaller naval cannon forward, the H.M.S. *Insubmergible*—a vessel described on the First Lord of the Admiralty's list as a "Frigate Escort"—had been a seaplane tender. She had just paid a two weeks' courtesy call upon the U.S. Navy at the Boston Navy Yard.

The official, announced intention of the visit had been to buttress the camaraderie between the fleets of the two Allied navies. In Sir Basil's studied opinion, the mission had been a failure.

Sir Basil was, despite the rough movement of the *Insubmergible,* nowhere near the present in his mind. He was reliving those grand and glorious days when Britannia did, indeed, rule the waves, and someone with his background, experience and length of naval service would be commanding a 120-gun ship of the line, not this rusty ex-seaplane tender. Instead of sneaking into Boston Harbor third in line behind an oil tanker and a tramp steamer, he would have arrived with all canvas aloft, the Royal Ensign snapping in the breeze and Her

Majesty's Royal Marines firing the required salutes, while the fife-and-drum corps played "Rule, Britannia!"

It was a pleasant picture, and Sir Basil did not at all like being recalled to the present. His arm was being tugged, ever so politely, by his First Officer, Lieut. Comdr. Elwood Heppingham, R.N.

"Beg your pardon, Captain?"

"What is it, Heppingham?" Sir Basil asked, somewhat icily.

"Mr. Woodburn-Haverstraw has had a spot of bad luck, Captain," Heppingham said. Mr. Woodburn-Haverstraw was one of two midshipmen aboard. He was not, in Sir Basil's judgment, a budding Nelson.

"Indeed?"

"Woodburn-Haverstraw has fallen down, sir," the First officer, known colloquially in the Royal Navy as "Number One," said.

"Mr. Woodburn-Haverstraw is always falling down, Number One," Capt. Sir Basil Vyvian Percy Smythe said. "Is there something out of the ordinary this time?"

"I'm afraid so, sir," First Officer Heppingham said.

"Dare I ask?" Sir Basil inquired.

"It seems Mr. Woodburn-Haverstraw was assisting Cookie, sir," the First Officer said.

"*Assisting Cookie?*" Sir Basil repeated. "Officers—even midshipmen—in Her Majesty's Navy do *not* assist the cook."

"Yes, sir," Mr. Heppingham said. "Young Woodburn-Haverstraw was carrying the roast beef to the wardroom, sir."

Sir Basil had a painful thought. The Roast Beef of Merrie Olde Englande seemed to have gone the way of a fife-and-drum corps playing "Rule Britannia." He could not recall the last time roast beef had come aboard as official rations. This splendid standing rib of beef had been a farewell gift from the U.S. Navy. It had arrived cased in plastic film, and for a moment, until he had actually touched it, Sir Basil had strongly suspected that he was about to be the butt of another American joke. The white fat-coated red meat had looked much too perfect to be real. But it was indeed real, and Sir Basil, who thought of himself as something of a gourmet, had issued orders that it be roasted immediately once they were at sea. Fresh beef, he announced, was always superior to frozen and thawed meat.

He had, furthermore, issued specific instructions as to how it, and the Yorkshire pudding which went, so to speak, hand in glove with roast beef were to be prepared: a very slow oven, for one thing; no salt until the roast was finished; a small amount of pepper; and a *soupçon* of garlic.

Sir Basil had made his way down narrow, slippery ladders from the bridge to the galley three times to inspect the beef as it roasted.

"Number one," Sir Basil said, very quietly, "give me a status report on the roast of beef."

"Sir," First Officer Heppingham said, coming to attention and stamping his foot on the deck. "I regret to inform you that the roast beef is over the side."

Sir Basil turned rare-roast-beef red. It took him a good forty seconds to gather control of his voice.

"Over the side, you say?" he asked. His voice was level and calm. "Now, how could something like that happen?"

"Mr. Woodburn-Haverstraw, as I said, sir, was carrying the beef from the galley to the wardroom."

"Go on, Number One."

"He lost his footing, sir. And the roast and the platter. . . ."

"The *platter?*" Sir Basil asked, nonchalantly. "Would that be, by any chance, the sterling-silver platter? The one presented to the vessel by Her Royal Highness Princess Margaret? Our *only* sterling-silver platter?"

"One and the same, sir," First Officer Heppingham said.

"Go on," Sir Basil said.

"Well, they slid down the deck, sir, when Mr. Woodburn-Haverstraw lost his footing . . . and . . . into the briny deep, sir."

"I see," Sir Basil said. He was now quivering, as if suddenly struck with a chill. When he spoke, little droplets of saliva sort of popped into the air. This phenomenon had occurred only rarely before, the last time when Mr. Woodburn-Haverstraw, who had the conn, had misunderstood an order and turned to port (and into an admiral's barge) rather than to starboard as Capt. Sir Basil Vyvian Percy Smythe had intended. But it had been remembered. This condition, known unofficially as "Rabbit-Tooth's Rage," had become part of the lore and tradition of the H.M.S. *Insubmergible.*

"Number One," Sir Basil said, "would you be good enough to tell Mr. Woodburn-Haverstraw that I would like a word with him?"

"That would, at the moment, be rather difficult to arrange, sir," First-Officer Heppingham said.

"I don't suppose, by any chance," Sir Basil asked, and for the first time a smile crossed his face, "that Mr. Woodburn-Haverstraw went over the side with the roast?"

"No, sir," Heppingham said.

"Pity," Sir Basil said.

"Mr. Woodburn-Haverstraw, sir," Heppingham said, "made an effort—one might even say a *valiant* effort—to save the beef. *And* the platter. As it was sliding down the deck, don't you see."

"No, I don't see. Explain yourself."

"He made what our American friends would call a flying leap at it, sir."

"You don't say?"

"But he missed it," Heppingham said.

"Obviously."

"What he did manage to do, sir, was break his arm."

"He broke his arm," the Captain said. "Well, I suppose that's something."

"He is in the wardroom, sir. It is the opinion of the medical orderly that he requires medical attention."

"See that he has it," Sir Basil said.

"What the medical orderly suggests, sir, is that he be evacuated to a hospital."

"You have the conn, Number One," Sir Basil said. "I will be in the wardroom."

Captain Smythe made his way to the wardroom. Hugh Percival Woodburn-Haverstraw, Midshipman, Royal Navy, was laid out on the wardroom table—in fact, strapped to it. His lower left arm was lying beside his body. There was evidence of severe bleeding, indicating a compound fracture. Mr. Woodburn-Haverstraw looked pale and wan and was obviously in great pain. Tears ran down his cheeks. He looked more, Sir Basil thought, like a sixteen-year-old boy than an officer in Her Majesty's Navy. He was, in fact, an eighteen-year-old boy, who looked sixteen, who happened to be an officer in Her Majesty's Navy.

"I'm sorry about the bloody beef, sir," Mr. Woodburn-Haverstraw said.

"Had a spot of bother with it, did you?" Sir Basil replied. "No matter."

"It's all my fault, sir," Mr. Woodburn-Haverstraw said.

"And what seems to have happened to your arm?"

"I seem to have broken it, sir," Mr. Woodburn-Haverstraw said. "I'm sorry."

"Put it from your mind," Sir Basil said. "Carry on, Mr. Woodburn-Haverstraw."

"Aye, aye, sir," Mr. Woodburn-Haverstraw said.

Sir Basil climbed the ladder to the radio room.

"Sparks, are you in touch with the American Coast Guard?" he asked.

"Yes, sir."

"Would you get me the commanding officer of the nearest Coast Guard aviation facility, please?"

"Aye, aye, sir," the radioman said. He pushed his microphone switch. "H.M.S. *Insubmergible* calling U.S. Coast Guard, Deer Isle."

An unmistakably American voice came back immediately.

"Go ahead, *Insubmergible*."

Captain Smythe took the microphone from the radio operator and said, "We are approximately fifty miles north-northeast your station. We have an injured officer aboard who requires hospitalization. Request that he be evacuated by helicopter."

"Roger, *Insubmergible,*" the radio replied. "Stand by." The operator neglected to switch off his microphone as he switched on another. Sir Basil could hear what he said: "Aviation, Deer Isle Radio. Crank one up. Details follow." Then he spoke to Sir Basil again: "*Insubmergible*, understand five-zero miles north-northeast of Deer Isle. Have you radio frequency 125.5 megacycles?"

Sir Basil looked at the operator, who nodded.

"We have 125.5," Sir Basil said to the radiotelephone.

"Switch to the frequency at this time. Stand by for further contact. Deer Isle Radio out."

The radio operator made the necessary adjustments. Another voice came over the radio.

"Coast Guard Four-Oh-Two off the deck at one-five past the hour," a voice said. "Vessel requiring assistance, come in, please."

"This is H.M.S. *Insubmergible,*" Sir Basil said.

"This is Coast Guard Helicopter Four-Oh-Two," the radio said. "Please give us a long count so we can get a heading."

Sir Basil looked baffled. The radio operator took the microphone and began to count up to ten and then down again.

"O.K., *Insubmergible,* we have a heading. We'll have you on radar in a minute or two. Who is speaking please?"

"This is Captain Smythe," Sir Basil said.

"What's the nature of the injury?" the Coast Guard inquired.

"Compound fracture of the left arm."

"Put the patient in a litter basket. If he can be sedated, sedate him," the Coast Guard said. "We have you on radar. We will be over your vessel in twenty minutes. We will hoist the litter aboard. Stand by for further instructions."

The Coast Guard pilot signaled for his copilot to take over the controls. He fished a clipboard from a net pouch

on his door and consulted it. He made adjustments to
his radio.

"Spruce Harbor International, this is Coast Guard
Four-Oh-Two."

"Go ahead, Coast Guard Four-Oh-Two."

"We are en route to H.M.S. *Insubmergible* to pick
up an injured officer. We ought to have him aboard in
twenty-five minutes. Spruce Harbor Medical Center is
the nearest medical facility. Would you please alert them
to receive a patient with a compound fracture of the arm?
We should be there in forty minutes."

"Coast Guard Four-Oh-Two, there is a helipad at
the hospital. I will notify them of your arrival."

It was conference time in the office of the Chief of Surgery of the Spruce Harbor Medical Center. Above the
door to the Chief Surgeon's office an illuminated sign,
reading IN CONFERENCE, had been turned on, testifying to that fact. When that sign was turned on, hospital
rules—promulgated by the Chief of Surgery, Benjamin
Franklin Pierce, M.D., F.A.C.S., himself—absolutely
forbade interruption, save, of course, in case of medical
emergency.

Conference time had just begun. That is to say that
Dr. Pierce and his longtime professional associate and
close friend John Francis Xavier McIntyre, M.D.,
F.A.C.S., had been in the room only a short time, barely
long enough to take the gin and vermouth and the on-
ions from the refrigerator. So short a time, in fact, that
they hadn't had time to do anything more than kick off
their shoes and raise their feet onto the coffee table.
They were still dressed in surgical greens.

"I have been giving the problem a good deal of thought
all day," Dr. Pierce, who was better known as Hawkeye,
said to Dr. McIntyre, who was better known as Trapper
John. "And I admit that I am at wit's end."

"Certainly," Trapper John said. "Someone of your
experience, wisdom and imagination—you are, after all,
the Chief of Surgery—should have some ideas." He
paused. "Easy on the vermouth, Hawkeye!"

"Sorry," Hawkeye said. "My hand isn't as steady as it was in medical school."

"Put some more gin in and get the percentages back where they should be," Trapper John ordered.

"Are you actually admitting that we should just give in?" Hawkeye asked, as he added a generous dollop of gin to the pitcher. He extended the mixer in both hands, and Dr. McIntyre took the stirring rod and made rapid, revolving movements with it.

"Your hand," Hawkeye said, "isn't a bit steadier than mine. You're going to bruise the gin!"

"You don't suppose," Trapper John said, "just thinking off the top of my head, of course, that if we just stayed right here and had a couple of more drinks than normal. . . ."

"I tried that," Hawkeye said, "year before last. Not only did my beloved bride escort me to the P.T.A. meeting in what she described as my 'disgusting condition,' but I got carried away and wound up as vice-chairman of the fifth-grade picnic committee. In short, no. That won't work."

Trapper John, having finished stirring the martinis, reached out to the coffee table and picked up two glasses. Hawkeye filled them. He set the pitcher down and took one of the glasses from Trapper John.

"We have fought the good fight," he said, solemnly, "and lost. As gentlemen and former officers, it behooves us to face a potluck supper, an exhibition of the graphic arts as performed in the third-through-sixth grades and the P.T.A. meeting itself with a stiff upper lip."

"There's no one, I suppose," Trapper John asked, "who requires our professional services?"

"The community we serve has failed us," Hawkeye said. "The sickest customer in the joint can be dealt with by a first-year student nurse."

"Speaking of first-year student nurses. . . ." Trapper John said.

"Yes, I saw her," Hawkeye said. "Her name is Beverly Chambers. I told you about her."

"She's the one on that phony scholarship? The one whose father took off for parts unknown?"

"Right. And what do you mean *phony* scholarship? Having come down with the clap like that, and having it cured permanently and *very* quietly before his wife got back from Rome, Banker Thomas was naturally very receptive to my suggestion that he make some small contribution toward nursing education."

"Especially since he could have the bank establish the scholarship and take it as a business deduction," Trapper John said.

"John F.X. McIntyre," Hawkeye said. "If I didn't know better, I might suspect that you are a cynic."

"Finest kind," Trapper John said.

"Which brings us back to our own problem."

"There is only one small ray of light, as I see. it," Trapper John said. "We won't be alone. Duke and Spearchucker are in this with us." Duke was Nathan Bedford Forrest, M.D., and Spearchucker was Oliver Wendell Jones, M.D.

"So they are," Hawkeye said. "If you think about it, it's like the old days; the V.D. lectures at the 4077th MASH. They were always scheduled during a lull in the war, to make sure we had our morality raised."

"I must be getting old, Hawkeye," Trapper said, solemnly, draining his martini and reaching for the pitcher. "Sometimes I look back wistfully, almost nostalgically, on the ol' 4077th Mobile Army Surgical Hospital."

"Me, too," Hawkeye confessed. "The lumpy cots. The leaking tents. The lousy food."

"Francis Burns, M.D.," Trapper said, picking up the stream of thought. "Margaret Houlihan!"

"Hot Lips!" Hawkeye said. "Here's to Hot Lips!"

At that, the door opened and Oliver Wendel Jones, M.D., who practiced the healing art of neurosurgery came in.

"I never really believed he could read," Trapper said, coldly. "Didn't you see the IN CONFERENCE sign all lit up?"

"That's why I came in," Spearchucker said. He helped himself to a glass and some of the contents of the pitcher with all the self-assurance of a six-foot-three-inch, 260-pound Negro neurosurgeon who had worked his way through college as a professional linebacker. "I need a drink. Unless there is some sort of instant medical catastrophe, I'm going to wind up at the P.T.A."

"We keep getting back to that, don't we?" Trapper said.

The door swung open again. Nathan Bedford Forrest, M.D., dressed for the street, strode in.

"We keep getting back to what?" he asked. Spearchucker handed him the martini pitcher. "Thank you," he said, and then he noticed it was empty. "The story of my life. When I need sick people and a drink, we are struck with an epidemic of disgusting, all-around good health and empty martini pitchers."

"I noticed you are wearing your Go-to-P.T.A. clothes," Hawkeye said. "Are you seeking office?"

Duke splashed gin liberally and vermouth very sparingly into the pitcher, added ice and stirred furiously.

"What do you say we all get plastered?" he said.

"That's been tried," Hawkeye said, getting to his feet.

"Where are you going?" Trapper demanded.

"To coin a phrase," Hawkeye said, "if at first you don't succeed, try, try again." He pushed a button on his intercom.

"Emergency room," a female voice responded.

"This is Dr. Pierce," Hawkeye said, formally. "Is there anything down there, any little thing, that I should know about?"

"Hardly anything at all, Dr. Pierce," the nurse said. "It's been as quiet as a tomb around here."

"I'm not sure I like your simile," Hawkeye said. "But define 'hardly anything at all' for me. That's not quite the same thing as 'nothing at all,' is it?"

"The only thing that's happening is that the Coast Guard is bringing in some sailor with a broken arm," the nurse said.

The three practitioners of the healing arts on the couch suddenly sat erect.

"A broken arm, you say?" Hawkeye said.

"That's right," she said. "Dr. Davis is on emergency-room call, and we're all set up for him."

"Far be it from me to suggest that Dr. Davis is anything but a most highly qualified physician," Hawkeye said. "But there are broken arms and then there are *broken arms.*" Dr. Davis was, in fact, two years out of medical school, not quite long enough to understand certain behavior on the part of the Chief of Surgery and his cronies. He had actually shown up at a late-afternoon conference with a pencil and notebook in hand, and had been shaken to learn that the medical discussion had been limited to professional judgments concerning a visiting surgical nurse—whether she did or did not wear anything under her greens.

"In fact," Spearchucker said, "the annals of medical science record more than one broken arm with neuro-surgical implications."

"Nurse," Hawkeye said, "please be good enough to inform Dr. Davis that Drs. McIntyre, Jones, Forrest and myself will be on hand to assist him in this hour of medical catastrophe."

"I heard about the P.T.A. meeting," the nurse said.

"Please telephone our wives, Nurse," Hawkeye said, "and tell them that medicine has called us to our duty." He broke the connection with his finger.

"Never abandon hope," he announced solemnly.

Spearchucker cocked his head to one side and then pointed toward the sky. The others listened, and then quickly left the chief of staff's office by a private door. They walked across the neatly cropped lawn to the helipad. From the emergency-room door, a small procession of nurses and technicians rolled out a hospital cart.

From out over the ocean, a Coast Guard Sikorsky helicopter, with the numbers Four-Zero-Two painted on its tail, raced toward them, seemed to settle back on its tail and then gently fluttered to the ground.

"Gee," Trapper said. "It's like old times, isn't it? A chopper fluttering down with an injured man aboard."

"All we need," Hawkeye said, "is Frank Burns coming out of Hot Lips's tent."

"With her shirttail caught in his zipper," Spearchucker said.

Midshipman Hugh Percival Woodburn-Haverstraw, R.N., looked up from his litter and decided that Captain Smythe had been right all along. The Americans overdid everything. All he had was a broken arm. There were enough doctors waiting for him to handle a train wreck in Waterloo Station. He decided he couldn't really be that badly injured, for all the doctors were smiling at him.

# Chapter Two

FROM COAST GUARD, DEER ISLE, MAINE
TO COMMANDANT, U.S. GUARD WASHINGTON
INFO: COMMANDANT, U.S. COAST GUARD DISTRICT,
       BOSTON, MASS.

AT THE REQUEST OF CAPTAIN SMYTHE, COMMAND-
ING, H.M.S. INSUBMERGIBLE, A HELICOPTER OF THIS
STATION EFFECTED AN AERIAL EVACUATION OF MID-
SHIPMAN H. P. WOODBURN DASH HAVERSTRAW, ROYAL
NAVY, FROM H.M.S. INSUBMERGIBLE AT 1645 HOURS
THIS DATE. WOODBURN DASH HAVERSTRAW SUFFER-
ING FROM COMPOUND FRACTURE LOWER LEFT ARM.
PATIENT TRANSFERRED TO SPRUCE HARBOR MEDICAL
CENTER, MAINE, WITHOUT INCIDENT. FURTHER MEDI-
CAL INFORMATION AVAILABLE FROM BENJAMIN F.
PIERCE, M.D., CHIEF OF SURGERY, SPRUCE HARBOR

MEDICAL CENTER. INITIAL DIAGNOSIS: SATISFACTORY
CONDITION.

> BRUCE SAFFERY
> LIEUT. COMDR., U.S.C.G.
> COMMANDING

The radio Teletype message, a fairly routine one, went
through the normal bureaucratic procedures. It was filed,
stamped, indexed and circulated. Among those agencies
to which it was circulated was the Coast Guard Bureau
of Public Relations. While as a fellow sailor, Lieut.
(junior grade) Homer Appleby, U.S.C.G., Deputy
Assistant Chief, Print Media-Relations Division, Bureau
of Public Relations, was naturally distressed to hear that
Midshipman Woodburn-Haverstraw had been injured,
there was sort of a silver lining to the cloud. He sat
down at his naval-grey I.B.M. Executive typewriter,
flexed his wrists and fingers and began to type:

NEWS BULLETIN:
FOR IMMEDIATE RELEASE:
A Coast Guard helicopter this afternoon swooped
down from the sky to pluck a seriously injured
officer of the Royal Navy from the deck of H.M.S.
*Insubmergible.* . . ."

Lieutenant Appleby stopped. Something bothered him.
*Insubmergible?* He had heard of the H.M.S. *Indomitable,*
and then he recalled the H.M.S. *Invincible.* But *Insubmergible?*

He picked up his Xerox of the radio Teletype message
and read it again.

He took out the Washington, D.C., telephone book
and found the number of the British Embassy. He dialed
the number. In less than a minute, a crisply efficient
British civil servant verified that there was indeed an
H.M.S. *Insubmergible* on the Admiralty rolls. Lieut.
(jg.) Homer Appleby thanked him, politely shrugged
his shoulders, flexed his wrists again and finished writing
his paean of praise to Anglo-American Cooperation on

the High Seas, courtesy of the U.S. Coast Guard. The draft of his story went upward through the Coast Guard public-relations bureaucracy, approval of its contents and slant initialed at every stage until it reached the chief, and then went into production. Two hundred copies of it were run off on a Multilith duplicator, and then distributed across the District of Columbia by three Coast Guardsmen who had left Iowa, Kansas and North Dakota respectively to see the world from the deck of a Coast Guard cutter and had found themselves instead facing Washington traffic on naval-grey Kawasaki motorcycles.

Most of the distribution, of course, went to the press and to what had become known as the Electronic Media; but distribution was also made to other governmental agencies, including the Office of Data Analysis and Research, of the House of Representatives.

ODAR, as it is popularly known on The Hill, is the agency charged with keeping the members of the House, and their staffs, fully aware of what is happening in the world. It has several functions, the most widely appreciated one being what is known as the Newspaper & Periodical Reference Service. Whenever a Congressman's name appears in any newspaper or magazine, he will shortly thereafter receive the clipping, neatly mounted on a board. If his name is mentioned on radio or television, he will shortly receive a tape recording of that momentous event. Congressmen like to see their names in the paper, just like other people.

Additionally, ODAR has what it calls its Information Service. Whenever it gleans from the press, or other sources, information which it feels would be of interest to House members, it distributes this information to each Congressman. Only the day before, for example, ODAR has issued an ODAR Information Service BULLETIN, classified Confidential, announcing that the District of Columbia Vice Squad was about to raid the premises of the Bali Hai Polynesian Massage Parlor and Lounge. Armed with that information, more than one Congressman decided to get his massage and midafternoon cocktail elsewhere, at least until things cooled off.

But not all of the work of ODAR was the stern, no-nonsense business of government. When something of human interest came along, something that might be used by a Congressman in his monthly newsletters to his constituents, this, too, was furnished to the House.

And so it was with the Coast Guard news release on the aerial evacuation of Midshipman Woodburn-Haverstraw from the H.M.S. *Insubmergible*. If plucking some broken Limey from his ship by helicopter wasn't human interest, what was?

Lieut. (jg.) Homer Appleby's release was fed into the ODAR's Xerox machine and five hundred copies run off. One copy was distributed to each Congressman's office. The extra copies were distributed to other agencies of government. One ultimately was delivered by a Congressional messenger to Lieut. (jg.) Homer Appleby, Deputy Assistant Chief, Print Media-Relations Division, Bureau of Public Relations, United States Coast Guard. It made his whole day. He had reached the Big Time, an ODAR Bulletin. A man could make his reputation that way. It could conceivably even lead to an offer from *The Washington Post*.

One of the four hundred copies which went to the House reached the desk of L. Bryan Fowler, Administrative Assistant to the Hon. Edwards L. "Smiling Jack" Jackson (Farmer—Free Silver, Arkansas). Congressman Jackson and Mr. Fowler had been professionally associated in government through all of Congressman Jackson's eleven terms. They had, over the years, established a smooth-running professional relationship. L. Bryan Fowler handled the bothersome administrative details which interfered with Congressman Jackson's political life. He was free, in other words, to pass his time pleasantly at the Burning Tree Golf Course, in preparing his memoirs (working title: "A Quarter Century on the Battle Line") and in giving inspirational talks to the Congressional Divine Inspiration League, of which he was a co-founder. He was spared the mundane matters of Congressional service. All he had to do was show up on the floor in time to vote. He was equipped with a Motorola Page-Boy, a tiny radio receiver he carried in his shirt pocket. It first set up a warbling noise to get his attention, then buzzed once for "yes" and twice for "no," according to Mr. Fowler's opinion of the issue to be resolved.

It had failed Smiling Jack only once, when the battery went dead between the first and second buzzes, and he had thereafter cast a resounding "no" vote against a bill intended to make Arkansas mules a "national treasure" and thus entitled to free mule feed from the Federal Government.

That had caused some waves (*The Swampy Meadows Arkansas Daily Farmer* had hysterically suggested lynching in its editorial); but Congressman Jackson was, after all, one of the boys, so he was able to have the House Clerk officially reprimanded for recording his vote incorrectly.

When the touching tale of Anglo-American Cooperation on the High Seas reached Mr. Fowler, even that ship with the funny name couldn't erase the gloom from Fowler's face. For the first time in his nearly quarter of a century on the battle line, spring had come and no junket had been laid on for him and Smiling Jack.

A junket is a little-known function of the Congress. That junkets (and thus "junketing" and "junketeers") are not on the tips of the public tongue is one more tribute to the overwhelming modesty of Congressmen generally. They are prepared to make the sacrifices entailed in spending, for example, three weeks on the sun-baked beaches of Bermuda in a study of Bermudan Crabs as just one more task laid on their overloaded shoulders by their constituents. If their constituents knew what agony it was to make their way in a government limousine through the snow-filled streets of Washington all the way to the airport and then spend twenty-one whole days away from the seat of government, they might decide that two years of such self-sacrifice is enough to demand of any one man and that someone else should be sent to Washington to pick up the burden.

It is enough, in the Congressional consensus, that the

government pay the bills for them and their staffs and families and advisers.* Public appreciation of their sacrifice is neither sought nor desired. A bill was passed in 1974 making publication of junketing costs a secret between the Congress and the Treasury Department.

L. Bryan Fowler had, in his twenty-two years on The Hill, made the sacrifice junketing requires at least twice each year. Once, in 1965, he had made the sacrifice four times, junketing to Tokyo, New Delhi, Angkor Wat and Kingston, Jamaica. It had been necessary for him to take two-weeks' sick leave to recuperate. Since he had, so to speak, fallen in his country's service, Congressman Jackson was able to arrange for the recuperation at Walter Reed Army Medical Center.

None of this had discouraged him. Fowler was fully prepared to make the sacrifice at this time and had, in fact, planned to make it. But something had gone wrong. The pressure of his many duties had apparently been too much for him. He had simply forgotten to volunteer, and now there didn't seem to be anything at all in the whole world which (a) needed Congressional investigation and (b) which hadn't already been spoken for.

The thought of staying home in Washington while his comrades were off on Congress Business in Tokyo, Paris, New Delhi and Kingston, Jamaica, was too much to bear. But then he did a double-take, and snatched Lieut. (jg.) Appleby's release from his wastebasket. His eyes lit up. He ran his finger down a list of telephone numbers and then punched the appropriate buttons.

"ODAR? This is Congressman Jackson's office calling." (The unwritten law has it that Congressmen's administrative assistants never use their own names except when collecting their paychecks.) "When was the last

---

* Advisers is a somewhat loosely defined term, junketing-wise. In the past, advisers have included waiters from the House restaurant, barbers, tennis and golf instructors and similar professionals. Most advisers, however, seem to be young women willing to share the Congressman's lonely vigil on foreign shores when the Congressman's wife, for one reason or another, is not able to make the trip.

time Congress investigated Anglo-American Cooperation on the High Seas?"

"I'll feed that to the computer immediately," the ODAR functionary replied. "May I call you back?"

"I'll hold," L. Bryan Fowler said. "I suspect this is a matter of the gravest importance."

In two minutes, the ODAR functionary came back on the line.

"I'm terribly sorry to have to tell you this," he said, shame in every tremor of his voice, "but the latest data we have on the subject of Anglo-American Cooperation on the High Seas is dated March 11, 1812. The title is 'Impressment of American Merchant Sailors into the Royal Navy.' "

"Thank you," L. Bryan Fowler said. "Thank you very much." He broke the connection and punched the button which summoned his secretary.

She opened the door and stuck her head in.

"Shall I bring my notebook?" she asked. "Or did you have something else in mind?"

"How does London grab you?" he asked.

"You mean you found some way we can go?"

"Call the Air Force and set it up," he said, with the pride of accomplishment in his voice. "But not right now. Come on in and latch the door."

"Poopsie," she said, a moment or two later, as they conversed on his couch, "am I allowed to ask something?" She blew in his ear. When she blew in his ear, she was allowed to ask him anything.

"Shoot."

"Do we have to take Smiling Jack along? He's such a drag!"

"I'll see what I can do," L. Bryan Fowler said. "But not to worry. If the Congressman feels that Anglo-American Cooperation on the High Seas is important enough to drag him out of Washington, we'll find something to keep him busy."

"There's this *darling* clerk-typist down in Public Dams & Highways," she said. "Even if she is a little long-in-the-tooth, she'd be good enough for Lard-belly. And I know she'd *love* to go to London."

"Well, see if she's free, but don't promise her anything yet. Maybe we can get Smiling Jack to stay home."

"All right," she cooed. She turned reflective. "London! Poopsie, I just knew you'd come through! Gee, I'm glad I decided to go into public service."

As Capt. Sir Basil Percy Smythe had waited aboard the H.M.S. *Insubmergible* for the U.S. Coast Guard helicopter to perform a medical evacuation of Midshipman Hugh Percival Woodburn-Haverstraw, four other men, under somewhat different circumstances, awaited the arrival of another aircraft to perform another medical evacuation. Three bearded men, standing on the shore of a tranquil and unnamed lake in the wilds of the Province of Quebec stared down with mingled horror and fascination (and in one case, barely concealed amusement) at a fourth bearded man, who was lying on his stomach.

The man on his stomach, who was alternately moaning piteously and taking healthy pulls at a quart bottle of Old White Stagg Blended Kentucky Bourbon, was enormous. He stretched six-feet-six from the toes of his camping boots to the top of his head. His chest and shoulders were massive. When he moaned in his pain, the gentle creatures of the wild in a half-mile circle fled through the brush in terror. His left buttock—from around which the cloth of his trousers and underpants had been cut away, and which was exposed to the crisp air of a Quebec summer—was in proportion to the rest of him. That is to say, it was enormous, without fat, and well-muscled. Almost precisely in the center, or apex, of the globular shape, there was what appeared at first glance to be a large, odd-looking insect. On closer examination, it became apparent that the purple-and-orange bug was in fact a fishing lure, to which were attached two large fishhooks. Both hooks were firmly imbedded in the flesh of the buttocks.

"Maestro," said His Royal Highness Prince Hassan

ad Kayam of the Kuwaitian Kingdom of Hussid, for the fifteenth time in as many minutes, "I'm so dreadfully sorry!"

His Highness was a plump little man, with a neatly trimmed beard that came to a point under his chin. He was wearing, over his L.L. Bean hunting boots, a flowing robe and a burnoose held in place on his head with the three golden cords signifying royalty.

"It wasn't Hassan's fault, Boris," a short, stocky man, whose beard was the result of not-shaving-for-a-week, rather than intent, said in a faint French accent. "This fishin's new to him."

"You're right," Boris said. "It's not the camel keeper's fault, and it's not your fault. It's my fault. Any sane man who voluntarily permits himself to be deposited in the wilderness with a crazy Cajun and a demented desert rat deserves whatever happens to him. Notwithstanding that, as soon as I am able to move, I'm going to drown the both of you."

"Does it hurt, m'sieu?" the third bearded man said. He was the guide.

The man on his stomach gave out with a heartrending moan, mingled rage and pain. "Where the hell is that airplane?" he screamed.

"It is on the way, Maestro," His Highness said. "In just a couple of hours, you will be receiving the finest medical attention money can buy."

"Has it occurred to you, you miserable little twerp, that in five days, presuming I am not dead of lockjaw or gangrene by then, I am supposed to sing *Otello* at the Covent Garden Opera? How am I supposed to sing the role of a king when I will be unable to sit on my throne?"

"And the finest nursing service that money can buy," His Highness went on. "Efficient, long-legged, firm-bosomed American nurses in stiff, white dresses." He and Boris had been friends for a long time. He knew the way to Boris's heart and it wasn't through his stomach.

"I shall have to enter the hospital incommunicado,"

Boris said, thoughtfully. "I wouldn't want something like this to become common knowledge. There are even those, lesser artists not blessed with my God-given talents, who would think it was amusing."

"You don't need no doctor," said the short, stocky man, whose name was Jean-Pierre de la Chevaux, and known to his friends as "Horsey." "I can get those hooks out of your ass by myself."

"The ingratitude of man!" Boris said, raising his hands as best as he could in an entreaty to Heaven. "Hassan, the man who would deny me medical attention in my hour of need—when God alone knows what foul poison is already spreading through my bloodstream; when God alone knows what agony I'm in; when the world is on the verge of losing forever the finest voice since Caruso, and probably of all time—is the same man I carried on my back through the shot and shell of the battlefield, through torrents of enemy fire, roaring cannons, crashing mortars, in the rocket's red glare. . . ."

"The gooks," said Horsey de la Chevaux, "didn't have no rockets, Boris, and you know it."

"Did I, or did I not," Boris asked, "carry your fat Cajun carcass, which was spouting blood like Old Faithful at the time, off Heartbreak Ridge? Thus saving your life, in what must rank as the greatest waste of effort in mine?"

"You carried me off the hill," Horsey said. "But Hawkeye saved my life."

"Hawkeye! Hawkeye! How *dare* you call the man who saved your life and who saved my incomparable voice for mankind, that superb healer, that prince among men, by his first name?"

"He told me to," Horsey de la Chevaux said. He, too, was an old buddy of Boris Alexandrovich Korsky-Rimsakov and one of the few people in the world who did not cower before a Korsky-Rimsakov emotional outburst. "And the last time you talked about him, you called him a broken-down chancre mechanic."

"I was out of my mind with pain at the time," Boris explained, reasonably.

There came the sound of an aircraft engine. Horsey and His Highness looked skyward. Horsey pointed toward a speck in the sky. "There it is," he said.

"Too late," Boris said. "I will die en route. Where is the nearest hospital, anyway?"

"Spruce Harbor, Maine," Horsey de la Chevaux replied.

"Oddly enough, the name of what certainly can be no more than a clutch of worm-eaten shacks occupied by drunken lobstermen rings a bell," Boris said. "Why is that?"

"The head chancre mechanic there," Horsey said, "is a superb healer, a prince among men, named Hawk-eye."

"Spare me your perverted sense of humor in my time of tribulation and agony," Boris said.

"Maestro," His Highness said. "It was to be our surprise. Before your unfortunate accident. . . ."

"*My* accident! You call your criminal assault on me 'my *accident*'?"

"Before this unfortunate incident," His Highness quickly corrected himself, "we had been in touch with Dr. Pierce and accepted his kind invitation to visit him and Dr. McIntyre at their home in Maine. It was to be a surprise for you, Maestro."

Boris moaned. He took another healthy pull at the bottle. He moaned again.

The speck in the air grew in size as the airplane approached and lost altitude. It became identifiable as a De Havilland Beaver, a large Canadian bush plane on floats. It made one pass over the campsite, while Horsey and His Highness and the guide waved their arms, and then swooped low over the trees and touched down on the lake. As it taxied to the shore, it was possible to read what was painted on the rear of the fuselage: CHEVAUX PETROLEUM CORPORATION, CANADIAN DIVISION.

The propeller stopped spinning and the plane floated up to the shore. A pilot climbed down to the float and threw a line to Horsey, who caught it and made it fast. The pilot jumped to the shore.

"Where's the dying man?" he asked, with concern in his voice. Horsey pointed to Boris. The pilot laughed.

"A couple of fishhooks in the ass never killed nobody," he said. Then he sobered. "Jesus, Buddy," he said. "There's going to be trouble about this. We got a priority call all the way from Louisiana to drop whatever we was doing and rush over here. Just wait till the big shots find out the big emergency is some drunken fisherman with fishhooks in his tail."

"Let's get him on the plane," Horsey said.

"I better call in," the pilot said. "And tell them the story. I'll need permission. This ain't no bona fide emergency."

"You won't have to do that," Horsey said.

"That's what you think, Mac," the pilot said. "This airplane belongs to Chevaux Petroleum. We don't run an aerial taxi service for drunken fishermen."

Horsey shrugged his shoulders. "My name is Chevaux," he said. "Jean-Pierre de la Chevaux. My friends call me Horsey."

The pilot's mouth dropped open. He stared for a moment at the somewhat grimy, badly-in-need-of-a-shave face before him. It didn't at first look much like the Bachrach photo of the chairman of the board and chief executive officer of the Chevaux Petroleum Corporation which hung on the wall of Chevaux Petroleum offices all over the world, but the longer he stared in disbelief, the more familiar it became.

"Charley," he called to the co-pilot, "come and help me load *Mr. Chevaux's* gentleman friend on the aircraft."

Horsey turned to look at Boris, more than a little surprised that Boris hadn't had something to say during the exchange. A sound very much like that a circular saw in a lumberyard makes when it hits a knot in a very large tree assaulted his ears. Horsey had heard the noise before. All was right with the world. Boris Alexandrovich Korsky-Rimsakov, having consumed all of a one-quart bottle of Old White Stagg Blended Kentucky Bourbon and most of a second, was sound asleep.

"He looks like he's smiling," the pilot said. A broad smile, indeed, was on his face. Another horrifying snore came out of him, but the smile didn't vanish.

"Hassan," Horsey said, "I wish you hadn't said that about the nurses."

# Chapter Three

The door to the lobby of the Spruce Harbor, Maine, Medical Center was suddenly flung open. A smallish, conservatively dressed woman marched inside, followed by three other women. They all wore looks of outrage and determination.

The smallish woman addressed the nurse on duty.

"Where are they?" she demanded, in icy tones. "And before you answer, I want you to consider that hell hath no fury like a physican's wife scorned."

"They're in the operating room," the nurse said.

"Playing poker, no doubt," Mrs. Benjamin Franklin Pierce said. She made a gesture of "follow me" to the other ladies, who formed up behind her in sort of a flying wedge. En masse, they marched down the polished corridor in the direction of the surgical wing of the hospital.

"Mary," the nurse called. "Really, they've got a patient in there."

"Suffering, no doubt, from a serious case of hangnail," Mary Pierce said, but she stopped. There were ground rules to the game. Innuendo, deceit, even fraud were permitted, but outright lies about medical necessity were not.

"It's a British Navy officer," the nurse said. "The Coast

Guard flew him in from his ship. He's got a badly broken arm."

Mary Pierce had heard the sound of the helicopter.

"All right, girls," she ordered, "to the exits. There's four ways out of here, and four of us. Keep in your minds the noble words, 'They shall not pass!' "

"There's only one way out of the operating room," the nurse said. She was after all, female, and knew where her basic loyalty lay. "They've been in there about an hour; they should be coming out any moment now."

"Good thinking!" Mary Pierce said. "With a little bit of luck, we can still make it to the P.T.A. meeting in time for the closing remarks and the potluck supper."

The ladies, who in addition to Mrs. Mary Pierce, were Madames McIntyre, Forrest and Jones, took up positions in the corridor outside the operating suite, through which, unless they chose to leave via the laundry chute in the dressing room, Drs. Pierce, McIntyre, Forrest and Jones would have to come. After ten minutes of inactivity, Mary Pierce walked into the scrub room and peered through a small window in the door to the operating room. She saw half a dozen figures, including her husband, all in surgical greens, laboring over a patient on the table. She returned to the corridor, located four chairs and a small folding table and took a deck of cards from her purse.

"Bridge, anyone?" she asked.

Broken bones are normally the responsibility of the orthopedic surgeon, and none of the doctors tending Hugh Percival Woodburn-Haverstraw were of that medical persuasion. This is not to say that the learned gentlemen were not familiar with broken bones and torn muscles. They had, in fact, more experience with the torn-up human body than most medical practitioners. They had all been surgeons of the 4077th Mobile Army Surgical Hospital, known to its members and clientele as the Double-Natural MASH. Long stricken from the active roll of the United States Army, the 4077th was remembered only vaguely by several thousand torn-up G.I.'s of the Eighth United States Army and with only slightly less vagueness by its former professional staff. But while it had lived, the doctors of the 4077th MASH had repaired more broken and torn limbs more frequently than any other medical facility anywhere.

While there was no question in their minds that they could properly reduce the fracture and tend to the torn ligaments and muscular structure of the patient, they proceeded, in the patient's interest, at a far slower pace than the swift precision with which Drs. Pierce and McIntyre would jerk a gall bladder, which was somewhat more complicated, or the rapid finesse with which Dr. Spearchucker Jones would remove a tumor from the cranial cavity, which was his usual line of work, or the practiced ease with which Dr. Forrest would open the chest to have at a malfunctioning human heart with his impressive array of tools and highly trained fingers.

But finally, they were finished. The wound was closed, the fracture reduced, the cast applied, and the accuracy of the whole procedure checked with X-rays. Midshipman Hugh Percival Woodburn-Haverstraw, R.N., his face the ghastly grey color of a patient coming out of anesthesia, was gently eased off the table onto a cart. With Hawkeye Pierce pushing and Trapper John McIntyre pulling, and with Spearchucker Jones and Duke Forrest hovering nervously at his side, he began the short trip to the postoperative recovery room.

Not expecting to find his bride in the act of announcing "three spades" in the middle of the hospital corridor, Trapper John McIntyre, who was pulling, backed into the card table. The card table and Trapper John went down in a flurry of pasteboard.

"I knew it!" cried Mrs. Benjamin Franklin Pierce, with mingled rage and regret in her voice. "The whole business in the operating room was a charade. Trapper John is obviously as drunk as an owl! They'll stoop to anything to avoid the P.T.A.!"

As her cronies rose to right this heinous wrong, however, Mary Pierce saw the ghastly grey face of Hugh Percival Woodburn-Haverstraw. His eyes were closed, of course, and his head lolled to one side. Even in that

condition, though, Hugh Percival had the face of a North
Country English youth: innocent, somehow vulnerable,
somehow silently but with great power calling out mutely
for tender, loving, female care of the maternal sort.

"What have you *done* to that beautiful child?" Mary
Pierce demanded.

"He is not a child," Hawkeye said.

"He is a midshipman in the Royal Navy," Trapper
John called up from the floor.

"He suffered a compound fracture of the lower left
arm," Duke Forrest said.

"Which we, ever faithful to the Hippocratic oath, have
reduced and otherwise cared for," Spearchucker Jones
said. "Even if this kept us from our heart's desire,
namely, attending the P.T.A. meeting and potluck supper
with our beloved wives and helpmeets."

"His mother must be frantic with worry," Mrs.
Spearchucker Jones said. "Where is she? I'll go tell her
he's all right. He *is* all right, isn't he?"

"My God, is that what they call death's grey pallor?"
Mrs. Duke Forrest asked. "The poor lamb!"

"Trapper, you worm," said Lucinda (Mrs. Trapper
John) McIntyre. "How *could* you get plastered when
this beautiful child needed your professional services?"

"I think," Hawkeye said, solemnly, "that we may
be able to pull him through, God-willing, provided you
ladies will get the hell out of the way and let us get him
into the recovery room."

Hugh Percival Woodburn-Haverstraw was wheeled
down the corridor to the recovery room, and gently off-
loaded into a bed. Spearchucker Jones raised his eyes
and saw four female heads peering in the door.

"Where, I asked," his bride said, menacingly, "is that
beautiful boy's mother? I want to go to her right now."

"Out of the question," Spearchucker said. "You can't
swim."

"What's that supposed to mean?"

"His mother is in England, I suppose," Spearchucker
said. "He's an English sailor. The Coast Guard picked
him off a ship out in the ocean."

"You mean that poor child is all alone, far from home?" Mary Pierce asked.

"And there is no one to comfort him in his pain?" Mrs. Trapper John asked in horror.

"No gentle hand to soothe his feverish brow?" chimed in Madame Forrest.

"We," said Mary Pierce, "will take care of him. It is our clear duty."

"What about the P.T.A. meeting?" Lucinda McIntyre asked. "And the potluck supper to follow?"

"To hell with it," Mary Pierce said. "Duty calls!"

"You may," Hawkeye Pierce said, with awesome medical solemnity, a technique he had learned from watching doctor programs on TV, "wait out in the corridor. The nurse will summon you when our patient regains consciousness. You may visit him briefly, one at a time, at that time."

"I know," Mrs. Spearchucker Jones said. "I will go home and bake some instant brownies. Boys always like brownies."

"Good thinking," Mary Pierce said, and then, her voice now suspicious, she turned to her husband. "And what are you going to be doing? You're not going to leave this darling child alone, are you?"

"The patient," Hawkeye said with great medical dignity, "will be entrusted to the capable hands of Nurse Chambers, who will watch over him while my medical associates and I confer in my office on post-operative treatment and things like that."

He closed the door in the faces of the ladies, picked up the telephone and instructed the head nurse to immediately dispatch Student Nurse Beverly Chambers to the post-operative recovery room.

"Why her?" Trapper John asked.

"If you were eighteen years old, would you rather wake up looking at you or me, or into the bright eyes and sparkling face of eighteen-year-old Beverly Chambers?" Hawkeye said. Miss Chambers appeared at that moment.

"Sweetie," said Hawkeye, "I want you to sit here and

watch this patient. If there are any frightening signs at all, any at all, you yell for the head nurse, and for us. We'll be in my office."

"Yes, sir, Dr. Pierce," Beverly Chambers said.

"And call me, in any event, the moment he wakes up."

"Yes, sir, Dr. Pierce," Beverly Chambers said.

They formed then into a column of twos and marched past their wives toward the office of the Chief of Surgery.

"Nurse Chambers has a delightful, respectful attitude, doesn't she?" Dr. McIntyre asked, approvingly.

"It's a shame to think that in just a few short years, she'll be just like the rest," Dr. Jones replied, "throwing her weight around and humiliating poor interns."

They made a column right into the offices of the Chief of Surgery, broke ranks, closed the door after them, snapped on the IN CONFERENCE sign and, a moment or two later, raised glasses holding freshly mixed martinis to each other in a mutual toast.

"Virtue," Hawkeye said, "is obviously its own reward!"

"Hear, hear," the others chorused.

At that moment there came a horrifying bellow of pain and outrage, filling every nook and cranny of the Spruce Harbor Medical Center. As one man, the senior medical staff of the facility laid their martini glasses down, rose to their feet and raced down the corridors to the emergency room.

A very large man was lying on his stomach on the treatment table, moaning piteously and quite loudly. Standing above him was the emergency-room nurse, triumphantly holding aloft, in a pair of forceps, a double-hooked fishing lure.

Mary Pierce, with her cronies in her wake, rushed into the room. She examined with distaste the man on the table, averting her eyes from the sight of his exposed, perforated and bleeding rump.

"My God, what's going on?" she asked. "I have as much sympathy for drunken derelicts as anybody, even one as ugly and foul-smelling as that one, but his drunken

ravings are going to disturb that beautiful boy in the
recovery room. Hawkeye, *do* something!"

"Mary," Hawkeye said, "you will recall that I promised, when the opportunity presented itself, to introduce
you to my good friend Boris Alexandrovich Korsky-
Rimsakov, the greatest living operatic tenor?"

"Don't you dare try to change the subject!" Mary
Pierce said.

"Boris," Hawkeye said, "stop moaning and say hello
to my wife."

"I am honored, madame," Boris said, and belched,
giving off a heavy cloud of Old White Stagg Blended
Kentucky Bourbon fumes. "As Hawkeye's wife, it will
not be necessary for you to kiss my hand. A small curtsy
will suffice."

"May I suggest that we take this patient to the operating room?" Trapper John said quickly, even as Mary
Pierce took in the very deep breath she would need to
further comment on the situation.

Before Mary Pierce could close her mouth, Boris
Alexandrovich Korsky-Rimsakov was slid off the work
table onto a cart and rolled out of the emergency room,
attended by the entire senior staff of the Spruce Harbor
Medical Center.

There was actually very little the assembled practitioners of the healing arts could do for Boris Alexandrovich Korsky-Rimsakov the emergency-room nurse
hadn't already done. But never one to pass up an opportunity to display his fine handwriting talent, Dr.
McIntyre personally attended to the application of the
antiseptic himself. For the next six days, until the
Merthiolate wore off, Boris's bottom would bear the
legend, "THIS SIDE DOWN. DO NOT FOLD, SPINDLE OR
MUTILATE."

Then they adjourned to Hawkeye's office, ordering
Boris installed in a semi-private room.

An hour later, the chief of the nursing staff of the
Spruce Harbor Medical Center stopped before the door
to the office of the Chief of Surgery and rapped on it

with her ring. Two raps. Pause. Three raps. Pause. Two final raps.

There came the sound of a lock being opened, and the door opened wide enough for an eye to peer out. Then the door swung wide open, the chief nurse stepped quickly inside, and the door closed and was locked again.

"I *gave* the secret knock," the chief nurse said, a touch of annoyance in her voice.

"Our wives are in the hospital," Hawkeye explained. "Extraordinary security provisions are necessary. Onion or olive?"

"Olive, please, and light on the vermouth," the chief nurse said. She was a lady in her forties, with bluish-white hair and a dignified carriage. Trapper John, with a flair, presented her with a martini.

"Trapper, is that big ape really an opera singer?" she asked.

"Finest kind," Hawkeye answered for him.

"He's quite a man," the chief nurse said.

"I feel sure that you will be able to control your baser urges," Trapper said. "But maybe you better go easy on the sauce. Calmer heads than yours have been lost over Boris."

"I could handle him," the chief nurse said. "But I would have to fight all the others, just to get close to him, and I'm too old for that."

"It's started already, has it?" Hawkeye said. "Well, in that case, just to maintain the high moral tone of the joint, maybe you better move the English kid with the broken wing in with him when he comes out of anesthesia."

"I anticipated your order, Doctor," the chief nurse said. "And I just looked in on that darling boy. He's stirring. That sweet little Chambers girl asked me to tell you."

"Welcome back to the world," Hawkeye said to Midshipman Woodburn-Haverstraw. "How do you feel?"

"Just fine, thank you, Doctor."

"And has Miss Chambers been getting you everything you need?"

"Miss Chambers has been most kind to me, sir," Woodburn-Haverstraw said. Beverly Chambers flushed prettily. "I've been very sorry to have put all of you to all this trouble."

"No trouble at all," Student Nurse Chambers and Dr. Pierce said, in perfect harmony. Nurse Chambers flushed even brighter, and Hawkeye went on. "As a matter of fact, you couldn't have timed it better. You saved me from a fate worse than death. My name is Hawkeye, by the way."

"Well, Dr. Hawkeye, I'm most grateful for all you've done for me."

"You can call me 'Hawkeye,' or you can call me 'Dr. Pierce'. I prefer Hawkeye," Hawkeye said.

"That's most gracious of you, sir," Woodburn-Haverstraw said.

"What should I call you?"

"My name is Hugh Percival Woodburn-Haverstraw," he said. "When I was at school, my chums called me Percy. I rather loathed that. Then when I went into the navy, I was generally called 'Hey, Hugh.' "

"How about me calling you 'Woody'?" Hawkeye asked. "That seems to fit, and that's what you'd be called if you lived here."

" 'Woody' sounds just jolly," Woodburn-Haverstraw said. "And begging your pardon, Doctor, where exactly am I?"

"*Hawkeye,*" Hawkeye corrected him. "You're in the Spruce Harbor, Maine, Medical Center, Woody."

"The last thing I remember clearly is leaping after that bloody roast of beef," Woody said. "On H.M.S. *Insubmergible.*"

"Well, you broke your arm," Hawkeye explained. "And the Coast Guard picked you up in a chopper and brought you here, and we've just finished fixing up your arm. In two months, all you'll have is the memory. Tell me about the bloody roast beef."

Woody Woodburn-Haverstraw explained how he had been carrying the Captain's standing rib from the galley to the wardroom, and how it had gone over the side. Hawkeye, who, in his younger years had had similar experience in earning the outrage of his military superiors, was naturally sympathetic.

"Woody," he said, "if you'll give me the name and address, I'll send a radio message to your mother and father telling them you're all right. I'm sure the Royal Navy is just as effective as the U.S. Army in sending terrifying telegrams to families."

"Oh, that won't be necessary, Doc . . . Hawkeye," Woody said. "Thank you just the same."

"I really think it would be a good idea," Hawkeye insisted.

"The thing is, you see, Hawkeye," Woody said. "My folks are dead."

"I'm sorry," Hawkeye said. "And there's no one else? Aunts, uncles. . . ."

"Just my Great-Uncle Hugh," Woody said. "And he's getting on a bit. He was ninety-three last birthday, and I'd hate to worry the old gentleman, you understand."

"Yes, of course," Hawkeye said. "Woody, would you do me a favor?"

"Anything at all, sir," Woody said. "It would be my great privilege."

"There is another . . . patient . . . in the hospital. He is suffering from . . . uh . . . lacerations of the epidermis in the vicinity of the gluteus maximus, if you follow me?"

"I think so, sir," Woody said.

"And, if it would be all right with you, I'd like to move you from the recovery room . . . where you are now . . . into his room. He doesn't like to be left alone. You could give each other some company."

"Smashing!" Woody said. "I'd jolly well like that."

"Great," Hawkeye said.

"Hawkeye, how long will I be here?"

"That depends," Hawkeye said. "Probably a week."

"Bully!" Woody said. "The *Insubmergible* won't wait around that long for me."

"That thought crossed my mind," Hawkeye said. "And we'll work out some way to get you back to England."

"I'm sure the British Embassy will arrange things," Woody said.

"I'm sure they will," Hawkeye said. "I'll go get the cart, and we'll have Miss Chambers roll you out of here."

"Hawkeye," Woody said. "I might not want to cross the Atlantic on H.M.S. *Insubmergible* with one arm in a cast, but I daresay I can make it from one room to another in here on my own two feet."

"Didn't your mother tell you never to argue with a doctor?" Hawkeye quipped, and immediately wished he could fall overboard from the H.M.S. *Insubmergible*.

"Actually, no," Woody said. "She died when I was rather young. Two months old, I've been told."

"I'll be right back," Hawkeye said. He went out into the corridor and nearly ran over Mary Pierce.

"How is he?" she asked.

"As well as can be expected under the circumstances," Hawkeye said, "which are that he's an eighteen-year-old orphan whose only kin in the world is ninety-three years old, and that he just dumped his captain's standing rib of beef into the North Atlantic."

"The poor lamb!" Mary Pierce said. "Is he awake? I'll go keep him company."

"He is already having his company kept by the Chambers girl," Hawkeye said. "You'd be a crowd, as in 'Two's company; three's a . . .' "

"That makes two orphans," Mary Pierce said, making reference to the absent Mr. Chambers and the shrillish, often-plastered wife from whom he had fled. "How's she making out here, Hawkeye?"

"Very well, from what I hear," Hawkeye said.

"Well, I hope that makes you feel terrible," Mary Pierce said. "She wouldn't be here at all except for the bank's generosity. And you're always saying those nasty and cruel things about bankers."

"You can visit him, if you like, when I get him moved in with Boris."

"What are you going to do about him, Hawkeye?" Mary asked.

"I'm going to keep him around here for a couple of days," Hawkeye said, "long enough to make sure his ship will have left without him, and to feed him up a little . . . he's as skinny as a rail."

"We have room enough at our house," Mary Pierce said. "Why don't you discharge him from the hospital and bring him home where I can get some food into him?"

"For the next day or two, you can sneak him a CARE package when you want to," Hawkeye said. "I want him officially in the hospital just as long as there's a chance that ship will come after him. And besides, you wouldn't want to interfere with young love, would you? I haven't seen a look like that on a girl's face since you used to look at me."

"I never looked at you that way," Mary Pierce said.

"What way is that, beloved, since you haven't seen her looking at him?"

"I'm going home and make him some stuffed pork chops," Mary Pierce said, not choosing to reply to Hawkeye's last statement.

"You better roast a whole pig," Hawkeye said. "I'm having him moved in with Boris."

# Chapter Four

"Mr. *John Smith*," Hawkeye said, significantly, to Boris Alexandrovich Korsky-Rimsakov, who was lying on one of the two beds, on his side, "this is Mr. Woodburn-Haverstraw. John, Woody."

"Oh, my!" Woody said, in shock. "Dr. Hawkeye, am I delirious?"

"I don't think so, why do you ask?"

"This gentleman bears such an uncanny resemblance to the world's greatest operatic tenor that, for a moment, I thought I was privileged to be in the presence of the great Boris Alexandrovich Korsky-Rimsakov himself."

"You don't say?" Boris said.

"That's impossible, of course," Woody said. "Not only would that be too much to hope for, but what would the world's greatest opera singer be doing in Spruce Harbor, Maine, suffering from fishhooks in the, excuse me, the can?"

"How did you know about that?" Boris demanded suspiciously.

"Dr. Hawkeye said you were suffering from 'lacerations of the epidermis in the region of the gluteus maximus.' That's what they put on my records when I hooked myself in the tail. It's excruciatingly painful, isn't it?"

"As only someone who has suffered through it can possibly know," Boris said. "Hawkeye, under the circumstances, you have my permission to tell this splendid young man who I really am."

"Midshipman Hugh Percival Woodburn-Haverstraw," Hawkeye said, formallly, "may I present Boris Alexandrovich Korsky-Rimsakov?"

"Oh, Maestro," Woody said. "It *is* you!"

"Yes, it is," Boris said. He bowed as well as he could lying on his side.

"Does your painful indisposition mean, Maestro," Woody asked, "that you won't be able to sing *Otello* at Covent Garden Opera House on Friday?"

"You know about that too, do you?" Boris said. "How interesting!"

"Maestro, I follow every step of your career," Woody said.

"Is that so?" Boris said. He turned to Hawkeye. "Do you think, Doctor," he said, "that you could find, somewhere in this quaint rural charnel house of yours, a bottle of good champagne with which my good friend

Woody and I can toast our fortuitous meeting in our time of pain and agony?"

"Would you settle for a six-pack of Schlitz?" Hawkeye asked. He quietly left the room. He thought that a six-pack would be medically indicated. Knowing Boris, the division of the six-pack between them would be on a ratio of five-to-one. One can of beer would settle Woody's stomach and make him drowsy. Five cans of beer would, in good time, work its way through Boris's digestive and urinary system, making it absolutely necessary for him to get out of bed and walk to the rest room. The walk would be slightly painful, but not as painful as it would be if he didn't—as he announced he would not—get out of bed at all until his near-mortal wound had healed.

He was somewhat surprised to find his wife in the corridor.

"I thought you were home roasting a whole pig," he said.

"I was going to," she said, "but as I passed the desk, I heard the nurses talking."

"Not, I trust, about the medical staff?"

"About the kitchen," she said. "You haven't heard?"

"I'm waiting with bated breath," Hawkeye said.

"There's a French chef in there," she said. "He chased Mrs. Fogarty out with a knife. He is preparing food for that opera singer friend of yours . . . if he really is an opera singer. He looks more like a cousin of the Godfather to me. . . ."

"He is, believe me, an opera singer," Hawkeye said. "Tell me more about the chow."

"Mrs. Fogarty told him she had patients to feed. He told her, if that was necessary, that he would feed them as they had never been fed before, just as long as it didn't interfere with his feeding your gangster friend."

"So?"

"Would you believe that chicken à la king has been scratched from the menu in favor of pheasant-under-glass?"

"I hope Antoine made enough for me, too," Hawkeye said. "He does it so well."

"You know about this? You *approve?*"

"Of course, I approve. You know how I hate chicken à la king," Hawkeye said. "Mary, Antoine, who was trained at the Ritz, and who was executive chef at Maxim's—which are a pair of fair-to-middling beaneries in Paris—is personal chef to Boris's bosom buddy, His Royal Highness Hassan ad Kayam."

*"Personal chef to whom?"*

"Him," Hawkeye said, pointing over his shoulder. "The sawed-off one." Mary Pierce turned to see where he was pointing. Her mouth dropped open.

Eight robed figures were coming down the corridor. Six of them were males, all about six feet tall, all bearded, and each carrying a chrome- (or perhaps silver) plated submachine gun. The seventh male was also bearded, but he was a foot shorter than the others, unarmed, and could best be described as roly-poly. He was, of course, His Highness, Prince Hassan ad Kayam. The eighth robed figure was in a powder-blue robe, on which had been embroidered, in gold thread, a huge Christian cross. The vertical staff ran from the neck of the garment to the hem; the horizontal staff ran, of course, horizontally, and was firmly supported at its outer ends by that glandular structure common to the female of the species.

"Hawkeye," the blonde-headed wearer of this extraordinary garment demanded, "what the hell is going on around here?"

"As I live and breathe," Hawkeye said. "Hot Lips!"

"Hawkeye," Mary Pierce demanded, "who *are* these people?"

"Mary, I would like you to meet my old friend, the Reverend Mother Emeritus of the God Is Love in All Forms Christian Church, Incorporated, formerly known as Major Hot Lips Houlihan, Army Nurse Corps," Hawkeye said.

"How do you do?" the ladies said to each other, and then added, in perfect harmony, "I've heard a good deal about you."

"And His Highness Prince Hassan," Hawkeye said.

"I am honored, madame," Prince Hassan said, bowing

deeply and kissing Mary Pierce's hand. Mary Pierce was unable to restrain a small giggle. Hand-kissing is not common among the normally practiced social amenities in Maine.

"We were right in the middle of the Semi-Annual Come to Jesus Revival and Crab Boil in Jackson Square," the Reverend Mother Emeritus said, "when Hassan's hooded hoodlums showed up, dragged me off the platform into a limousine, pushed me aboard one of Horsey's jets and flew me up here."

"I fear the misunderstanding is entirely my fault," Prince Hassan said.

"Really?" Hawkeye said. "How could that be?"

"It was I who spoke on the radio from the lake in Canada," Hassan said, "to order the airplane, you understand."

"O.K. So what?" Hawkeye asked.

"I think that perhaps in the excitement of the moment, I may have given the impression that Boris Alexandrovich was more seriously injured than he really was. When I said that he urgently needed medical attention, the members of my bodyguard sought out the only medical person they knew: the Reverend Mother."

"What's wrong with the big ape, Hawkeye?" Hot Lips asked.

"He's suffering from lacerations of the epidermis in the region of the gluteus maximus," Hawkeye explained.

"Fishhooks in the can, huh?" Hot Lips asked. She laughed a nasty little laugh. "I suppose it's too much to hope that he did it to himself?"

"I am responsible," His Highness said. "In extenuation I can only say that there is no body of water, either fresh or salt, in my native land. I had never before held a fishing rod in my hand when tragedy struck."

"I suppose that since I'm here," Hot Lips said, "I might as well say hello to him."

"Right in there," Hawkeye said.

"Are you going to permit this . . . person . . . to go in there with Poor Woody?" Mary Pierce asked.

"Madame," Hot Lips said, "you may rest assured that my interest in Boris Alexandrovich is purely professional. I will remind you that I am a registered nurse."

That wasn't the truth, the whole truth, and nothing but the truth. Hot Lips and Boris were friends. She was, in fact, Boris's only true friend of the opposite gender.

The reason for this was quite simple. Each of them, in his own way, had a rather unusual effect on those of the opposite sex, a certain animal magnetism. If Hot Lips, for example, entered a restaurant alone, havoc was sure to follow as she was spotted by male diners. Husbands, blind to everything but Hot Lips's rather conspicuous charms, would spill soup into their wives' laps; fall out of their chairs; and physically remove potted palms, headwaiters, busboys and other patrons from their lines of vision.

In a similar situation, with Boris Alexandrovich entering a restaurant alone, the results were much the same. So many handkerchiefs would be dropped in front of Boris's table by normally respectable wives, mothers and P.T.A. chairpersons that it resembled the bottom of a hotel laundry chute after a busy weekend. Orchestras would be drowned out by the sound of heavy breathing and by the massed roar of feminine sighs. In most European opera houses, there was a heavy wire mesh device (known to the trade as the Korsky-Rimsakov Protective Curtain) which—in order to protect the cast from the typically enormous European hotel keys, sure to sail stageward from the audience—was put in place whenever the Maestro was performing.

They had, oddly enough, no physical interest in each other; and this was the seed on which their friendship had grown over the years, nurtured and fertilized by their interest in good food and drink. Their friendship, too, dated back to the 4077th MASH, where Boris Alexandrovich Korsky-Rimsakov (having adopted the *nom de guerre* of "Bob Alexander") had been treated for wounds suffered on Heartbreak Ridge. Boris/Bob had gone to then Major Houlihan and begged her in the name of

Florence Nightingale to keep her nurses from tending to him, rather intimately, in the wee hours of the morning, lest he should never regain his strength. Since he was the first patient ever to pass through the 4077th who had not attempted to corner her in a dark area of the medical facility, Major Houlihan had investigated the complaint and found that it was not only completely justified, but proof that on the other side of the sexual fence, there was another soul tormented by unwanted attention.

They had remained in touch over the years. Boris Alexandrovich Korsky-Rimsakov had made one of his few American appearances when, at a moment's notice, he had flown to New Orleans to sing at Hot Lips's wedding. At the solemn nuptials celebrating the joining together in holy wedlock of Margaret Houlihan Wachauf, R.N., (she had been briefly married to and widowed by a Mr. Wachauf) and the Rev. Buck Wilson, founder of the God Is Love in All Forms Christian Church, Inc., Boris had sung "I Love You Truly" and "There's Nothing Like a Girl" with such skill and artistry that even certain exquisitely graceful and well-perfumed male members of the Reverend Buck's Flock had wept over *both* selections.

And he sang again, three days later ("We Will Gather at the River" and "When the Roll Is Called up Yonder"), at the funeral rites for the Rev. Mr. Wilson, who had expired (it was rumored of overexertion) on the nuptial couch. Sufficient revenue had been obtained from the sale of church seats to hear him perform to pay for both the wedding reception and the second-largest cemetery memorial (a white Canberra-marble tomb topped with a twelve-foot statue of the Reverend Wilson sculpted as St. George slaying a dragon) in New Orleans Parish.

For the part, the Rev. Mother Emeritus Wilson (who had been named to that post in the religious body founded by her husband immediately after his death) had been the only person with courage enough to tell Boris Alexandrovich that his marriage to Congressperson

Hortense V. Clumpp (Radical-Liberal, California) was
foredoomed to failure. When the marriage had indeed
been rent asunder, it had been the Reverend Mother
Emeritus who had consoled the singer, although not, as
foul rumor had it, by pressing him to her breast. Truth
being stranger than fiction, they had spent two weeks
touring the Greek Islands on Prince Hassan's yacht in
separate staterooms and unsullied chastity. (The source
of the nasty rumors was probably the press. Boris had
indeed been seen and photographed boarding the yacht,
the 190-foot *Diana,* with the Reverend Mother Emeritus,
somewhat dishabille, slung over his shoulder. But this
was because the Reverend Mother Emeritus had somehow
mistakenly gotten the impression that Ouzo, the 160-
proof Greek *vin de pays,* was nothing more than licorice
soda and had consumed two bottles over lunch.)

The Rev. Mother Emeritus Margaret H.W. Wilson
entered the hospital room of Boris Alexandrovich Korsky-
Rimsakov without knocking. Midshipman The Hon.
Hugh Percival Woodburn-Haverstraw, R.N., stopped
talking in the middle of a word. He was struck with the
same vision that had caused, early that day, an extraordinary number of sinners to accept the invitation
to come. to the Platform and Jesus in New Orleans's
Jackson Square. The Reverend Mother Emeritus, fully
aware of how hot it got under the blazing sun in Jackson
Square, had worn under her ecclesiastic gown only the
lightest of Ladies' Unmentionables; to wit, a nylon bras-
siere of the Outward & Upward pattern and matching
bikini panties. The gown itself was nylon. In Jackson
Square, as in the doorway to room 302 of the Spruce
Harbor Medical Center, rear lighting served to rather
effectively reduce the light-stopping characteristics of the
nylon cloth. In other words, with the light behind her,
as it was now as she entered the room, the gown was
nearly invisible; and for a moment, Woody Woodburn-
Haverstraw thought that he had died and gone to heaven
and was being greeted by a broadly smiling angel whose
idea of eternal bliss had nothing to do with riding around
on a cloud playing a harp.

Boris, turning to see why Woody had stopped talking, saw the Reverend Mother Emeritus. His mouth opened too, and he just had time to say "Hot Lips!" before the Reverend Mother shoved a thermometer into his mouth and grabbed his wrist to take his pulse.

Hot Lips smiled at Woody, and his pulse rate increased by thirty percent.

"Hello there, young man," she said. "I am Nurse Wilson. I'll be with you in a minute."

"Yes, ma'am," Woody breathed, laying his head back on his pillow, in blissful anticipation.

## Chapter Five

"The Secretary will see you now," the Secretary's secretary said in the tastefully appointed outer office of the Secretary of State. Quincy T. Westerbrook, Deputy Assistant Secretary of State for Northern and Central European Culturo-Political Affairs, a plump little man with gleaming skin, stood up, ran his fingers lightly over his head to make sure his hair was in place, and marched up to the Secretary's door.

Mr. Westerbrook, whose hairline had receded completely, except for a sparse band an inch wide in the vicinity of his ears and the three hairs he patted into place as he stood up, was more than a little nervous about being summoned to the Secretary himself.

Aside from television, on which the Secretary appeared as often as "I Love Lucy," Deputy Assistant Secretary of State Westerbrook had seen the Secretary of State only once, that is in person, since he had assumed office. They had met in the senior staff washroom on the fifth floor late one afternoon. (Assistant Secretaries and up, of course, had their own private toilet facilities; one seldom if ever encountered them meeting nature's calls amongst the underlings.) Quincy Westerbrook had been so surprised at the Secretary's cheerful greeting (*"Wie steht's mit Dir Liebling?"*), that he had quite forgotten where he was and what he was doing. He had, in fact, attempted to readjust his clothing before the matter at hand had been concluded. In so doing, he managed to enmesh a certain delicate portion of his flesh into the teeth of the zipper.

The Secretary, who had expected to receive in reply to his friendly greeting either a polite smile and a nod or a "Good Afternoon, Mr. Secretary," had gotten, instead, a bloodcurdling howl of pain and what looked like an impromptu performance of the Chiricahua Apache fertility dance. (Which dance, as all students of Indian lore know, is performed by jumping about on one leg in a bent-over position with the hands in a cupping position in the vicinity of the junction of the legs.)

So, while Westerbrook could say—and of course, did— that he had personally spoken to the Secretary himself in the men's john, the truth was that their interchange of ideas had been somewhat one-sided. As a matter of fact, after flashing his world-famous smile at Quincy Westerbrook, the Secretary had apparently decided he could wait a little longer to accomplish what he had entered the senior staff washroom to accomplish, and had fled. With dignity, of course.

Westerbrook knocked at the highly polished oak door.

"So, come in already," the Secretary's familiar voice called.

"Good afternoon, Mr. Secretary," Quincy T. Westerbrook said.

"So, vat's good about it?" the Secretary replied.

"I beg your pardon, Mr. Secretary?"

"I'm a busy man, Quincy," the Secretary said. "You believe that? It's all right, I should call you Quincy?"

"Yes, of course, Mr. Secretary," Westerbrook said.

"I know you," the Secretary said, suddenly remembering their last meeting. "You're the one who makes with the funny dances in the men's room."

"I can explain that, Mr. Secretary," Westerbrook said, flushing bright red.

"I vouldn't vant you should do that, Quincy," the Secretary said. "Dat's between you and your family physician. More important problems, I got."

"How may I be of assistance, Mr. Secretary?"

"I got here an urgent radio from London," the Secretary said. "Maybe you seen it?" He passed to Westerbrook a top-secret radio Teletype message from the U.S. Embassy in London.

FROM U.S. EMBASSY, LONDON
FOR THE SECRETARY OF STATE, WASHINGTON

FOLLOWING MESSAGE WHEN DECODED IS CLASSIFIED TOP SECRET—EYES ONLY FOR ASSISTANT SECRETARIES OF STATE FOR POLITICO-MILITARY AFFAIRS AND HIGHER OFFICIALS:

BRITISH GOVERNMENT THIS AFTERNOON WILL ANNOUNCE THE DEATH OF VICE ADM. LORD HUGH PERCIVAL, THE DUKE OF FOLKESTONE. INFORMATION FROM INVARIABLY RELIABLE SOURCES INDICATES THAT HIS GRACE DIED OF A HEART SEIZURE BROUGHT ABOUT BY OVEREXERTION. AT THE TIME OF HIS DEATH, HIS GRACE, WHO WAS NINETY-THREE YEARS OF AGE, WAS BEING PURSUED THROUGH HYDE PARK BY LIEUT. GEN. SIR ARCHIBALD SOMMERSBY, RETIRED, AGED EIGHTY-EIGHT, WHO HAD DISCOVERED HIS GRACE IN FLAGANTE DELICTO WITH LADY SOMMERSBY, AGED SIXTY-FOUR, IN AN APARTMENT HIS GRACE MAINTAINED IN THE DORCHESTER HOTEL.

SIR ARCHIBALD, WHO WAS ARMED WITH A SHOTGUN, WAS UNSUCCESSFUL IN HIS ATTEMPT TO SHOOT LORD HUGH, ALTHOUGH A TOTAL OF ELEVEN SHOTS WERE FIRED BEFORE SIR ARCHIBALD COULD BE RESTRAINED BY OFFICIALS OF SCOTLAND YARD. HE IS BEING DETAINED INCOMMUNICADO AT THE VICTORIA & ALBERT MEMORIAL RESIDENCE FOR DISTURBED GENTLEFOLK. IT IS BELIEVED THAT THE AFFAIR WILL BE HUSHED UP.

THE LATE LORD HUGH PERCIVAL, DUKE OF FOLKE-
STONE, IS FIRST COUSIN, TWICE REMOVED, TO THE
QUEEN. HE WAS OWNER OF EAST ANGLIA BREWERIES,
LTD., AND OF THE YORKSHIRE AND NORTHUMBER-
LAND LIFE AND CASUALTY ASSURANCE COMPANIES,
LTD., AND HAD EXTENSIVE OTHER HOLDINGS, INCLUD-
ING THE VILLAGE OF HERSTEAD-ON-HEATH.

HIS SOLE LINEAL DESCENDANT, TO WHOM BOTH TI-
TLE AND PROPERTY PASSES, IS HUGH PERCIVAL
WOODBURN-HAVERSTRAW,      PRESENTLY      SERVING
ABOARD H.M.S. INSUBMERGIBLE. H.M.S. INSUBMERGI-
BLE IS PRESENTLY PAYING COURTESY CALL TO U.S.
NAVY YARD, BOSTON, MASSACHUSETTS.

IT IS STRONGLY RECOMMENDED THAT A SENIOR
STATE DEPARTMENT OFFICIAL VISIT THE NEW LORD
HUGH PERCIVAL, THE DUKE OF FOLKESTONE, ABOARD
H.M.S. INSUBMERGIBLE TO CONVEY OFFICIAL CON-
DOLENCES OF THE U.S. GOVERNMENT. IT IS FURTHER
STRONGLY RECOMMENDED THAT ALL RESOURCES
AVAILABLE TO U.S. GOVERNMENT BE PLACED AT THE
DISPOSAL OF HIS GRACE IN ORDER TO ENABLE HIM TO
RETURN TO ENGLAND IN TIME TO PARTICIPATE IN
BURIAL SERVICES OF HIS UNCLE, WHO WILL BE IN-
TERRED, FOLLOWING SERVICES IN WESTMINSTER AB-
BEY, IN THE FAMILY CRYPT AT FOLKESTONE
CASTLE, NORTHUMBERLAND.

> S. ISAAC RONALD
> DEPUTY CHIEF OF MISSION FOR
> POLITICO-MILITARY AFFAIRS

"I'm familiar with it, Mr. Secretary," Westerbrook
said, glancing at it.

"So maybe you can tell me vat's all the excitement?"

"I'm afraid I don't understand the question, Mr.
Secretary," Westerbrook said.

"Flowers, maybe," the Secretary said. "Between you
and me, Quincy, I got to respect a guy—vat, ninety-three
years old?—who's getting a liddle on the side. It should
happen to me when I'm ninety-three. Vat a vay to go!
But vat's all this business about us sending somebody

in person to offer official condolences, and 'putting the entire resources of the U.S. Government at the disposal' of the nephew?"

"I think I begin to understand the nature of your inquiry," Westerbrook said.

"Tell me, Quincy," the Secretary said. "You vent to school vhere?"

"Yale, as a matter of fact, Mr. Secretary," Westerbrook said.

"At Yale, they don't teach you to talk plain?" the Secretary inquired.

"Mr. Secretary," Westerbrook said, "do you know what takes place in the village of Herstead-on-Heath?"

"So tell me."

"Herstead-on-Heath is the supply point for our Polaris submarines," Westerbrook said. "We rent the entire village for offices and living quarters and warehousing purposes."

"So? Ve throw a liddle business their way, they throw a liddle our way. It all vorks out in the end. I hate to think vat they got to pay for dat Rolls-Royce showroom on Park Avenue."

"The Defense Department is very interested in renewing the lease on the same favorable terms, Mr. Secretary," Westerbrook said.

"The English got ports they never use," the Secretary said. "We can chisel them a liddle. Vat's so special about Herstead-on-Heath?"

"We negotiated a contract with the late Duke to last during his lifetime, Mr. Secretary, which gives the U.S. Government complete control of the village and the port, for an annual rental of one pound."

"One pound of vat? Diamonds? Uranium?"

"One pound sterling, Mr. Secretary. About $2.28."

"I vouldn't like it, Quincy," the Secretary said, "for you to kid around with me. It's not nice to fool the Secretary of State."

"The contract was negotiated, Mr. Secretary, by Rear Admiral Davies, U.S.N., and members of his staff. They had a chance, fortuitous encounter with His Late Grace in the South of France."

"Tell me more," the Secrtary said. "Try to use liddle vords."

"As I understand it, Mr. Secretary, Rear Admiral Davies and his staff were making a personal inspection . . . with an eye to placing them off limits, of course . . . of certain establishments known as *Maisons Tolerées*. The actual meeting took place, I understand, in an establishment known as *La Maison des Toutes Les Nations* in Marseilles."

*"Oy vay iz mir!"* said the Secretary.

"His Late Grace, was, as you know, Vice Admiral, Royal Navy, Retired. When he saw, so to speak, his comrades-in-arms, he offered a toast to the U.S. Navy. Admiral Davies had no choice but to return the courtesy. One thing led to another. Two or three days later, there was apparently a young lady present who, for one reason or another, required some financial assistance."

"And?"

"In the playful spirit of the moment, His Late Grace paraphrased that memorable line from English history, 'My Kingdom for a Horse'. He didn't actually have a kingdom, of course, but he did have a village; and Admiral Davies felt it his duty to advance him a pound, which was all they had left, to lease the village for our government."

"And vat happened ven they all sobered up?"

"The Duke of Folkestone, Mr. Secretary, in or out of his cups, was an English Gentleman. He honored his verbal agreement. The lease, however, expired with His Late Grace. A new lease will have to be negotiated with His New Grace."

The Secretary of State looked very thoughtful for a moment. Then he pulled the red telephone on his desk toward him, and lifted the receiver. It was a direct line, and it was not necessary for him to dial the party he was calling.

"Turn off the tape recorder," he said. "Ve got a liddle problem. I vouldn't vant it should get oudt."

The chief nurse of the Spruce Harbor Medical Center let herself into the Chief of Surgery's office, locked the door, flipped on the IN CONFERENCE sign, poured two fingers of Benedictine and brandy into a glass, lowered herself onto the couch, kicked off her shoes, raised her feet onto the coffee table, sipped the B & B and gave off with a mighty sigh of satisfaction.

Esther Flanagan, R.N., had seen it as her duty to remain on duty beyond her normal tour in order to properly supervise the medical attention being paid to both that nice English kid and to Boris Alexandrovich Korsky-Rimsakov.

The pheasant-under-glass had been just as good as Dr. Pierce had said it would be, and Mr. Korsky-Rimsakov had been right when he said the only way to eat pheasant like that was to wash it down on a flood of champagne. The only problem she had had with the whole affair was with the nurses. There had been a fistfight in the nurses' lounge over whose turn it was to perform unscheduled volunteer night duty, with three nurses vieing for the honor, and she had to speak a good deal more sharply than she liked to Student Nurse Chambers in order to get her out of the room. In the corridor outside the room, she had had to point out rather sternly that while Tender, Loving Care has its place in a hospital, it does not entail sitting by the patient's bed holding his hand and staring soulfully into his eyes.

There came a knock at the door. Chief Nurse Flanagan was surprised, because she knew that Doctors Pierce, McIntyre, Jones and Forrest had left the hospital for the evening. She elected to ignore the knock. Getting up to answer the door would mean putting her shoes back on, and there was no one in the hospital worthy of that sacrifice. The chief nurse was even more surprised when she heard the sound of a key slipping into the study lock, and then saw the door start to swing open.

The cockamamie dame in the flowing robe, with Christian cross, who had appeared with the Arabs, stepped into the office. The chief nurse got to her feet, both embarrassed and annoyed.

"Keep the load off," the dame said, smiling broadly at her.

"May I ask what you're doing in this office?" Chief Nurse Flanagan demanded icily.

"Same thing you are," the Rev. Mother Emeritus Wilson said.

"How, may I ask, did you come into possession of a key to the office of the Chief of Surgery?" the chief nurse demanded, warming to the whole subject of this outrageous, illegal invasion of the sanctum sanctorum of Spruce Harbor Medical Center.

"Hawkeye gave it to me," the Reverend Mother said. "Ah, here it is," she said, opening one of the file drawers and coming out with a bottle of Old White Stagg Blended Kentucky Bourbon. "Right where he said it would be. Can I fix you one?"

"I have one, thank you," Chief Nurse Flanagan said, less severely. There was something about this blonde's make-yourself-at-home attitude that did not smack of the unlawful intruder.

"You really have to hand it to Hawkeye," the Reverend Mother Superior said. "There was only one way to get Boris out of that bed, and Hawkeye knew what it was. It took two six-packs of beer and two bottles of champagne, but the Great Man just lurched across the floor, bladder about to burst, moaning every step of the way, to the john."

"How long have you been addressing Dr. Pierce, our beloved even revered, Chief of Surgery, as Hawkeye?"

"Ever since I was his chief nurse in Korea," the Reverend Mother said.

"You're a nurse? A *registered* nurse?"

"You mean, you couldn't tell?" the Reverend Mother asked in surprise. She had splashed about four inches of Old White Stagg into a glass. She raised it to the chief nurse. "Over the teeth and over the tongue; watch out, ventriculus, here it come!"

"Mud in your eye," the chief nurse responded. "And now that I think about it, why don't you freshen this up a little?" As the Reverend Mother poured B & B in her glass, the chief nurse asked, "Army nurse, were you?"

"Lieutenant Colonel, Retired," the Reverend Mother said.

"I always wondered if I made a mistake getting out," the chief nurse said.

"Were you an Army nurse?"

"Navy," the chief nurse said.

"I'll drink to the Navy," the Reverend Mother said, reaching for the Old White Stagg.

By the time the telephone rang, about an hour-and-a-half later, they had become good friends. Chief Nurse Flanagan, who had been known to keep a record in her neat hand about who had borrowed aspirin tablets, individual packets of sugar and the like, was positively firm in her insistence to lend to the Reverend Mother, R.N., suitable nursing garb for just as long as she needed it; and the Reverend Mother, R.N., was just as emphatic in insisting that Esther Flanagan spend her next vacation with her in New Orleans where, she said (and the chief nurse believed) she could have her choice of gentlemen escorts—ranging from those (essentially the vestry of the God Is Love in All Forms Christian Church, Inc.) with whom her virtue was absolutely safe for reasons having nothing to do with churchly morality to those (bachelor members of the Bayou Perdu Council, Knights of Columbus) where the precise opposite situation would prevail.

"And anything in between. Whatever you want, pal," Hot Lips said. "You come to New Orleans, Esther, and Ol' Hot Lips'll show you some real Southern Hospitality."

At that point, the telephone rang. Both nurses reached for it. The Reverend Mother, R.N., misjudged both the distance and her balance on the couch, and slid to the floor. The chief nurse wagged a finger at her.

"Reverend Mother, old buddy, if I didn't know better, I'd shay you were shmashed."

"Don't be ridiculum, redililikous," the Reverend Mother said, firmly, and reached for the Old White Stagg. "If you're sho shober, you anshwer the phone."

The chief nurse braced herself for the ordeal, and managed to pick up the phone on the second try. When she spoke, however, there was no suggestion in her voice that she had so much as sniffed a cork.

"Spruce Harbor Medical Center," she said, with perfect clarity. "Office of the Chief of Surgery. Chief of nursing services speaking."

She looked to her new buddy for approval, and got it. Hot Lips nodded, smiled encouragingly and gave her a broad wink of approbation.

"Why, yes," the chief nurse said. "We do have a patient named Woodburn-Haverstraw." She covered the microphone with her hand. "Nicest kid in the world, ol' Woody. And he's sort of sweet on one of my student nurses. How 'bout dat?"

Hot Lips expressed her appreciation of youthful love by applauding, or attempting to. She had a little trouble getting the palms of both hands to come together, which is necessary to make the expected clap-clap sound, but managed, on the third try, to come up with one loud clap. Her face beamed its self-satisfaction.

"Atta girl, Reverend Mother," the chief nurse said. "If at first you don't . . . " She stopped in the middle of her sentence, took her hand from the telephone mouthpiece, and quite clearly said, "I'm sorry, that sort of information would have to come from the attending physician. We are not at liberty to divulge it without permission." She covered the microphone with her hand again. "You ought to *hear* this guy! Sounds like Schultzie on 'Hogan's Heroes'."

"I only know one guy who really talks like that," the Reverend Mother said, thoughtfully.

"If you insist," the chief nurse said to her caller, each syllable clear and bell-like. "The attending physician is Benjamin Franklin Pierce, M.D., F.A.C.S. Dr. Pierce is not in the hospital at the moment, and I have no way of knowing when he will return. May I suggest you try his answering service?" There was a slight pause. "Well, if you tried the answering service already, what are you calling here for?"

"Won't take no for an answer, huh?" the Reverend Mother said. "Sounds like Tubby!"

"If you insist," the chief nurse said to the telephone, "the reason that Dr. Pierce cannot come to the telephone is that he is performing a sex-change operation on Premier Kosygin, who checked in incognito this afternoon. Good-bye, sir." She slammed the phone in the cradle.

"Kosygin really here?" the Reverend Mother asked. She sounded fascinated.

"Nah, I just said that," the chief nurse said.

"Why'd ya say something like that, ol' buddy?" the Reverend Mother pursued, very carefully picking up the Old White Stagg bottle in both hands, holding it over her head and dribbling a stream of its contents into her open mouth. "I watched the Greeks do this in Greece," she said. "I had a whole bunch of 'em teaching me how."

"Why not?" the chief nurse said.

"Why not what?" the Reverend Mother replied.

"Why not tell 'em some wild yarn about Kosygin?"

"Oh, yeah, that," the Reverend Mother said, remembering with some difficulty.

"He said he was the Secretary of State," the chief nurse said.

"Is that so?" the Reverend Mother said, lowering the Old White Stagg bottle. "Tell me, ol' buddy," she asked, "vas duh falla vat called haffing an haccent like dis?"

"Very good," the chief nurse said. "That's just the way he sounded."

"I wonder what Tubby wants with Woody?" the Reverend Mother asked thoughtfully.

"Tubby? Who's Tubby?"

"The Secretary of State, who else?" the Reverend Mother said.

# Chapter Six

The news of the passing of Vice Adm. His Grace Hugh Percival, the Duke of Folkestone, was brought to the English people on the six P.M. Home Service telecast of the British Broadcasting Corporation.

There are no commercial messages on the B.B.C. Viewers are not required to wait while three unctious males and one disgustingly cheerful female extoll the virtues of aspirin, hemorrhoid suppositories, friendly, small loan companies and miracle-fabric fat-restrainers with clever names before getting the news. An off-camera voice announces "And Now the News"; and the camera immediately focuses upon a gentleman, usually wearing a dinner jacket, who begins to read the news.

The only similarity between British news telecasts and American news telecasts, aside from the fact that both are in approximately the same language, is that neither of them feels obliged to present the news by means of telling the truth, the whole truth, and nothing but the truth.

At 6:30 a black-framed photograph (taken in 1939) of Vice Admiral His Grace the Duke of Folkestone in full naval uniform was flashed onto the tube as the announcer said:

Buckingham Palace this afternoon announced the passing of Vice Adm. His Grace Hugh Percival, the Duke of Folkestone. His Grace expired unexpectedly while taking his regular afternoon constitutional jaunt in Hyde Park, near the apartment he maintained in the Dorchester Hotel, apparently of a heart attack. He was ninety-three and had never married. With him at the time of his death was his old comrade-in-arms, Lieut. Gen. Sir Archibald Sommersby, Retired, who was so unnerved by the event that it was considered best for him to temporarily enter the Victoria & Albert Memorial Residence for Disturbed Gentlefolk.

Her Majesty has decreed five days of official mourning for His Grace, who was Her Majesty's first cousin, twice removed. While funeral arrangements have not been completed, it has been announced that His Grace's remains will be placed in Westminster Abbey tomorrow, to remain there until his funeral, which will be a formal state and naval affair. Final interment will be at Folkestone Castle, Northumberland.

It was announced that the uncertainty regarding burial arrangements was made necessary by the fact that His Grace's great-nephew, The Hon. Hugh Percival Woodburn-Haverstraw, to whom the title passes, is presently serving aboard the H.M.S. *Insubmergible*, which is now somewhere in American waters. It is expected that as soon as he can be located, and arrangements can be made, the new Duke of Folkestone will be flown to London.

During his long and distinguished naval career, which spanned forty years, His Grace served all over the world, and it is expected that his final rites will be attended by many foreign dignitaries and military groups. It has already been announced that first position in the marching order for the funeral procession has been assigned to the H.M.S. *Indefatigable* Association, membership in which is limited to those who survived the sinking of the H.M.S. *Indefatigable* which His Grace commanded at the time of her sinking in World War II.

Indeed, even as the dulcet Oxfordian diction of the announcer brought the news of the passing of His Grace

to the English people, the Hon. General Secretary of
the H.M.S. *Indefatigable* Association, Chief Gunner's
Mate Alf Whattley, Royal Navy, Retired, was in the
Sword, Crown & Anchor Hotel in a section of London
known as Canningtown, attempting to run down the one
man, Sgt. Angus MacKenzie, Royal Marines, who,
although not a member of the H.M.S. *Indefatigable*
Association, certainly would want to participate in His
Grace's last parade.

Sergeant MacKenzie had been marine orderly to His
Grace aboard the H.M.S. *Indefatigable* and had been
awarded the Victoria Cross for keeping His Grace (who
had been seriously wounded) afloat during the sixteen-
hour period between the sinking of *Indefatigable* and
their rescue by another vessel.

Over the years, Alf Whattley had frequently tried to
get in touch with MacKenzie and failed. Only after His
Grace had died had he been able to get any information
at all from the Royal Marines about MacKenzie, and
that hadn't been much—just that his pension check had
been mailed to, and apparently picked up at, the Sword,
Crown & Anchor.

One does not rise to become a chief gunner's mate
in the Royal Navy unless one can demonstrate an entirely
fearless character. And among peers, Chief Gunner's Mate
Alf Whattley enjoyed a reputation not only for fear-
lessness, but for a certain facility in barroom-brawling
ability. In the old days, Port Said, or Hong Kong, or
even Brooklyn, New York, had held no fear for Alf
Whattley. But when he stepped out of the cab in front
of the Sword, Crown & Anchor, he had to remind himself
that duty called, and that, under the circumstances, he
probably didn't have to worry much.

Still, he fixed a smile on his face, took off his hat and
knocked politely at the door before stepping into the
public rooms of the Sword, Crown & Anchor. There was
no sense in asking for trouble.

The Sword, Crown & Anchor, by virtue of the length
of its continuous operation (214 years), if for no other
reason, was a British Institution. It had been, ever since

the birth of the Royal Marines, where Royal Marines had gathered for conversation and a cheering cup. For some reason, however, it had seldom received any attention at all from the photographers of the Visit Beautiful & Historical Britain Tourist Assn., Ltd. The whole Canningtown area, truth to tell, is neither beautiful nor especially historical in the usual, tourist-attracting sense. It was generally agreed that few American tourists would want to come all the way across the Atlantic to have a look at the spot, for example, where No. 8 Company, Royal Marines, had sent 103 members of HM Warwickshire Rifles to the hospital following a disagreement over a lady. The photographers took more photos of the Tower of London.

The Sword, Crown & Anchor Hotel is a three-story building: the lower floor is occupied entirely by the public rooms, which is what the English call their saloons (often referred to as "pubs); and the second floor has six rooms (including the bridal suite) available to rent. The proprietor and his brood occupy the third floor.

The public rooms are public only in the sense that any member of the public who happens to be a Royal Marine (active or retired) may avail himself of the bar services. Others, whether civilians or members of other branches of Her Majesty's Armed Forces, are well advised to quench their thirsts elsewhere. The only exception to this Royal Marines Only custom is that members of the United States Marine Corps are welcome, as sort of nonvoting members in good standing. There is a Marine detachment at the United States Embassy, of course, and there are usually Marines aboard U.S. ships-of-the-line which call at London. Both waitresses at the Sword, Crown & Anchor know all six verses of the U.S. Marines Hymn.

The bridal suite is the only room in the hotel with a private bathroom and water closet. For that reason, over the years, it had become the room insisted upon by Royal Marines who have a bride and are in need of a connubial couch. Hence the name.

It was rented on a monthly basis now, however, by

a bachelor, known to the proprietors as Company Sgt. Maj. Angus "Black Dog" MacKenzie, Royal Marines, Retired.

Black Dog MacKenzie did not actually live in the bridal suite. He was employed (the general impression was that he was employed as a night watchman; no one dared press for details) by the East Anglia Breweries, Ltd., of East Anglia, and occupied the bridal suite only when he could get off from work to spend a few days in London with his old comrades-in-arms—an event which took place about once a month, and generally coincided with the arrival of his pension check.

It was understood between MacKenzie and the proprietor of the Sword, Crown & Anchor that the bridal suite could be rented out if he wasn't in London. All Black Dog asked was that when he was in London, there would be no honeymooners in his suite, and that it be entirely reserved for him and his wee black doggie. (The dog, a 180-pound Scottish wolfhound, had no other name. It answered to Doggie or Wee Black Doggie without discrimination.)

This arrangement had been going on for twenty-five years, with the only variant the wee black doggie. There had been a number of wee black doggies in that quarter of a century. As one wee black doggie got a little long in the tooth, and the shadow of the Grim Canine Reaper appeared on the horizon, the old wee black doggie was joined by a wee black doggie puppy; and for a while there were two 180-pound wee black doggies curled up and snarling at Angus's feet as he had a wee cup or two at the bar.

The proprietor had, he thought, deduced Angus MacKenzie's true story. Like other good-men-gone-wrong, poor Angus had gotten himself married off to some female (there had been references, when Angus was somewhat in his cups, to The Old Biddie of the Castle) who sent him and his dogs off to work each night as a night watchman, and from whom he managed to conceal the fact of his pension. On some pretext or another, Angus was able to slip away from The Old

Biddie of the Castle every now and again (probably when the Old Biddie visited her mother, or her sister, or something like that) and come to London to drink up his pension check.

Angus MacKenzie was not the sort of man into whose private affairs one dared snoop, and the proprietor asked no questions. Angus was not a subject of pity. The proprietor knew a hundred or more Good Marines who had their own Old Biddies, and who never got a chance to slip off for a couple of days with the boys.

"Excuse me, sir," said Chief Gunner's Mate Alf Whattley. "I am Chief Gunner's Mate Whattley, Royal Navy, Retired."

"Yer in the wrong place, swabbie," the proprietor said. "But because you're an old salt you can have one drink before ye shove off."

"That's very kind of you," Whattley said. "As a matter of fact, sir, I am looking for a retired marine gentleman."

"Is that so?"

"Company Sgt. Maj. Angus MacKenzie, Retired," Whattley said. "He is sometimes known as Black Dog MacKenzie."

"So what?"

"I understand he gets his pension check here."

"What are you, some kind of bill collector?"

"I am the executive secretary of the H.M.S. *Indefatigable* Association," Whattley said. "We are to march in the funeral procession of His Grace the Duke of Folkestone."

"Good for you," the proprietor said. "Drink up and start marching."

"I would like to get in contact with Sergeant Major MacKenzie," Whattley said.

"What for?"

"We would like to have him march with us in the funeral parade," Whattley said.

"What makes you think a retired Royal Marine would be seen in public with a bunch of swabbies?"

"The thing, you see, is that Sergeant Major MacKenzie

was with us on the *Indefatigable*. He kept the Captain from drowning when she went down."

"Me, personally, I have never held what a man does when he's drunk against him," the proprietor said. "Even keeping a swabbie afloat."

"The Captain was His Grace the Duke of Folkestone," Whattley said. "I wonder if you would be kind enough to give him that message."

"If I happen to see him, I will," the proprietor said, and snatched the glass from Whattley's hand.

"Thank you very much," Whattley said.

"Think nothing of it," the proprietor said, watching Whattley flee.

But once Whattley had gone, the proprietor had a chance to think. Black Dog did have the V.C., for keeping some officer afloat, and it was just possible that he would be interested. He pulled the telephone from under the bar, and asked the operator to connect him with East Anglia Breweries, Ltd.

"East Anglia Breweries, Ltd.," a cheerful female voice announced. "May I help you?"

"You got a guy what works there named MacKenzie," the proprietor of the Sword, Crown & Anchor said. "Right?"

"Would that be Mr. Angus MacKenzie of whom you inquire?" the girl said, and sounded as if she were giggling.

"That's the one. Can you call him to a phone somewheres?"

"Whom should I say is calling?" she asked, and again she tittered.

"Just tell him Sgt. Amos Davis, Royal Marines, Retired," the proprietor said.

"One moment, please."

It was a very long moment, and Amos Davis naturally assumed this was because Black Dog MacKenzie had to be summoned from some remote warehouse. That wasn't quite the case.

Early in his Royal Marine Corps career, during the late 1930's, Angus MacKenzie had become enamored of a black mongrel puppy he had found behind the Governor General's palace in New Delhi, India, around which edifice he was marching with a rifle on his shoulder, a member of the Marine Guard.

He took the mongrel with him when he went off duty, saw to it that it was fed, groomed and eventually fitted out with a marine uniform of its own. The dog—a photograph of which now hung in a place of honor over the bar of the Sword, Crown & Anchor—which had grown enormous, had gone off with MacKenzie to World War II. He had been assigned to the ship's company of the H.M.S. *Indefatigable,* a cruiser of the Kellogg class, which went down in the China Sea from four torpedoes in early 1942, taking with her sixty-five officers and five hundred other ranks and the enormous black dog. (It was for his heroic action in keeping the *Indefatigable*'s Captain, His Grace the Duke of Folkestone—who had been badly injured when the ship blew up—alive for the sixteen hours they spent in the water, that Sergeant MacKenzie had been awarded the Victoria Cross.)

Sergeant MacKenzie had been summoned to the bunk holding His Grace aboard the H.M.S. *Wellington,* the destroyer which had found them, and plucked them from the sea.

"Awfully good of you, Sergeant," His Grace had said, "to have kept me from going down."

"My pleasure, Captain," MacKenzie replied.

"And I'm dreadfully sorry about that dog, Sergeant," His Grace had said. "He was obviously a canine of incredible intelligence. I share your loss." His Grace was not just making polite remarks suited to the occasion. He had liked the dog. Not only had the dog provided many a jolly moment on a long and dull voyage, but he and Sergeant MacKenzie were the only two persons aboard the H.M.S. *Indefatigable* whom the dog had not tried to eat.

"I'm going to miss the little bugger, all right, sir," Sergeant MacKenzie had said. Tears ran unashamed down his already grizzled cheeks.

"When this war is over, Sergeant, I'll make it up to you," the Duke had said.

"Yes, sir, thank you, Your Grace," Sergeant Mac-Kenzie had said, and had promptly forgotten about the whole thing.

In a later action in the war, MacKenzie had been wounded and invalided out of the service. He had been in his home village in the Scottish Highlands three days when an ancient, but still glistening, Rolls-Royce had rolled up outside, flying a Vice Admiral's official flag from the right front fender.

"I say, MacKenzie," the Duke of Folkestone had said, "is that you in that hovel?"

"What's on your mind, Admiral?" MacKenzie had replied, somewhat impatiently.

"I have something for you," His Grace had replied.

"If I can't eat it, drink it or smoke it, Your Grace," MacKenzie had replied, "you can shove it."

"Have a look, my dear fellow," His Grace had insisted. MacKenzie had opened the door, and was promptly set on his tail by an enormous, jet-black dog who held him down with his front paws while he washed his face with an enormous, sandpapery tongue.

"Friendly little beastie, ain't he, Your Grace?" MacKenzie, visibly delighted, had said.

"I understand," His Grace had said, as he and the chauffeur had pulled the hundred-pound animal off MacKenzie, "that when they get their growth, they calm down somewhat."

"How old is he?"

"Five months," His Grace had said. "They grow till they're a year-and-a-half old."

"What kind of a dog is it?"

"It's a Scottish wolfhound," His Grace had said. "They're more intelligent than the Irish kind."

"And he's for me?"

"To replace the other one," His Grace had said, coming to attention, "who gave his life for King and Country!"

"Gone but not forgotten, Your Grace," MacKenzie

had said, snapping to attention himself. "Would Your Grace do me the great honor of hoisting a wee cup in memory of me wee black doggie?"

"I would be honored, MacKenzie," His Grace had said. "He was a credit to the Royal Marines."

"Aye, that he was, Your Grace," MacKenzie had said, reaching for a bottle and two glasses.

Two days later, when Vice Adm. His Grace Hugh Percival left the small village in the Scottish Highlands, Company Sgt. Maj. Angus MacKenzie, Royal Marines, Retired, and his wee black doggie were with him in the back seat of the Rolls.

And two weeks after that, there was a small note in the *British Brewers Journal* to the effect that Angus MacKenzie, V.C., had been elected to the office of general manager, East Anglia Breweries, Ltd., by unanimous vote of the stockholders, replacing Vice Admiral His Grace the Duke of Folkstone in that position. Since it was generally known that the Duke of Folkstone was East Anglia Breweries, Ltd.'s, sole stockholder, Angus MacKenzie had very little trouble taking the reins in his hands.

Very few of his associates at East Anglia Breweries, Ltd., had any idea that he was a retired sergeant major. When the rumor popped up from time to time, it was quickly discounted. Certainly, the closest friend of Vice Admiral His Grace the Duke of Folkstone, his boon companion stalking deer on the moors, Cape Buffalo in Kenya, and, it was whispered, certain two-legged game on various beaches and promenades around Europe, could not possibly have been a common enlisted man.

"Are you still holding for Mr. MacKenzie, sir?" the operator asked.

"This is an emergency," Amos said. "Otherwise I wouldn't bother him at work. Thank you kindly."

"Amos?" MacKenzie's voice came on the line.

"That you, Black Dog?"

"What can I do for you, Amos?" MacKenzie asked. "You in some sort of trouble?"

"Black Dog, there was a swabbie in here just now, looking for you."

"What did he want?"

"He wants you to march in the funeral parade of the Duke of Folkestone. I didn't know how you'd feel about that, but I figured I'd better let you know. I didn't tell him where you was, or anything. He belongs to the H.M.S. *Indefatigable* Association, or something like that."

"I appreciate the call, Amos," MacKenzie said. "How did you know where to reach me?"

"I knew you worked for East Anglia," Amos said. "I hope I didn't get you in trouble with your boss, Black Dog."

"Don't worry about that," MacKenzie said. "Don't rent out my room, Amos. I'll be going to the funeral. I'll be in London just as soon as I take care of a few things around here."

"If it's money that's bothering you, Black Dog, just say the word and I'll telegraph you a couple of pounds."

"It isn't the money, Amos, but I'm grateful for the offer."

"The Old Biddie in the Castle is the problem, huh?"

"How," asked Angus "Black Dog" MacKenzie in utter surprise, "do you know about her?"

"Sometimes, when ye've had a few, Black Dog, you let things slip. Are you sure you can get off from work?"

"I can fix that all right, Amos," Black Dog said. "I'll see you in a day or so. And thank you for calling."

He broke the connection with his finger, and then paused thoughtfully, holding the telephone in his hand. For the first time in his life, since he was eighteen years old and had been named corporal of the Royal Marine Corps, Angus MacKenzie had two problems to solve without the foggiest idea about how to solve either.

The first problem was the boy. Black Dog MacKenzie could clearly hear in his memory the Duke of Folkestone's high, piercing, somewhat adenoidal voice: "Should anything ever happen to me before he's a man, Black

Dog, I'll want you to keep an eye on him for me. I know I can trust you."

Black Dog MacKenzie willingly accepted the responsibility. The problem was that he had no idea how to discharge that responsibility.

The second problem was The Old Biddie in the Castle, otherwise known as Miss Florabelle Jenkins, Executive Castlekeeper, Folkestone Castle.

He lifted his finger from the telephone switch. Immediately, his secretary came on the line.

"Yes, Mr. MacKenzie?"

"Have them bring the Rolls around," he said. "I'll be going up the Castle, and then if I live through that, I'll be going into London." He hung up. He straightened his shoulders, as if in anticipation of his meeting with Miss Florabelle Jenkins, and then marched toward the door, thirty-five feet across the room from his desk.

"Come along, Wee Black Doggie," he said, and snapped his fingers. A 184-pound Scottish wolfhound stretched luxuriously, over about eight feet, nose-to-tail, and then trotted after him, tail wagging slowly from side to side.

# Chapter Seven

At Andrews Air Force Base, just outside Washington, D.C., the United States Air Force maintains an organization known as the 3505th Special Missions Wing. While the name suggests, probably on purpose, some sterling military purpose, such as dropping spies behind enemy lines or flying courageously into the eye of a hurricane, what the 3505th really does is far less romantic, although far more costly to the taxpayer.

The mission of the 3505th Special Missions Wing, which received Congressional approval by "unanimous voice vote," states in part that it is to "maintain aircraft and other facilities necessary to provide essential aerial transportation to the President of the United States, the Vice President of the United States and other senior governmental officials in the execution of their official duties."

It is generally agreed on Capitol Hill that everyone connected in any way with the Congress of the United States (with the possible exception of the public servant in charge of filling Congressional inkwells) falls within the category of a "senior governmental official."

Most people are under the erroneous impression (possibly because a good deal of high-priced public-relations effort is expended to give the erroneous impression) that the 3505th Special Missions Wing is concerned mainly with the fleet of DC-9's plushly fitted out to ferry the President hither and yon. (Fleet is correct: The last time someone counted there were four DC-9's reserved for the President and his staff. Whichever one happens to be airborne with the President is Air Force One; the others are kept in reserve for important, official governmental purposes, such as carrying in-favor California Congressmen across the nation to mend political fences.)

There are, in addition, other aircraft, ranging from small jet Aero Commanders, carrying only six people and costing no more than a million dollars each, to intermediate-sized (ten to twenty passengers) airplanes of the type normally used to transport tycoons of industry about their empires. These aircraft are those in most frequent use, especially around Congressional recess time. Arriving at the hometown airport in a glistening Air Force Sabreliner serves not only to remind constituents of the high regard in which their Distinguished Solon is held by the Defense Department, but is also considerably more economical than using, for example, Eastern Air Lines.

For this reason, what was called the "high usage factor," the United States Air Force was not able to immediately respond to the request of the Hon. Edwards L. "Smiling Jack" Jackson (Farmer—Free Silver, Arkansas) for aerial transport for himself and key members of his staff to London, England, where the Congressman planned to look into the manifest problems involved with Anglo-American Relations on the High Seas.

The Congressman and his staff had to wait two whole hours until a plane could be freshly fueled, stocked with booze and food, rolled up to the plushly appointed V.I.P. waiting room at Andrews and made available to him. The Congressman, who had been serving his nation for nearly a quarter of a century and had risen high on seniority, was not used to such an outrageous delay in his planned travel. The Congressman's ill mood, morever, was heightened when L. Bryan Fowler, his administrative assistant, told him where they were going and what they were supposed to be doing. The Congressman had somehow gotten the idea that they were going to Bali again to investigate, on behalf of American Womanhood, the long-range effects of going without upper undergarments. The Congressman had liked Bali. From what he remembered of London (he had been there three times before, but never entirely sober), it was rainy and foggy and most of the women were fully clothed.

But anything, L. Bryan Fowler reminded him, was better than going home to Swampy Meadows, Arkansas, and Mrs. Jackson, which was the only viable alternative to going to London. That thought cheered the Congressman somewhat, and he was only mumbling his displeasure, rather than orating his outrage, when he was led out of the V.I.P. Lounge and helped up the stairway to the glistening Sabreliner.

The door was closed and the engines started. The Sabreliner moved away from the V.I.P. Terminal to the threshold of the active runway. The pilot, who had long experience in the hauling about of Congressional personages and knew their little likes and dislikes rather well, switched his radio so that his conversation with the tower could be heard inside the passenger compartment.

"Andrews Departure Control," he said. "V.I.P. Flight

Three-Oh-One. Direct London, with Congressman
Jackson aboard. Request take-off permission."

There was something about that message which brought
a smile to the Congressman's face. There were some
benefits which accrued to those who served their country
long and well. Fog and rain or not, going to London
on a private jet sure beat hell out of spending the next
two weeks with all those dummies back in Swampy
Meadows, Arkansas. Then the Congressman's smile faded
as Andrews Departure Control spoke back.

"Three-Oh-One, hold in position. We have two more
passengers for you."

"What's this? What's this? I'm far too busy a man
to cater to aerial hitchhikers," Congressman Jackson
spluttered. "Fowler, straighten this out!"

L. Bryan Fowler, who had been checking to see that
this particular Sabreliner did indeed convert into aerial
*chambres séparées,* rushed forward to the cockpit. The
last thing he himself wanted was to share the Sabreliner with a bunch of party poopers. He had once been
on a junket with a Senator who, previously a rational
man, had been saved by an itinerant Evangelist just before
take-off time, and had spent the twelve-hour flight to
Hong Kong on his knees reading aloud from the Bible
and exhorting the others to repent. It had been a ghastly
experience, and Fowler was determined that it should
not happen again.

"What's going on here?" Fowler demanded of the
pilot. "Congressman Jackson is expected in London right
now."

"I don't know, Mr. Fowler," the pilot said. "All I
know is what came over the radio."

"Well, get on the radio and tell them Congressman
Jackson waits for no man."

The pilot nodded and picked up his microphone.
"Andrews Departure Control, V.I.P. Flight Three-Oh-
One. Congressman Jackson says he can't wait."

"Roger, Three-Oh-One," the radio replied immediately. "Message understood. Hold your position.
Passengers are on the way to you from the terminal."

Smiling Jack heard this of course. He got somewhat unsteadily to his feet and lurched up the aisle to the cockpit.

"Pilot," he announced pontifically, "you inform whomever it is that you're talking to that unless this airplane starts moving immediately and without further delay that the third-ranking member of the House Subcommittee on Sewers, Subways and Sidewalks will complain personally to the Secretaries of State and Defense."

The pilot dutifully repeated the message, verbatim.

"Andrews Departure Control advises V.I.P. Flight Three-Oh-One to hold in position to facilitate transmission of official complaint," the radio responded.

"What the hell does that mean?" Congressman Jackson asked.

At that moment, the door in the rear of the cabin opened and two men climbed aboard.

"Andrews Departure Control advises V.I.P. Flight Three-Oh-One that your flight is now designated Air Force Three," the radio said.

"Mr. Secretary!" Smiling Jack Jackson said, in shocked surprise, as the Secretary, breathing hard, staggered up the aisle, trailed by a puffing, red-faced Quincy Westerbrook.

"You look like a bright boy," the Secretary said to the pilot. "You think maybe you can find Spruce Harbor, Maine?"

"Yes, sir, Mr. Secretary," the pilot said. "If it's on the map, we'll get you there."

"Dat may pose a liddle problem," the Secretary said. "Fly to Maine. Ve'll ask somebody."

"Andrews Departure Control," the radio interrupted, "clears Air Force Three for immediate take-off, for direct flight wherever the Secretary tells you he wants to go."

"Mr. Secretary," Congressman Jackson said, very respectfully, "may I ask, presuming the national security will permit a reply, what pressing business of state requires the presence of our distinguished Secretary of State in Spruce Harbor, Maine?"

The radio was still plugged into the public-address system. The Secretary had to wait before replying as the loudspeaker boomed: "Andrews Departure Control, Air Force Three rolling!"; and then, slumped in a chair, his chest heaving from the exertion of the long run from the terminal building, the Secretary of State replied. "Lissen, Jackson," he said, "confidentially, if I vas to tell you, you vouldn't believe it, believe me." He looked up at the steward who was hovering anxiously over his seat. "Maybe you could find me a little glass Manischewitz Concord? You vouldn't believe vat a day dis has been."

L. Bryan Fowler, whose face had been wreathed in what looked like mourning when he feared their junket would be spoiled, was now smiling from ear to ear. It wasn't every day that Smiling Jack could get into the same building with the Secretary; and now, here he was, flying off God-knows-where with him alone! The possibilities for news releases which would really get Lard-belly on the front page instead of buried between fertilizer prices and Sears, Roebuck Foundation Garment advertisements on page 34 were boundless:

> *Congressman Jackson, the Secretary of State's trusted adviser in the House* . . .
> *With Congressman Jackson at his side, the Secretary of State arrived here today* . . .
> *After conferring with the Secretary of State, Congressman Jackson announced* . . .

Fowler made a few quick notes on his ever-present notepad, and then decided to take a chance

"Mr. Secretary," he said, "I am L. Bryan Fowler."

"You should excuse me, I got enough of my own problems," the Secretary said.

"Mr. Secretary," L. Bryan Fowler pursued, "have you been giving much thought recently to Anglo-American Relations on the High Seas?"

At that moment, as the Secretary of State's mouth dropped open in surprise, Peggy-Lou Kastenmeyer, administrative assistant to Administrative Assistant L.

Bryan Fowler, stuck her head into the aisle and opened hers. "Poopsie," she announced coyly, "Peggy-Lou's got the bed unfolded. Does that give Poopsie any ideas?"

"Not now, you dumb broad!" L. Bryan Fowler shouted. "Cool it!" From the look of pain on the Secretary's face, he knew he was on to something.

"Vy do you ask?" the Secretary said, noncomittally.

"Congressman Jackson is en route to England to fully investigate the matter," L. Bryan Fowler said.

The Secretary of State put his hands to his eyes. "Security, schmurity," he said. "Ve got the F.B.I., ve got the C.I.A., ve got security people for the security people, and still that place leaks like a sieve." He raised his eyes and met L. Bryan Fowler's. "You vouldn't vant to tell me how you found oudt?"

"Let me say," L. Bryan Fowler said, "speaking for Congressman Jackson, of course, that we're in this with you, Mr. Secretary, to the end."

"My mama warned me," the Secretary said. " 'Stay where you are,' she said. 'You got a nice steady job teaching school. So why give it up to take a temporary, no-future job with the government?' " He looked up at Fowler. "I used to think I was a pretty smart fella. So maybe you can tell me vy I didn't lissen to my mama?"

Nymphomania, as some wise man once wrote, is no respector of position or class. It affects the common folk as well as those born to high social position. In the case of Lady Chastity Cheppingwhite-Browne, only daughter of the late Duke of Crimley and his Duchess, it could be fairly said—and indeed was said—that Lady Chastity was a chippy off the old blockheads.

At twenty-four, Lady Chastity had been around. She knew, for example, in the Biblical sense of the word, every officer of the Household Cavalry save the Colonel Commanding. The Colonel Commanding was sixty-two and moreover had never displayed more than a casual interest in the opposite sex—a Freudian barrier that even Charity, seeking a perfect record, could not overcome.

She was similarly well acquainted with the officers and ranks of other royal military organizations. She was probably the only woman in the world personally privy to the answer to that age-old question concerning what the Scotsmen of *all* the Highland regiments wear under their kilts.

Having working her way through the military services by the age of twenty-two, Lady Chastity had next turned her attention to politics. It was generally agreed that she knew more intimate secrets about Members of Parliament than her Majesty's Prime Minister and Scotland Yard combined. Lady Chastity, however, had quickly become bored with affairs of state and had moved into the world of art. She quickly came to *know*, as it were, most of the familiar names in belles lettres and fine art (those, of course, who were interested in the female, say, not more than fifty percent) and then became, at twenty-four, enthralled with modern music, especially that kind exported from the United States of America.

When the Duke of Folkestone had made his final exit from the Dorchester Hotel, Lady Chastity was in the building. She did not hear the shots fired at His Grace by Lieut. Gen. Sir Archibald Sommersby, neither those in the corridors and lobby nor those in the park across the street. She was at the time intimately engaged with Dongo the Great, a tall, wild-haired, mustachioed youth, born Elmer Wilson in Apple Valley, Kansas, and now employed as lead guitarist for the hard-rock musical ensemble known to the world's youth as Porky Pig & The Swine.

It was only when they took off the earphones they had been wearing (Dongo the Great prided himself on never being far from the sound of his own music) and untangled the cords that Lady Chastity learned from the rest of The Swine (actually from Porky Pig himself, who had been leading the cheering) that His Grace had moved on to that great Maison Tolerée in the Sky.

She didn't think much about it at the time, and was rather surprised when her mother, Her Grace the Duchess

of Crimley, appeared at The Swine's suite at half-past
nine the next morning.

"Darling," Her Grace said, "I hate to tear you from
your little friends, but we must have a little mother-
daughter chat."

"At this time of the morning?" Lady Chastity asked.
"I just got to sleep."

"Trust Mommy, darling," Her Grace said. "This is
important."

"It better be," Lady Chastity said, menacingly. She
dressed (in a headband; a T-shirt on which was printed
the Japanese flag and the word NIPPONESE; and a cutoff
pair of ten-year-old Levi's) and stepping over Porky
Pig, who was alseep on the floor, followed her mother
out of the suite, down the elevator and out of the lobby
of the Dorchester to the familiar Rolls-Royce.

"What's with the Rolls?" Lady Chastity asked as she
got into the back. "The last time you came around
mooching money, you complained you couldn't afford
to buy gas for it."

"It is sometimes necessary, as your American friends
put it so aptly, to spend money to make money," Her
Grace said.

"What's that supposed to mean?"

"Darling," her mother said, "are you aware that the
Duke of Folkestone is no longer with us?"

"I heard about it," Lady Chastity said. "What's that
got to do with me?"

"I'm sure you remember, darling, the Hon. Hugh
Percival Woodburn-Haverstraw?"

"No," Lady Chastity said. "I don't."

"Yes, you do," her mother said, firmly. "He is that
simply darling boy you met at the Furness Hunt two
years ago."

"You mean that pimply faced kid who kept falling
off his horse? What about him?"

"On the death of His Grace," Her Grace said, "that
poor child is all alone in the world . . ."

"That's the way the cookie crumbles," Lady Chastity
said.

"With an income, after taxes, of about three thousand pounds."

"You can get by on three thousand a year," Lady Chastity said. "I do. You have to watch yourself, but you can get by."

"A *week,* darling," Her Grace said.

"Mommy," Lady Chastity said, "we must rush to poor whatsisname's side, to stand by him in his hour of need."

"I was thinking precisely the same thing," Her Grace said.

"Is that where we're going now?" Lady Chastity asked, rather eagerly.

"No. The poor orphaned lamb is in America . . . "

"What the hell's he doing in America? He's liable to be snapped up by some American bird before . . ."

"His Grace is serving aboard the H.M.S. *Insubmergible,*" the Duchess of Crimley said, "but I understand from friends in the Admiralty that he will be rushed home for the funeral."

"Then where are you going now?"

"To Harrods," the Duchess said, "to get you some appropriate clothing."

"I thought Harrods shut off your credit?" Lady Chastity said. "And what's wrong with what I'm wearing?"

"I think we must keep in mind that His Grace has led a rather sheltered life," the Duchess said. "And dressed that way, precious, Mommy is afraid you might come on a little strong."

"He's in the navy, is he? Sailors spend a lot of time away from home, don't they?"

"No sacrifice is too great in the service of the Queen," the Duchess said.

"Three *thousand* a *week!*" Lady Chastity said. "And him gone most of the time!"

"That is a conservative estimate," the Duchess said.

"I always suspected," Lady Chastity said, "that one day I would be swept off my feet by someone, someone of my own position and class. Mommy, have you seen him lately? Does he still have that ghastly acne?"

"I think the acne will pass with the love of a good woman," the Duchess said. "I've noticed that none of your little friends seem to suffer with it."

"How are we going to get close to him?" Lady Chastity asked.

"I have taken the liberty of sending a radiogram in your name," the Duchess said. She handed a carbon to Lady Chastity.

CRIMLEY CASTLE
NORTHUMBERLAND

MIDSHIPMAN HIS GRACE HUGE PERCIVAL,
  THE DUKE OF FOLKESTONE
ABOARD H.M.S. INSURMERGIBLE AT SEA

MOMMY AND I ARE WAITING WITH OPEN ARMS,
DEAR HUGH, TO COMFORT YOU IN YOUR HOUR OF
SORROW. ADVISE TIME AND PLACE OF ARRIVAL BY
RADIO SO THAT WE MAY MEET YOU AND STAND BY
YOU WITH ALL OUR LOVE AND UNDERSTANDING.
WE YEARN TO TAKE YOU IN OUR ARMS.

                              YOUR CHASTITY

"What's this 'we yearn to take you in *our* arms' business?" Lady Chastity demanded. "You keep *your* arms off my darling whatsisname, Mommy, or you'll walk down the aisle in Westminster Abbey with both of them in casts!"

"Merely a figure of speech, precious," the Duchess said. "A figure of speech."

"Yeah?" Lady Chastity snarled. "Well, don't get any funny ideas."

"Here we are, darling," the Duchess said. "At Harrods."

Her Grace the Duchess of Crimley and Lady Chastity Cheppingwhite-Browne made it all the way to Finer-

Quality Ladies' Garments before word of their arrival reached the credit department and a representative of management could rush to intercept them. In Harrods's files, the Duchess and her daughter were classified as D.B.E., or Dead Beats Extraordinary.

"Good morning, Your Grace," the man from the credit department said. "Lady Chastity, you're looking well. Just browsing, I trust?"

"My daughter, my good man," the Duchess said, "will require a complete outfitting."

"That, unfortunately," he said, "as much as we value your patronage, brings up the unpleasant matter of your account, Your Grace."

"What about my account?" the Duchess asked, in high umbrage.

"Oh, shut up, Mommy," Lady Chastity said. From the hip pocket of her blue jeans, she extracted and handed over a small plastic card, reading AMERICAN EXPRESS. "We'll use this," she said.

"Excuse me, Lady Chastity," the credit manager said, "but this card is made out to 'Dongo the Great'."

"That's my professional name," Lady Chastity said, smoothly, "for tax purposes, you understand."

"I see," the credit manager said. "I'll just verify that, if you don't mind." He walked away.

"I suppose the card is legitimate," the Duchess said, "but how are you going to explain this to Mr. Dongo?"

"As the Duchess of Folkestone," said Lady Chastity, "I will not have to explain very much of anything to anyone," she said.

"How right you are, darling," the Duchess said, and in a burst of maternal pride, leaned over and kissed Lady Chastity on the cheek. "Blood always tells, I always say."

# Chapter Eight

The next regularly scheduled flight into Spruce Harbor International Airport was not until the day after tomorrow at three in the afternoon, so normally there would have been no one on duty in the Spruce Harbor International Airport Control Tower.

But the morning's mail had brought to Wrong Way Napolitano, proprietor of the Spruce Harbor Air-Taxi Service, in a plain brown wrapper, that month's issue of *Playboyo Italiano,* and past experience had taught him that it was best to peruse this journal of Romanish pulchritude somewhere far from the family hearth. The deserted control tower, which was equipped with several stout locks, as well as ominous warnings to the unauthorized to make themselves scarce, was ideal for this purpose.

Wrong Way was not especially surprised to see from his glass-walled reading room in-the-sky that there was some transient traffic. Parked on the field were an amphibious De Havilland Beaver and a sleek North American Sabreliner, each bearing some oil company's insignia on its fuselage. He paid little attention to them. Oil-company aircraft were a fairly common sight, bearing either workers into the Canadian wilds in search of oil, or oil-company executives into the Canadian wilds in search of fish.

Wrong Way had just turned to that month's feature article, an historic, photographic re-creation of Pompeii's places of amusement two days before the ashes fell, when the radio loudspeaker sputtered into life.

"Spruce Harbor International, this is Air Force Three."

Wrong Way picked up the microphone without taking

his eyes from a detailed re-creation of a Pompeiian massage parlor.

"This is Spruce Harbor," he said. "We're closed for the day."

"Spruce Harbor," the radio barked, "Air Force Three is fifteen minutes from your station. We have an in-flight advisory message for Benjamin F. Pierce, M.D. Can you handle?"

"Roger, Air Force Three," Wrong Way said.

"Message follows, quote: 'Urgent you meet me on arrival Spruce Harbor concerning matter of national importance. Signed, the Secretary of State.'"

"Roger, message received," Wrong Way said. He had, without taking his eyes from the magazine, slipped a sheet of paper into a typewriter and typed out the message, This is, as odd as it sounds, a character trait fairly common among radio operators. They develop, over the years, an ability to function at two or more levels. They can, for example, receive radio messages (even those in Morse code) and perfectly transcribe them with a typewriter, while simultaneously carrying on a conversation, eating lunch or, as in Wrong Way's case, staring bug-eyed at an historical photo re-creation of what Nero was actually doing, with what and to whom, while Rome burned. The only flaw in this multilevel functioning is that they have no idea what the message which they have faultlessly transcribed said. The contents do not register, in other words, on their own consciousnesses.

Neither was Wrong Way really aware that he had responded to a request—"Please give landing instructions"—from Air Force Three. He had, for a brief, reluctant moment, lifted his eyes from the magazine and quickly scanned the array of instruments in front of him. His eyes were already back on the magazine before his mouth opened and he said, "Spruce Harbor clears Air Force Three as number-one to land on Runway Two-Seven. The winds are from the north and negligible; the altimeter is two-nine-nine and the time is one-five past the hour. Instrument flight plans should be closed out with Rockland Central. Fuel, minor repairs, and home-cooked Italian food, featuring lasagna and veal scallopini, are available at the Napolitano Aviation Service, which may be found by turning right off the active runway at Taxiway Three. Welcome to Spruce Harbor."

He had made a similar announcement a thousand times before and was, to put it bluntly, rather bored with the whole business, especially since he now had the opportunity to fill in certain blanks in Roman history which, for some reason, had been excluded from the curriculum of his alma mater, Blessed Virgin Junior High School.

Thirteen-and-a-half minutes later, as he was vicariously enjoying the fringe benefits of a gladiator of two thousand years ago (which fringe benefits, according to the historians in the magazine, made the fringe benefits of even Joe Namath look pretty dull), he was rudely brought back to the twentieth century: first, by the radio suddenly blaring the message "Spruce Harbor, Air Force Three turning on final to Runway Two-Seven" in his ear; and then, by the whistling roar of a North American Sabreliner whooshing by the tower with the speed brakes and landing gear out and screaming in the wind.

His eyes fell upon the typewriter and, for the first time, he read what he had typed thirteen-and-a-half minutes before. He shook his head, and read it again. He hadn't made a mistake in transcribing a radio message since he had been, in World War II, Pfc. Napolitano, Army Air Corps radio operator; so he would have to accept the message as fact.

The fact was confirmed visually. There was a U.S. Air Force Sabreliner on the ground out there. The sound of its powerful engines in reverse thrust reached his ears, and the plane slowed and swung around on the runway and started taxiing back toward the terminal.

Wrong Way grabbed for a telephone and dialed a number.

"Finest-Kind Medical Center and Fish Market," a charming female voice said. "May I help you?"

"I got to speak to Hawkeye right now!" Wrong Way said.

"I'm very sorry," the voice cooed, "but Dr. Pierce is in consultation at the moment and not available. Would you care to leave a message?"

"Where is he?"

"I'm sorry, I am not at liberty to give out that information," the voice said, oozing sincere regret.

"What would you say if I was to tell you that the Secretary of State has just landed out here at the airport and wants to see Hawkeye right away on a matter of national importance?" Wrong Way demanded.

"If you were to tell me that," the voice said, "I would be forced to the reluctant conclusion, Wrong Way, that you've been hitting the Chianti again," the charming female voice said.

"Mabel, for God's sake, let me talk to Hawkeye!" Wrong Way pleaded.

"Hold on, please," she said. There was a pause, some clicking noises, and then a male voice, not at all charming.

"Yeah?"

Wrong Way thought the voice was familiar and he listened a moment before saying anything. Sure enough, in the background, he could hear the sounds of shrill female laughter and breaking glass and male voices joined in bawdy song. He was connected with the Bide-a-While Pool Hall/Ladies Served Fresh Lobster & Clams Daily Restaurant and Saloon, Inc.,* and indeed talking to its proprietor.

"This is Wrong Way, Stanley," he said. "Let me talk to Hawkeye."

"Nobody here by that name," Stanley said.

"For God's sake, Stanley, tell him the Secretary of State is here," Wrong Way said.

There was a long pause, the silence punctuated only by the sound of Stanley K. Warczinski sucking thought-

---

* The name of the establishment, which was posted outside in its entirety, was the result of a free offer from the Coca-Cola people. They told the proprietor he could put any name at all on the sign, just so it also said "Coke." Stanley K. Warczinski knew a bargain when one came his way.

fully on his loose dentures. But then, finally, Wrong Way heard Stanley bellow.

"Hey, Hawkeye," he called, "Wrong Way's on the phone. Drunk as a lord. Says the Secretary of State is here."

Hawkeye came on the phone a moment later. "What's up, Wrong Way?"

"Hawkeye, you're not gonna believe this . . ."

"You're pregnant?"

"The Secretary of State just landed out here," Wrong Way said.

"Is that so?"

"He wants to see you," Wrong Way went on, "on a matter of national importance."

"In that case, send him right over," Hawkeye said. "I'll try to squeeze him in between the steamed clams and the lobster." The phone went dead in Wrong Way's ear. He removed it, looked at it disbelievingly, and then glanced out the plate-glass windows of the control tower again. The Air Force Sabreliner was now stopped in front of the terminal building. As Wrong Way watched, the rear door opened, a stairway unfolded, and the Secretary of State appeared and began to walk down it.

Wrong Way ran down the stairs from the control tower, taking them three at a time. He knew his patriotic duty when he saw it.

The Hon. Edwards L. "Smiling Jack" Jackson (Farmer—Free Silver, Arkansas) had, while waiting in the V.I.P. Room at Andrews Air Force Base, taken a little bourbon-and-branch to pass the time. He had taken a little more, once aboard the aircraft, to settle his stomach against the rigors of the flight. He'd had two more to ease his disappointment about going to London instead of Bali; and then one more after Ground Control had ordered the plane to hold its position to wait upon two more passengers. And then, of course, it had been necessary to celebrate with a cheering cup his fortuitous meeting with the Secretary of State.

All in all, Smiling Jack had consumed very nearly all

of the Congressional size (quart-and-a-half) bottle of
Wild Turkey bourbon* he had with him. Under the
circumstances, L. Bryan Fowler realized, this was a
blessing in disguise. Sober, Congressman Jackson might
have objected to being driven through some God-forsaken
fishing town on the rock-bound coast of Maine in the
bed of a battered and rusty pickup truck, perched
somewhat precariously atop a lobster trap.

The Secretary of State, ever the gentleman, had insisted, of course, that Ms. Peggy-Lou Kastenmeyer ride
up front with the driver, a wild-eyed Italian who had
rushed breathlessly up to the plane to announce that none
of the town's three taxicabs were available (they had
been engaged, on a 24-hour-a-day basis, the Italian had
said, without further amplification, "by the Arabs") but
that he would be honored to put his truck at their service,
without charge, in order that the Secretary of State could
be taken to his rendezvous with Benjamin Franklin Pierce,
M.D.

The Secretary, again manifesting that unshockable
*savoir faire* which had made him world-famous, had
immediately accepted the offer, bowed Peggy-Lou into
the front seat and then helped Fowler push, haul and
drag Congressman Jackson into the back of the truck
and prop him up on the lobster trap.

The trip from the airport to a long, rambling, ominous-
appearing roadhouse on the other side of town had been
accomplished with only minor incident. The truck had
skidded to a stop for a red light in what was apparently
downtown Spruce Harbor. Smiling Jack, who had been
dozing, was awakened by the scream of the brakes and
squeal of the tires. When he saw the gathering (the town's
youth, gathered outside the Ajax Billiard Parlor), he
had instinctively risen to his feet and begun his standard

---

* It was part of a case presented to him, in small token of the respect and
affection in which he was held, by lobbyists of the American Association of
Sweet-Potato Growers. Although sweet potatoes had never been grown in
Arkansas, Congressman Jackson was conversant with, and sympathetic to,
the problems of sweet-potato growers. He could be counted upon, in other
words, to faithfully vote to perpetuate the government payment to farmers
in Mississippi, Louisiana and Texas not to grow sweet potatoes.

speech ("I am privileged and deeply honored to be with you all tonight . . . ") and had almost gone over the side when the Italian put the pickup truck in gear and raced off when the light turned green.

At the roadhouse, however, L. Bryan Fowler came to realize how little even someone in his in-the-know position really knew about secret diplomacy. Standing outside the roadhouse, glistening submachine guns held menacingly in their hands, were two Arabs, in flowing robes. His already deep respect for the Secretary's ability to cope with explosive situations rose when the Secretary jumped nimbly from the bed of the pickup, embraced each Arab in turn, and then chatted briefly with them in what sounded like Arabic. (The only word that Fowler thought he recognized was "Hawkeye" which was obviously the code name of some super-secret mission.)

"You vant to take a chance," the Secretary called, "you can come in."

L. Bryan Fowler had desperately wanted to accompany the Secretary inside the building to become part of this top-level hush-hush international confab, but he was realistic enough to think the time wasn't ripe; that he would first have to convince the Secretary that he was the sort of man who could be trusted with the nation's most sacred secrets. Truth to tell, if he were the Secretary, there weren't very many Congressional administrative assistants he would trust with the time of day.

But the invitation had been extended. This was obviously his lucky day. He pushed Smiling Jack out of the truck and got him on his feet. As he led him toward the roadhouse, Peggy-Lou Kastenmeyer stuck her head out of the pickup cab and whined, "Poopsie, I thought you said we were going to London?"

"Shut up, you dumb broad," L. Bryan Fowler said, without thinking.

"I don't know where you're from, Mac," the wild-eyed Italian shouted at him, "but in Spruce Harbor, Maine, we don't talk to lovely little ladies like that. You looking for a fat lip?"

L. Bryan Fowler fixed a smile on his face. "I apologize," he said.

"You're cute!" Peggy-Lou Kastenmeyer said to Wrong Way Napolitano, who blushed.

The Secretary of State pushed open the swinging doors to the Bide-a-While Pool Hall/Ladies Served Fresh Lobster and Clams Daily Restaurant and Saloon, Inc., and stepped inside.

His way was barred by six-feet-four-inches and 260 pounds of Polish muscle, sinew and loose dentures named Stanley K. Warczinsky, who inquired, "Something for you, Doc?"

"I understand that Hawkeye is here," the Secretary said, flashing the smile that had melted the hearts of Syrians, Israelis, Chinese, Russians and Egyptians. It didn't do a thing to Stanley K. Warczinski.

"Nobody here by that name," Stanley announced flatly. It was the key to his business success. When his now-sprawling establishment had been nothing more than a frame shack offering nothing but steamed clams and draft beer, Stanley had seen the light. No one wanted to be interrupted by wives, friends, insurance salesmen or anyone else when engaged in something as important as eating clams and drinking beer. His first rule as an innkeeper would be, henceforth and forever more, he had vowed, that his customers should not be disturbed. Keeping that vow had seen his business prosper beyond his wildest dreams.

"Is there the slightest chance," the Secretary asked, "that you could be mistaken? I have it on good authority that Hawkeye . . . perhaps you know him as Doctor Pierce? . . . is in this splendid establishment."

"I thought you looked familiar," Stanley K. Warczinski said. "You're that shyster lawyer from Portland. If there's one thing I can't stand, it's a Canuck ambulance chaser bothering my customers."

"Perhaps you would be good enough to permit me to look around?"

"Get out of here, you bum!" Stanley said, and picked up his well-used Louisville Slugger Joe DiMaggio Home

Run King baseball bat. "And take your drunken pals with you." This last observation made reference to Congressman Jackson and L. Bryan Fowler, who were now standing behind the Secretary.

"It's O.K., Stanley," a familiar voice said. With enormous relief, the Secretary saw the face of John Francis McIntyre, M.D., F.A.C.S.

"So, Trapper, how's by you?" the Secretary said.

"You know this creep?" Stanley asked, reluctantly lowering the Louisville Slugger.

"Stanley, you are addressing a very well-known public servant," Trapper said. "This is the Secretary of State."

Stanley K. Warczinski began to tremble. His face took on a strange contorted appearance. His chest heaved. His massive abdomen jiggled like a bowl of Jell-O. A strange noise came out of his throat, a deep, burbling growl. Tears began to run down his stubbled cheeks. The Secretary looked at him with horror and concern, as he collapsed helplessly into his chair, his hands gathered around his massive belly. Stanley K. Warczinski was laughing.

As Trapper led the Secretary, the Congressman and Fowler toward a table in the rear of the room, Stanley K. Warczinski spoke. "Trapper, you ought to go on the TV! You're a lot funnier than even Walter Cronkite."

His Royal Highness Prince Hassan ad Kayam, a large white bib reading COURTESY SPRUCE HARBOR FUNERAL HOME hung around his neck, laid down the lobster claw from which he had been sucking the meat and bowed.

"Your Excellency," he said. "What an unexpected pleasure. Will you join us?"

"Your Highness," the Secretary said, returning the bow. "What brings you . . . wherever we are?"

"Whatever you want, Chubby," Hawkeye said, by way of greeting, "the answer is no."

"More lobsters," Trapper John called over his shoulder, "and more suds."

"You're looking vell, Hawkeye," the Secretary said.

"So how's the practice? Making a liddle money, are you?"

"Unless you've taken over the Internal Revenue, too," Hawkeye said, suspiciously. "You didn't come all the way up here to ask how's my practice. What's on your mind, Little Man? Out with it."

"So, all right," the Secretary said. Mrs. Stanley K. Warczinski suddenly appeared. She was an inch taller and forty pounds heavier than her husband. In her left hand, she balanced a trayful of steaming lobsters, at least eight. In her right hand, she easily grasped three half-gallon pitchers of beer. She laid the tray of lobsters on the table, put her massive paw on the Secretary's head, pushed him into a chair, laid the schooners of beer on the table and firmly knotted a COURTESY SPRUCE HARBOR FUNERAL HOME bib around his neck. All this took no more than fifteen seconds.

"Any friend of Hawkeye's is a friend of mine," she said. "Pleased to meetcha."

"You were saying?" Hawkeye said.

"Hawkeye," the Secretary said, "you got a patient, I understand, by the name Woodburn-Haverstraw?"

"You came all the way up here about Woody?" Hawkeye asked. The Secretary nodded. "Mr. Secretary, I owe you an apology," Hawkeye went on. "I take back all those nasty things I've been saying all these years about our insensitive government."

"Excuse me?" the Secretary said.

"Under these circumstances, I'm glad to see you," Hawkeye said. "Have a lobster. And put your mind at rest."

"Maybe you could explain?"

"Just as soon as Woody's fit to travel . . . which will be two hours after we're sure nobody's going to put him back on the boat with Captain Bligh . . . we're going to fly him home to England," Hawkeye said. "Boris has to be in London in a couple . . . "

"That vouldn't, God forbid, be Boris Alexandrovich Korsky-Rimsakov?"

"None other," Hawkeye said. "I've got Woody in

with Boris in a room at the hospital. He and Boris and Hassan here will fly to England in one of Horsey de la Chevaux's airplanes. . . . "

"So slow down already," the Secretary said. "Ledt's get back to vat's wrong vit him."

"He broke his arm on an English ship," Hawkeye said. "Would you believe H.M.S. *Insubmergible?*"

"So how's the arm?"

"In a cast, all set," Hawkeye said. "The arm is not the problem. That poor kid . . . he's only eighteen, you know . . . is all alone in the world, except for a ninety-four-year-old uncle!"

"I got bad news, Hawkeye," the Secretary said. "He's all alone, period."

"You mean the uncle . . . the uncle is . . ."

"Like a mackerel," the Secretary said.

"Then we're all the family he has," Hawkeye said. "Is that why you came up here, to tell him?"

The Secretary nodded.

"That's very *nice* of you," Hawkeye said, "considering all you have to do."

"Things has been a liddle slow," the Secretary said.

"As I was saying," Hawkeye said, "we've been talking. Hassan just got off the phone from talking to the Royal Hussid Embassy in London."

"Vy did he call London?"

"To ask around. He found out that you can buy your way out of the Royal Navy. We're going to buy Woody out of the navy. Then we're going to bring him back over here to . . . he'll live with Mary and me . . . and I'll see what I can do about getting him into my alma mater, Androscoggin College. We were even talking about you."

"I can't vait to find out vy," the Secretary said.

"To work out the immigration visa."

"So vy not?" the Secretary said. "Vat are friends for? You agree?"

"I agree to what?" Hawkeye said, suspiciously.

"You agree that when friends have a liddle problem, friends should help out, right?"

"Right," Hawkeye said. "Have some lobster."

"I already got some lobsters," the Secretary said. "Tell me, you think the boy would like to go to his uncle's funeral?"

"I'm sure he would. And we . . . we formed a little organization, known as The Friends of Woody . . . will even make sure the old guy gets planted in style."

The Secretary closed his eyes. Suddenly, very loudly, but very clearly, the following philosophical observation filled the Lobster Room of the Bide-a-While Pool Hall/Ladies Served Fresh Lobster and Clams Daily Restaurant and Saloon, Inc.

"If there is one thing more revolting than a dumb Polack, it is an ugly dumb Polack." There was a pause. "So put that baseball bat down, and get out of my way, you ugly dumb Polack, or I'll impale you on it like an olive."

"I guess Boris is feeling better," Hawkeye observed, dryly. All heads turned to the door. Stanley K. Warczinski and Boris Alexandrovich Korsky-Rimsakov were standing at the entrance (Boris dressed in a hospital bathrobe six sizes too small) clutching opposite ends of Mr. Warczinski's Louisville Slugger, held vertically between them. Each had one hand on the bat.

"Why are you grunting, you ugly Russian ape?" Mr. Warczinski inquired. "Getting tired?"

"Grunting? Who's grunting?" Boris grunted. "That's the sound of your muscles snapping. When I get this thing away from you, would you prefer that I make you eat it? Or perhaps you would prefer to complete your resemblance to a monkey sitting on a stick?"

"When I tire of toying with you," Mr. Warczinski replied, "I will stick this bat through that hollow bone between your ugly ears and then roast you over a slow fire to extract the only worthy thing in your entire existence: whale blubber."

They both grunted, simultaneously. There was a sudden sharp crack, very much like the noise a high-powered hunting rifle makes. They fell into each other's arms and, for a moment, Hawkeye actually feared someone had been shot. But then the two broke from each other's embrace. Each held half of the bat, which had shattered neatly in the middle, in his hand.

Stanley K. Warczinski looked at the bat half in his hand and then at Boris. "I don't know who you are, you ugly, bearded ape," he said, admiringly, "but I tell you one thing. You got one hell of an arm. That bat busted two hundred, maybe *three* hundred, of the thickest heads in Maine and never got so much as a scratch."

"What do you mean," Boris asked, incredulously, "you don't know who I am?"

"Just what I said, fat-boy," Mr. Warczinski said. "I don't know who you are. You look a lot like my favorite opera singer, the great Boris Alexandrovich Korsky-Rimsakov, but I know you're not."

"Why are you so sure?" Boris asked, charm oozing from every syllable.

"What would the great Boris Alexandrovich be doing in my joint in Maine?"

"Hawkeye!" Boris bellowed. "Come over here and introduce me to this splendid Polish gentleman and inn-keeper. Not only is he almost as strong as I am, but he is evidently a man of great culture and esthetic sensitivity."

"That's him, Stanley," Hawkeye shouted.

Mr. Warczinski's reply made reference to the product of the defecating function of the male of the bovine species, or "bull".

Boris put his right hand on his chest and thrust his left ahead of him at arm's length. Mr. Warczinski, mistaking the gesture, dropped quickly into a fighting crouch, hamlike fists at the ready.

"Aïda!" Boris burst into song. *"Celestiale ai—*EEEEEEEEE—*Da!"* Cups rattled. A plaster bust of President Warren G. Harding crashed to the floor; and then, suddenly, the row of beer mugs hanging from hooks above the tap shattered simultaneously, showering Stanley K. Warczinski, Jr., the bartender, with broken glass.

"Maestro!" Stanley K. Warczinski said. He grasped

Boris's outstretched hand. "Welcome to my establishment!"

"You are most kind, Innkeeper," Boris said. "Not too bright, but kind. Now, if you will stop that slobbering over my hand, I will join my friends."

"Mama," Stanley K. Warczinski shouted, "bring in some of the good, fresh lobsters. And the bottle of real vodka!"

## Chapter Nine

At eight o'clock that same evening, in London, in the oak-paneled Board of Directors' Room of the Yorkshire and Northumberland Life and Casualty Assurance Companies, Ltd., in the Northumberland Building, there had gathered the firm's six senior executives in emergency session, made necessary by the untimely passing that afternoon of His Grace the Duke of Folkestone.

It was a solemn gathering. An era, they all mournfully, even tearfully agreed, had passed. The Duke was dead. The firm now belonged to a new owner. New owners posed problems. The new owner, for example, might wish to examine more closely the expense-account reports of the senior executives, something His Grace had not found the time to do in twenty-seven years. There were in addition a number of other things which the new owner, unless the matter was handled with delicacy, might find interesting. On the payroll, for instance, were six actuarial consultants at an average annual compensation of four thousand pounds sterling (a little under $10,000), plus expenses. There is nothing wrong with actuarial consultants, of course; but these particular consultants all happened to be female, in their early twenties and falling into that category of lady known as "amply endowed". Of their number only one could spell the word "actuarial"; none knew for sure what it meant.

This fact had been determined at the time with high hilarity, at a meeting of the actuarial consultants and the six senior officers of the company who now gathered to mourn their lost leader. The meeting had been held at the Mamoumian Hotel in Marrakech, Morocco, and all the participants had traveled to and from Marrakech in the company jet. There had been another burst of laughter, the reason of which two of the actuarial consultants had actually understood, when someone pointed out that never in the history of the company had anything or anyone in Morocco been placed under the protective umbrella of the Yorkshire and Northumberland Life and Casualty Assurance Companies, Ltd.

So far as anyone knew, His Grace, who had demonstrated a lifelong distaste for the bureaucratic, had not left a last will and testament.

"The legal term for that," said the Hon. Lester Hyde-Jekyll, Queen's Counsel, barrister at law, "is 'intestate.'"

"Get to the point," Bruce J. Ludwell, chairman of the board of Yorkshire and Northumberland said.

"What that means, old boy, is that while the grand-nephew, Midshipman Woodburn-Haverstraw, will eventually, I'm sure, be named sole heir, the key word is eventually."

"Go on, go on, spell it out," Ludwell said, impatiently.

"It will take some time."

"How much time?"

"A year, at least."

There were five quite audible sighs of relief around the conference table. A year was plenty of time not only to cover some unpleasant tracks, but to milk a few final dishonest drops from the corporate teat.

"Of course," the Hon. Lester Hyde-Jekyll went on, "as the heir-apparent, he can go to court at any time and ask that a receiver, or protector, be appointed to guard the assets of the firm until such time as the courts get around to naming the final heir."

There were five quite audible groans around the conference table.

"If I understand you correctly," Bruce J. Ludwell said, "unless he goes to court and requests that a protector be appointed, one need not be appointed? Is that right?"

"That is correct," Hyde-Jekyll said.

"Then all we have to do is keep him out of court!" Ludwell said.

"We must," said the assistant general manager, J.K. Crumpet, "simultaneously gain his confidence and keep his mind off the business."

"That shouldn't be hard," said Algernon Kidde, director of public relations. "We have a well-established reputation for integrity."

"Gaining his confidence or keeping his mind off the business?" Ludwell asked.

"The two go hand in hand," Kidde said.

"I think Kidde's onto something," Ludwell said. "The boy is only eighteen."

"Right!" the others chorused.

"And what is first and foremost in the mind of an eighteen-year-old male, especially one with the Duke's red blood coursing through his veins?" Ludwell asked, rhetorically. With the exception of J.K. Crumpet, who couldn't understand what Riding to the Hounds could possibly have to do with their predicament, the others immediately caught Ludwell's meaning.

"I should think," Hyde-Jekyll said, "that Daphne would be ideally suited for the task."

"Why Daphne?" Ludwell asked, indignantly. Daphne Cooper was the actuarial consultant, assigned, so to speak, to the chairman of the board. "Why not Hortense?" Hortense Calibash was the actuarial consultant who worked very closely with the general legal counsel.

"Just so long as you're not thinking of Penelope," said the Vice President, Death Benefits (Natural Causes).

"Or Heloise," said the Vice President, Death Benefits (Accidental).

"Or Pamela," said the Vice President, Investments.

"Or Geneviève," said the Vice President, Casualty Benefits.

"Gentlemen," Chairman of the Board Ludwell said, "these are desperate times, when a sacrifice for the common good is called for."

"Bully for you, old boy!" said J.K. Crumpet, who had finally come around to understanding. "I'm sure that Daphne can do the job."

"What I am saying, my dear chap," the general manager said, "is that we must *all* be prepared to make a great sacrifice."

"Eighteen years old or not, I don't think the kid . . . I beg pardon: *His Grace* . . . can take on all six of them," the Vice President, Death Benefits (Accidental) said.

"What I'm saying, you simpleton, is that we will let His Grace make the selection himself. I'm sure that we can find a replacement, so to speak, for the winner."

"My dear fellow," said the Executive-in-Charge, Investments, "are you saying that we are simply going to line the girls up and let His Grace go Eeney, Meeney, Miney, Moe?"

"That puts it rather neatly," the general manager said. "When His Grace steps off the plane, a delegation, including all the actuarial consultants, as well as ourselves, will be on hand to offer our most profound condolences and to render whatever service we may to him."

"I say," J.K. Crumpet said, "that *does* express it rather neatly. 'Service' really *is* the word, isn't it?"

As soon as the word of his passing reached the Duke of Folkestone's ancestral residence, Folkestone Castle, Plan A was ordered into execution by Miss Florabelle Jenkins, executive castlekeeper.

First, the castle would be draped in black mourning crepe. There was a sufficient supply on hand from the very successful promotion "Spend Halloween in a Genuine Haunted Castle!" which had seen twenty-six busloads of jolly merrymakers arrive at Folkestone on the All-Expenses-Paid Scheme. For only ten pounds (tax included), Folkestone Castle, Motel and Amusement Park, Ltd., provided two days and one full night of Halloween Thrills, which included: choice of a boat ride around the moat, or a tour of the dungeon; lunch; dinner (with complimentary cocktail); the traditional *Assault on the Castle* Passion play; a motel room; Continental breakfast the next morning; and a box lunch on boarding the bus to leave.

The bleachers which had been erected for the See Knighthood in Flower Pageant (featuring real jousting by knights in armor) were ordered taken down and moved to the Great Pathway, where seats from which a good view of the arriving dignitaries would be placed on sale at a flat one pound each. A pound a seat was a little high, Miss Jenkins realized, but it wasn't every day that the "guests" would have the chance to watch the "host" being carried to his final resting place, accompanied by both a Royal Naval delegation and the Household Cavalry.

The actual burial services would be private, a decision which had been forced on the management by the location of the family crypt. There was simply no way they would get enough people into the third subbasement of the castle to make it pay.

As a mark of respect to His Grace, all the rides except the Ferris wheel would be taken out of action during the burial ceremonies. It was felt that the Dodgem and The Whip and the like would get little play anyway. The Ferris wheel, however, rising as it did above the ground, would give its passengers a splendid, if brief, view of the goings-on, and would probably be jammed.

The Jungle Park would be closed. While there might be those who would be more interested in the sight of lions and tigers stalking around than in the funeral ceremonies, Miss Jenkins had arranged to lease the elephants to Maj. Gen. Sir Percy Ungalodohr, the military attaché of the Indian Embassy. Sir Percy, who would be representing the Indian Government at the funeral, thought that the arrival of himself and his staff on elephant back would be a nice touch. His Grace had spent some time in India.

There were six Duke's Taprooms on the estate. They would be closed for a period beginning an hour before the funeral services and ending a half-hour after the official party had entered the crypt. The bartenders and the waitresses, in full costume, would be deployed to the bleachers area where they would sell beer and ale in paper cups. The bleachers would be in the sun, and the bleacher customers would obviously be thirsty.

But it wasn't all good news. The Tour of the Castle itself would have to be canceled. The castle was large enough for both the paying guests and the official, non-paying guests; but there was no good way to keep the two separated, and Miss Florabelle was determined that no freeloaders should pass the castle gates.

Miss Florabelle Jenkins did not suggest canceling the Tour of the Castle. When it came up at the staff meeting, she even called for a show of hands to see if the others thought it was necessary. When the vote went eight-to-two to close, Miss Florabelle, although of course there was nothing in her face to indicate this, was delighted.

When she had taken over Castle Folkestone as "housekeeper," that's all there had been, a lousy little tour of the castle itself, one little mob of glassy-eyed tourists paying a shilling for the privilege of shuffling through the castle with a guide.

Miss Forabelle had changed all that, gradually, but inexorably. Her first innovation had been the installation of the first of the Duke's Taprooms halfway through the castle (and thus halfway through the tour). They were soon making more money selling the tourists a glass of beer than they were from the entrance fees.

The boat rides around he moat really suggested themselves, and she didn't really feel that she was due a lot of credit for instituting the very popular tour of the dungeon. But the other things were all hers. First had come the Game Park. She had been able to make a very good deal with a bankrupt circus for the first wild animals, a couple of moldy lions and one tiger. The only

expense beyond that had been to fence in both ends of
a rocky canyon. From there on in, it had been all gravy.
The "guests" paid a shilling a head to drive through the
canyon in their cars so they and the lions and tigers could
look at one another through the windshield. She had
plowed the profits from the operation right back into
it, so that the Game Park now had more lions and tigers
than the Serengeti National Park in Africa.

It was almost self-contained, ecologically. The garbage
from the Duke's Taprooms (hot-dog, hamburger and
fish-fillet remnants, plus of course, the uneaten buns and
chips (french fries) were fed to a herd of pigs and the
pigs were fed to the lions and tigers.

She had, frankly, been a *little* leery of the Dodgem,
The Whip, the Ferris wheel and the rest of that. But the
carnival owner's price had been hard to resist, and she
took the chance. She immediately realized how wrong
she'd been. People didn't really want to see the castle.
What they wanted to do was have a couple of cold beers
and some hot dogs, and *say* they'd been out raising their
culture by visiting the castle. By the installation of some
discreetly worded signs (with an arrow pointing CASTLE
TOUR in one direction and BEER in the other), it had
been a simple matter to get 85 percent of the castle
tourers out of the castle and back out spending money
within five minutes of their having passed through the
castle-tour turnstiles.

And the *Assault on the Castle* Passion play was Miss
Florabelle's idea from beginning to end. It was held inside the castle walls, in the courtyard, and any would-be
freeloaders would have to swim the moat to avoid buying
a ticket. For three shillings, the "guests" got a forty-five-
minute performance based "loosely" on the history of
the castle, and featuring knights in armor galloping
around, a maiden in a low-cut dress high up in a castle
turret, a sword fight in the center of a spotlight on the
castle wall and, for the pièce de résistance, the Greek
Fire Sequence. What this was was two gallons of kerosine
poured down from the top of the wall and then ignited
by a pilot light. The whole wall looked like it was on

fire. It was spectacular, it didn't hurt the wall (which was, after all, eleven feet thick) and it was a lot cheaper than the fireworks display with which the performance had originally ended.

With the profits from the Passion play, Miss Florabelle had started construction of the first motel unit. There were now 180 rooms in use and another 300 under construction. When they were up, their garbage would make the Jungle Park entirely self-sufficient food-wise, and there would probably be enough pork left over to go into the Castle Hickory Smoked-Sausage Business. Miss Florabelle had learned that once she got the "guests" onto the estate, she could sell them practically anything, just as long as it had the Folkestone Ducal Crest stamped on it somewhere.

One might well be asking oneself, "And what did His Late Grace think of all this?"

Miss Florabelle Jenkins had no way of knowing what the Duke of Folkestone thought about it. She had seen His Grace only once in her life. Her dealings with His Grace after that had been through the most despicable male chauvinist sexist pig, Angus MacKenzie, V.C., she had ever had the gross misfortune to encounter.

Fifteen years before, Miss Florabelle Jenkins, late assistant headmistress of St. Agnes's School for Girls, Midnapore, West Bengal, had come to England rather down on her luck. St. Agnes's School, which for two hundred years had educated the female offspring of the middle-level British colonialists, had gone under. There simply were not enough English girls left in India to support it. (It was now the Karl Marx School of International Revolution.)

Miss Jenkins's mother, the late Ernestine Ward Jenkins, widow of the late Maj. Homer P. Jenkins, Eighteenth Bengal Lancers, had told Florabelle as a girl that if she ever required assistance, she was to contact His Grace the Duke of Folkestone. His Grace had been in India on several occasions during his lifetime and had apparently developed a sort of paternal relationship with Mrs. Jenkins. There had been, in Mrs. Jenkins's bedroom beside the traditional pictures of recent English monarchs, two pictures of His Grace. One showed him standing over a tiger and carried the inscription: "For Ernestine Jenkins, In Appreciation of Splendid Hospitality, Folkestone." The other showed His Grace standing in the Great Hall of Folkestone Castle (on the spot where Souvenir Stand No. 14 now stood) and was inscribed: "For Ernestine Jenkins, In Anticipation of Sometime Again Enjoying Her Magnificient Hospitality, Folkestone."

Both photographs were old, as old as Florabelle herself, and Florabelle was half-afraid that the Duke might have forgotten his friend in far-off India, but she was desperate.

She wrote His Grace a letter immediately on arrival in England, and told him, with discretion, of course, of her present plight, and let him know that she would be quite grateful for anything that he could do to secure for her suitable employment.

Three days later, the visibly impressed proprietor of the Prince Edward's Arms Boarding Residence for Returned Colonial Servants knocked on her door to announce that His Grace the Duke of Folkestone and another gentleman waited upon her in the salon.

His Grace, truth to tell, had reeked of spiritous liquors, as had the quite ugly and wholly offensive Scotchman with him. The Scotchman, furthermore, had with him an enormous, vicious black dog who had mistaken the base of a bust of Prince Edward for a fireplug and had subsequently disrupted the tranquillity of the card room by racing through it, barking loudly, in hot (but fortunately unsuccessful) pursuit of a cat.

The interview, in other words, in Florabelle's later assessment of it, had not gone well. She had, and was now somewhat shamed of the memory, actually thought that His Grace's comment ("I'll do what I can to work out something for you, my dear.") had been a polite evasion of her request for help.

The following day, however, the Scotchman, Angus

MacKenzie, and his damned dog, had come back to Prince Edward's Boarding Residency.

"I suppose, at that school, you've had some experience with herding people from one place to another?" he had asked.

"I suppose that it could be put that way," she had replied, rather icily.

"Just from looking at ye," MacKenzie had said, "I can clearly see that ye enjoy pushing people around," he said. "I think ye'll do."

"I do not follow you, sir."

"The job of running the castle is open," MacKenzie said. "It's yours, if you want it, for as long as you stay honest. Yes or No?"

She had been tempted, of course, to refuse. But she had made other inquiries regarding employment and had quickly realized there was not much demand for a former assistant headmistress of a minor, and now-defunct girls' school in India. She had never really liked teaching school anyway.

On the three-hour ride to Folkestone Castle in Mac-Kenzie's Rolls-Royce—during which his damned dog had (a) a half-dozen times and always without warning licked her ear; (b) fallen asleep with his head in her lap; and (c) playfully chewed the head off the silver-fox neck-piece which was her one fur—MacKenzie had briefly outlined her duties.

Her mission was to get as many "guests" through the place at a shilling-a-head as possible and, simultaneously, to insure that the "guests" didn't strip the place to the walls for souvenirs. The income from the "guests" was to be used for maintenance of the castle and its grounds. The Duke, through MacKenzie, would make up the deficit which, MacKenzie said, was presently enormous.

Miss Florabelle was not stupid. She realized that a castle, properly run, was a potential money-maker. MacKenzie was perfectly willing to give her, in addition to the salary agreed upon, a percentage of net profits, if any, because he thought there was about as much chance that there would ever be a profit as there was that he should suddenly sprout the wings of an angel.

It took ten years before there was black ink in the ledger, but there had been black ink ever since, and each year's profit had been larger. Miss Florabelle had a tidy little sum socked away. Her expenses were negligible. She ate her meals at the castle, of course, so they were free. Also free were her living quarters, the apartment last occupied by the last Duchess of Folkestone, the mother of the present Duke. Any of the cars in the Ducal Garage (admission, one shilling, the Finest Collection of Antique and Classic Motorcars in Great Britain) were at her disposal whenever she wanted to go anywhere.

She was, however, naturally a little uneasy about the future now that His Grace had passed on. She had come to love Folkestone Castle. She had permitted herself, in her conscious fantasies, to think of it as hers, to imagine that the Ducal blood flowed in her veins, that she was in the place, so to speak, by the *droit du seigneur*. (It should be noted parenthetically that whatever her other virtues, Miss Florabelle Jenkins was not very strong in French. What she meant by *droit du seigneur* had nothing to do with the quaint medieval custom when Knighthood Was in Flower of giving the Laird of the Manor first shot, so to speak, at the local brides. She was under the impression that *droit du seigneur* made reference to the right of possession by inheritance. In her conscious fantasies, in other words, she dreamed that her great-grandfather, the first of the Jenkinses to go to India, was really a Folkestone deprived of his rightful inheritance; and that one day the Truth Would Come Out and she would be recognized as the rightful heir to Folkestone Castle, and the man who had all these years been known as the Duke of Folkestone would be exposed as an imposter.)

(It should also be noted parenthetically that Miss Jenkins's fantasies-in-her-sleep, dealing as they did with being carried off to the castle's lowest dungeon for the purposes of foul and imaginative ravishment by a huge

Scotsman in his kilt, deserve no place in a high-toned, morally uplifting volume like this.)

There was more than enough money socked away, in other words, for Miss Florabelle to buy a little house in the South of France, which for years had been her ambition. But now that the ambition seemed likely to be realized, she didn't like the idea at all. She wanted to stay at Folkestone Castle, and she was afraid that the new owner, the new Duke, would have plans for the castle which did not include her.

When the security guard at Entrance 4 telephoned her office to announce that a Mr. Angus MacKenzie was at the castle gates, demanding to see Miss Jenkins and flatly refusing to pay the admission fee, there was a sinking feeling in her stomach. Nothing would please that miserable Scotchman more than to be the bearer of bad tidings to her.

"You may admit Mr. MacKenzie," she said, her heart in her throat. "Ask him to come to the Duchess's apartment."

# Chapter Ten

FROM HER MAJESTY'S ADMIRALTY
TO CAPT. SIR BASIL V.P. SMYTHE
H.M.S. INSUBMERGIBLE AT SEA

REFERENCE TO OUR INSTRUCTIONS TO PROCEED AT FLANK SPEED TO SPRUCE HARBOR, MAINE, U.S.A., TO CONVEY PERSONAL CONDOLENCES OF HER MAJESTY TO THE DUKE OF FOLKESTONE. H.M. ADMIRALTY HAS RECEIVED NO MESSAGE FROM YOU ANNOUNCING ACCOMPLISHMENT. ADVISE.

DESMOND TERWILLIGER
REAR ADM., ROYAL NAVY
FOR H.M. ADMIRALTY

FROM CAPT. SIR BASIL V. P. SMYTHE, R.N.
COMMANDING H.M.S. INSUBMERGIBLE
TO H.M. ADMIRALTY, LONDON

DELAY IN REACHING SPRUCE HARBOR, MAINE, IN COMPLIANCE WITH ORDERS DUE TO FAILURE BOTH ENGINES. H.M.S. INSUBMERGIBLE AT THIS TIME (ZERO-FIVE-FORTY-FIVE HOURS MAINE TIME) APPROACHING SPRUCE HARBOR, MAINE, U.S.A., UNDER TOW BY U.S. ARMY TUG GENERAL MAD ANTHONY WAYNE. SGT. ALPHONSE Z. GONZALES, COMMANDING U.S.A. TUG WAYNE ADVISES WE HAVE AUTHORITY TO ENTER PORT IMMEDIATELY AFTER STRING OF GARBAGE-DISPOSAL BARGES ABOUT TO GET UNDER WAY EXITS PORT. HER MAJESTY'S CONDOLENCES WILL BE OFFERED IMMEDIATELY UPON DROPPING ANCHOR. SGT. GONZALES FURTHER ADVISES THAT THE JOLLY ROGER MARINA ONLY MARINE-REPAIR FACILITY AT SPRUCE HARBOR, OPERATES ON CASH BASIS ONLY. PLEASE ADVISE BRITISH EMBASSY, WASHINGTON, AND REQUEST DISPATCH OF APPROPRIATE OFFICIAL WITH NECESSARY FUNDS.

CAPT. SIR BASIL V.P. SMYTHE, COMMANDING

At this precise hour, Mary (Mrs. Benjamin Franklin) Pierce was realizing, sort of, a dream of her girlhood. At sixteen, or thereabouts, when the prospect of maturity and marriage were ever more frequently in her thoughts, she had allowed herself to dream wistfully of being married to a professional man—a lawyer, or maybe even a doctor. She would stand by his side as he rose in his chosen profession. She had had dreams of herself in formal dress, standing by her mate's side, offering her hand to be kissed by leaders of the government, by world-famous diplomats, as she entertained them in her home.

Neither the Secretary of State, the Deputy Assistant Secretary of State for Northern and Central European Culturo-Political Affairs, Congressman Edwards L. "Smiling Jack" Jackson, or the Congressman's administrative assistant, had offered to kiss her hand, but there was no question that she was entertaining them in her home. They were sitting at her kitchen table, unshaved, bleary-eyed, their hands supporting their chins, gloriously hung over, as Mary Pierce, in a bathrobe, her hair in curlers, poured cup after cup of black coffee.

What made things even worse was the condition of her husband. He was freshly shaved, neatly dressed, reeking of cologne and of both professional and human concern for his fallen-from-grace brothers.

"If I had suspected," Hawkeye said, piously, "that you intended to stay in that disreputable roadhouse, I would not, of course, have left you there."

"So shut up already," the Secretary of State said.

"You should be ashamed of yourselves," Hawkeye went on. "What are people going to think?"

As one man, they raised bloodshot eyes at him and glowered.

"Certainly," Hawkeye went on, "you must have known that the law would have to step in on behalf of the sober, hard-working, early-to-bed and early-to-rise citizens of this fine community. We are not used to four-in-the-morning-pickup barbershop quartets singing bawdy songs on the steps of our city hall."

"That was Smiling Jack's idea," the Secretary said. "Another brilliant inspiration from Capitol Hill."

"And what are the good citizens of Swampy Meadows, Arkansas, going to think when they hear that you, Mr. Jackson, their *Congressman* was hauled off to the slammer as a common drunk?" Hawkeye went on. "Not to ask what *The Washington Post* is going to say when they hear about you, Mr. Fowler. What are your fellow administrative assistants on The Hill going to think when they hear you were jailed for making indecent proposals to one of our fair waitresses?"

The Secretary shrugged his shoulders in a mighty heave. He sighed mightily.

At this point, John Francis Xavier McIntyre, M.D., like Hawkeye the picture of the satorially splendid, clear-eyed, responsible member of the medical profession and leader of his community, came into the kitchen.

"I just heard about this, Doctor," he said. "I came as soon as I could."

"Very good of you, Doctor," Hawkeye said.

"I could hardly believe my ears," Trapper said. "Arrested as common drunks!"

"Words cannot describe my pained surprise and disappointment," Hawkeye said. "What *is* the world coming to?"

"*Somebody* called the cops," the Secretary said, painfully. "I think I know who."

"We must all meet our civic responsibility," Trapper John said. "Certainly, Mr. Secretary, you of all people, should understand that."

"You're vant to tell vy?" the Secretary said. "You're through maybe with the needle?"

"Dr. McIntyre," Hawkeye asked, "do you, perchance, recall the last time we had a high-ranking State Department Official in our fair village?"

"Why, yes, Dr. Pierce," Trapper said, "now that you mention it, I do seem to recall that momentous event."

"And do you recall, Doctor, what that distinguished governmental functionary had in his fat little paw?"

"Rather clearly, Doctor," Trapper said. "He carried with him a document signed by our distinguished Secretary of State."

"And what did that document say, Doctor, do you recall?"

"With perfect clarity, Doctor," Trapper said. "It said unless we went along with the Secretary's Machiavellian plans, we would be called back into the Army, and sent, as I recall, to a remote atoll in the Pacific."

"And what did we do, Doctor?"

"Why, Doctor, we rather naturally gave into the shameless blackmail. We allowed ourselves to be dragged from the bosoms of our loved ones, and sent far across the sea."

"And what did we decide at the time, Doctor?" Hawkeye pursued.

"We vowed that it would never happen again," Trapper said.

"Are we getting through to you, Chubby?" Hawkeye asked.

"So you had a week in Paris,"* the Secretary said. "And the Frenchies gave you a medal. So what's so bad about that?"

"Quite aside from the agony of being torn from our beloved wives," Hawkeye said, with a side glance at Mrs. Pierce, "to spend a week of miserable loneliness, racked with homesickness, in that very wicked city, we rather objected to the system of recruiting. We had already been drafted once, and once a lifetime is more than enough."

"Let's stop with the diplomatic fencing," the Secretary said. "Vat's the bottom line?"

"You mean, what's it going to cost you for us to have a word with the Chief of Police in your behalf?"

"Spell it oudt," the Secretary said.

"May I respectfully suggest, Mr. Secretary," said the distinguished solon from Arkansas, "that we be prepared to make any sacrifice, to pay any price . . . "

"Shut up, Jackson," the Secretary said. "I'm the diplomat. If you hadn't started to sing, none of us would be here."

"First," Hawkeye said, "we want your word that we don't have to go anywhere we don't want to go."

"And then we want an explanation, the truth, the whole truth, and nothing but the truth, about what you're doing here," Trapper John said. "Specifically, what is your real interest in our friend Woody Woodburn-Haverstraw?"

"Believe me, the farthest thing from my mind is that you should go anywhere," the Secretary said. "You want to stay here, stay here—with my blessing."

"One for our side," Hawkeye said.

* The details of this rather interesting tale of high-level diplomacy have been splendidly reported in a scholarly work entitled *M*A*S*H Goes to Paris*, Pocket Books, New York, 1975.

"Watch out," Trapper said. "He's outwitted smarter people than you."

"And what's with Woody?" Hawkeye asked.

"I told you about Woody's uncle?" the Secretary asked.

"The one who croaked?"

"Right. Vat I didn't tell you was that his uncle was a Duke."

"A Duke? You mean a Deke, like in college?" Trapper said. "I was Kappa Alpha, myself."

"I mean a Duke, like in England," the Secretary said. "He was the Duke of Folkestone. Which means that your Woody is now the Duke of Folkestone."

"I knew," Mary Pierce, who had been listening very, very carefully, said, "that there was something *noble* about Woody."

"I'll be damned," Hawkeye said. "So he's not the poor little orphan we thought he was, huh?"

"Liddle, maybe. Orphan, positively. Poor, no," the Secretary said.

"Go on," Hawkeye said. "I'm always suspicious of people who take a sympathetic interest in rich orphans. What are you after, Chubby?"

"From the old Duke, the Navy leased a place to park their submarines," the Secretary said. "The lease expired when he did."

"And the Secretary of State and three other public servants fly all the way up here to sign a new lease?" Trapper asked, his voice dripping suspicion.

"Ve hoped, frankly," the Secretary said, "to bring the matter up at some time during the trip to England."

"Tell me about the lease," Hawkeye said.

"Ve rent a seaport, complete with village," the Secretary said.

"What's unusual about that?"

"We've been paying a very good price, from our viewpoint."

"How much?"

"About $2.28 a year," the Secretary said.

"Per square foot?"

"For the whole shmeer."

"I don't know what a port like that is worth," Hawkeye said. "But it's more than a couple of bucks."

"I vouldn't lie to you. A million, maybe a million and a quarter," the Secretary said.

"And you're going to try to cheat that nice boy out of all that money? Well, forget it. I won't let you do it," Trapper John said.

"*We* won't let you do it," Hawkeye joined in. "Shame on you, Chubby!"

"Vait a minute," the Secretary said. "It's not as bad as it looks. If ve paid him what it's worth, in his tax bracket, it all goes to the British Government. Which is probably why the old Duke made the deal in the first place. If ve pay him a million and a quarter—and you know where that million and a quarter is going to come from—he doesn't make a dime."

"What you are suggesting, then, is that we are shamelessly cheating the English Government?" Trapper asked. "Her Britannic Majesty the Queen is actually getting stuck with the bill?"

"I vouldn't phrase it exactly that way . . . " the Secretary said. "But, yes."

"In that case," Hawkeye said, "tell us how we can help, Mr. Secretary."

"You mean dat?"

"Cross my heart and hope to die," Trapper John said.

"Boy Scout's honor," Hawkeye said, solemnly, raising his right hand above his shoulder, three fingers extended.

"All I vant you should do," the Secretary said, "is nothing."

"Nothing?"

"Absolutely nothing," the Secretary said. "Ve'll take it from here."

"Take what from here?" Hawkeye asked suspiciously.

"Just as soon as I feel a liddle better," the Secretary said, "ve will go to the hospital. I will extend to His

Grace, on behalf of the President, our most profound condolences on his loss."

L. Bryan Fowler jabbed Congressman Jackson with his elbow. Smiling Jack looked at him in surprise. L. Bryan Fowler nodded his head significantly. The message finally got through.

"And I will offer the same on behalf of the Congress of the United States," Smiling Jack said. The Secretary of State didn't look exactly overjoyed at this offer but said nothing.

"I will inform His Grace," the Secretary said, "that, as a token of our respect for his late uncle, and for himself."

"And as a symbol of Anglo-American Cooperation on the High Seas," L. Bryan Fowler added.

"Didn't your mama teach you not to interrupt?" the Secretary said to Mr. Fowler, and then went on: "As soon as he is able to travel, he will be flown to England for the funeral services of his uncle by the United States Government."

"He can travel now," Hawkeye said. "I stopped by the hospital on the way to bail you out of the pokey. Assisted by three other nurses, Hot Lips was feeding him breakfast."

"What kind of a person is he, Hawkeye?" the Secretary asked.

"He's a good kid," Hawkeye said. "That's what worries me. Putting you guys around a good kid."

"Doctor, I'll remind you," L. Bryan Fowler said, "that you are referring to a distinguished member of the United States House of Representatives."

"You get my point, then," Hawkeye said. He looked at Trapper. Trapper shrugged. Hawkeye shrugged. "O.K., Chubby, so be it."

"*I*," said Mary Pierce with a regal imperative which would have done credit to Her Britannic Majesty, "absolutely forbid it!"

"I beg your pardon?" the Secretary said.

"Hawkeye, I absolutely forbid you to hand over that brave, tragedy-struck child to these . . . these . . . "

"Common drunks?" Trapper offered. "These singers of bawdy songs in public places?"

"Exactly," Mary Pierce said.

"She has a point," Hawkeye said. "Trapper, how would that fit into the Hippocratic oath?"

"Madame," the Secretary asked, "just what do you have in mind?"

"There is nothing going on at the hospital right now," Mary Pierce said. "There is no reason, Hawkeye, why you can't go with poor Woody and stand by his side—at least through the funeral."

"But that would take your husband from what he insists on calling the bosom of his loved ones," the Secretary replied.

"I am prepared, in that child's interests, to make that sacrifice," Mary Pierce said.

"Mary, you are actually suggesting that I should go off alone with these disreputable people all the way to England?" Hawkeye asked. "By myself?"

"Of course not," Mary Pierce said. "Trapper will go with you. Trapper will keep *you* out of trouble."

"I'm afraid that's out of the question, Mary," Hawkeye said. "I cannot permit myself to be torn again from my humble hearth and home."

"Let me put it this way," Mary said. "Either you go with Woody, or nobody goes with Woody."

"You could maybe explain that?" the Secretary asked.

"One word from me to the Chief of Police and you four will spend the next thirty days in the slammer," Mary Pierce said. "I know what went on at the Police Chiefs' Convention, and Ernie Kelly knows I know."

"She'd do it, too, Chubby," Trapper said. "Don't try to handle Mary the way you handled Golda."

"I have come to see that my duty, as painful as it may be, is to go to London," Hawkeye said.

The telephone rang. Mary Pierce answered it on the first ring.

'Oh, it's you, Ernie," she said. "We were just talking about you." Congressman Jackson and the Secretary looked pained. "How's your charming, unsuspecting, wife?"

Chief Kelly's reply, whatever it was, was lengthy and unintelligible. "Yes, I'll tell him," Mary Pierce said finally. "And thank you for calling, Ernie." She hung the telephone up and turned to face the Secretary.

"Another of your friends from last evening's debauchery has just become a guest of the city," Mary Pierce said. "Stanley K. Warczinski was just arrested as he raced around Courthouse Square in his Jeep, blowing the horn and yelling, 'The British are coming! The British are coming!'"

"Stanley always likes to sing," Trapper said. "How come he wasn't with you guys?"

"Chief Kelly investigated," Mary Pierce went on. "A British Naval vessel has indeed appeared in the harbor. The Chief thought you should know, Mr. Secretary."

"That must be the H.M.S. *Insubmergible*," the Secretary said.

"What else could it possibly be but the good ship *Insubmergible*?" Hawkeye asked. "Mr. Secretary, if you think a shave and a shower would remove at least some of the signs of your debauchery, we can stop by your motel en route to the hospital."

"I'll do something nice to you, Hawkeye," the Secretary said, "ven the time is ripe."

The Rev. Mother Emeritus Margaret Houlihan Wachauf Wilson, R.N., had gotten back into uniform to better fulfill her nursing responsibilities to both Boris Alexandrovich Korsky-Rimsakov and Midshipman Hugh Percival Woodburn-Haverstraw. Her borrowed nurse's whites were fairly standard: a stiffly starched white dress, white stockings and white shoes—topped off by her nurse's cap, a crisply starched square of linen folded in the peculiar manner of her nursing school. Nurse Wilson was a graduate, summa cum laude, of the first class of lay nurses ever to graduate from Blessed Mary and Joseph Hospital School of Nursing. Her nurse's cap (the design was changed for subsequent lay graduates) reflected the previously ecclesiastical nature of the institution. It was, in fact, identical to the headgear worn by the Nursing Order of the Nuns of Blessed Mary and Joseph and, when worn without the black coif which the nuns wore, bore a striking resemblance to a B-58 Hustler nuclear bomber, poised to take off.

Nurse Wilson, moreover, knew from her own experience that whenever a, so to speak, "new girl" appeared in a hospital ward, there were often unspoken questions regarding her past experience, and thus her ability. To tactfully advise one and all that she was no Margaret-Come-Lately, Nurse Wilson had pinned to her uniform certain small pins. Perched on her left bosom, at the apex, was an official U.S. Army name tag, which read LIEUTENANT COLONEL HOULIHAN, CHIEF NURSE. On her right bosom, one above the other, was a miniature Expert Combat Infantryman's Badge and a representation of a four-and-a-half-inch-tall sterling silver bear—erect, snarling, ready to fight. Both of these had been presented to then Major Houlihan, chief nurse of the 4077th MASH, in grateful appreciation for professional services rendered, by the officers and men of the 223rd Infantry Regiment, "The Grizzlies". In the emotion of the moment, Major Houlihan had vowed to the Regimental Colonel that whenever she wore her nurse's uniform, she would wear the insignia of an Honorary Grizzly. If nothing else, the Reverend Mother Emeritus was a woman of her word.

She had, finally, been similarly touched, and made a similar vow to never take it off, when the vestry of the God Is Love in All Forms Christian Church, Inc., had, on the day her late husband (founder of the G.I.L.I.A.F.C.C., Inc.) had been put to his final rest, named her the Reverend Mother Emeritus and presented her with the symbol of that office, a gold Christian cross, large enough to have "Mother" spelled out in diamond chips on the left horizontal member and "Emeritus" spelled out in diamond chips on the right horizontal member. The word "Reverend" was spelled out in rubies on the vertical portion of the cross. The device, in all, weighed just over a pound, not counting the weight of the chain; and when suspended from her neck, it served to accentuate the fact that the female torso has two prominent topographical features.

Capt. Sir Basil Vyvian Percy Smythe, R.N., had, since the first radio message from H.M. Admiralty arrived aboard the H.M.S. *Insubmergible,* been preparing himself to carry out the orders of his monarch. His full dress uniform had been taken out of its stout, oak-and-brass sea chest. It had been pressed and the buttons polished. His decorations (and there were many) had been taken from their little boxes and shined. His sword, which he had not worn, or for that matter seen, in eight years was taken from its case and lightly oiled. And for the first time ever (there being no more formal occasion in H.M. Navy than carrying out the personal orders of Her Majesty Herself), he took from its box and clamped upon his head his dress cap. This item (known unofficially as the "Trafalgar model"), which was three-cornered, had come down virtually unchanged from the headgear worn by Admiral Nelson at the Battle of Trafalgar.

And as he and his Number One, Lieut. Cmdr. Elwood Heppingham, R.N., came ashore from the H.M.S. *Insubmergible* in a Boston whaler the sides of which were emblazoned JOLLY ROGER MARINE COURTESY BOAT, Captain Smythe studied for the final time a pocket-sized edition of *Royal Navy Protocol for All Occasions*.

It was all spelled out in detail. He would be announced by a "suitable person" (Commander Heppingham seemed suitable enough) who would say (in a firm, audible voice, which might pose some problems for Heppingham), "Captain Sir Basil Vyvian Percy Smythe, Royal Navy."

Captain Smythe would then, sword drawn, held erect and touching the right shoulder, enter "the audience room, or other place" and state, "I come on the Queen's business. God save the Queen!"

Then, "following the response from the person attended," he was to state the nature of his business "briefly and with dignity."

There were three things to be stated briefly and with dignity.

First, that Vice Admiral His Grace the Duke of Folkestone had gone on to his reward. Second, that Her Majesty wished to convey her personal condolences to the next of kin (which was to say, Woodburn-Haverstraw). And finally, as the senior officer present of H.M. Navy, he was to offer the official condolences of H.M. Admiralty to Midshipman His Grace the Duke of Folkestone.

He was apparently expected at the Spruce Harbor Medical Center. A stout nurse met them at the door and insisted on pinning a small sign (VISITOR, NONFAMILY) on each of them. They then followed her down a long corridor to a door.

"You may go in," she announced.

Lieutenant Commander Heppingham flung the door open, stepped inside and announced, in as deep tones as he could muster, "Captain Sir Basil Vyvian Percy Smythe, Royal Navy!"

At this point, Lieutenant Commander Heppingham's eyes fell upon the Rev. Mother Emeritus Wilson, R.N. Nurse Wilson at that moment had leaned over the bed of Midshipman Woodburn-Haverstraw to take from his hands the glass from which he had been drinking. The weight of the sterling-silver grizzly bear and the name tag pulled the material of her nurse's uniform away from her body, giving Lieutenant Commander Heppingham a clear view of the Reverend Mother's upper undergarments. The Rev. Mother Wilson was partial to black lace. It was a spectacular sight.

"Jesus Christ!" Lieutenant Commander Heppingham added; and then he remembered where he was and came to attention, his right hand on the seam of his trousers, his left hand (as *Royal Navy Protocol for All Occasions* decreed) "firmly grasping the saber hilt in a vertical position."

Lieutenant Commander Heppingham was five-feet-three-and-one-half-inches tall. When he firmly grasped the saber hilt in a vertical position, this served to place the bottom of the curved saber scabbard some six inches in front of him, about three inches off the floor.

"I come on the Queen's business," Captain Smythe announced, and stepped into the room with a firm tread which was interrupted when his foot encountered Lieutenant Commander Heppingham's saber scabbard. Proudly crying, "God save the Queen!" Captain Smythe fell flat on his face. The sword which he had been carrying, according to regulations, unsheathed and held vertically against his shoulder, flew from his hand, sailed through the air and imbedded itself, quivering, into the wall two feet above Midshipman Woodburn-Haverstraw's head. Captain Smythe, meanwhile, skidded across the highly polished floor on his stomach and disappeared under the high hospital bed, coming to a halt only when his "Trafalgar model" dress hat encountered the wall of the room.

Captain Smythe next became aware that he was being pulled out from under the bed by firm hands on his feet. He was put back on his feet and found himself looking at a tall, lanky man wearing a doctor's white medical jacket.

"You all right?" Hawkeye asked.

"Quite all right, thank you," Captain Smythe replied with as much dignity as he could muster.

"You're sure?" Hawkeye persisted.

"Quite sure," Captain Smythe said.

"In that case, then," Hawkeye said. Something large, heavy and cold was thrust into Captain Smythe's arms. He looked down at it. It was a very large, solidly frozen, standing rib of beef.

"Compliments of the house," Hawkeye said.

"Good morning, Sir!" Midshipman Woodburn-Haverstraw said. "Are you all right, Sir?"

"Just fine, thank you, Mr. Woodburn-Haverstraw," Captain Smythe said. Then he remembered his mission. "I regret, sir," he said, "to be the bearer of sad news."

"About Uncle Hugh, you mean, Sir? Dr. Pierce has already told me."

"I bring the condolences of Her Majesty on your loss," Captain Smythe said.

"That's very gracious of Her Majesty," Woody said. "Thank you very much, Sir."

"Your Grace," Captain Smythe went on, "I come, too, to offer the condolences of Her Majesty's Admiralty on your loss."

"Thank you, Captain," Woody said.

"And as a practical matter," Captain Smythe went on, "to arrange for your transportation home as soon as you are able to travel."

"We have just been discussing that," Woody said, "with the Secretary of State."

"With *whom?*" Captain Smythe asked in disbelief.

"A pleasure to make your acquaintance, I'm sure," the Secretary said, putting out his hand. "Eat the roast beef in good health."

"And with Dr. Pierce's permission, we're flying to England this afternoon."

"*We're* flying, Your Grace?" Captain Smythe asked.

"Yes, Sir. Drs. Pierce and McIntyre . . . "

"That's very kind of you, gentlemen," Captain Smythe said, "to take yourselves from your practice."

"Our pleasure," Hawkeye and Trapper said in unison.

"And Congressman Edwards L. Jackson, Captain," the Secretary said, "who is to represent the President at the funeral of the Duke."

"I see," Captain Smythe said.

"And Boris here, and Horsey," Woody went on. "And the Reverend Mother, too, of course."

The Secretary of State looked pained. "Your Grace," he said, "I'm afraid there just won't be room on the aircraft we have available for all your friends, as much as I personally would like to see them go with you."

"Not to worry, Chubby," Horsey de la Chevaux said. "I got a plane at the field, too."

# Chapter Eleven

The Secretary of State's decision to have the Hon. "Smiling Jack" Jackson, member of Congress, serve as the President's official representative at the funeral of the Duke of Folkestone had come early that morning. Specifically, it had been the last decision made before the decision to go caroling through downtown Spruce Harbor had been reached.

L. Bryan Fowler, however, hadn't kept his feet on the higher steps of the Capitol by letting opportunity slip between his fingers. As the others searched for Congressman Jackson's shoes (he had bunions, and frequently took off his shoes when among friends), Fowler had found a dime and, with a good deal of trouble, had managed to get it into the slot of the pay phone. He telephoned collect to Ms. Iris Jackson, the Congressman's spinster sister, who served as the Congressman's press secretary.

Ms. Iris, as she was known (she was forty-six), maintained her press secretary's office at her home. This was not only more convenient for her (she said it permitted her to keep her ear to the ground of the district), but the U.S. Government sent her a nice little check each month for the use of her front porch for what was described in the budget as "official Congressional business". Ms. Iris was a little annoyed at being wakened at two-fifteen (Arkansas time) in the morning but, when she finally understood what Fowler was saying, she was overjoyed.

"I'll catch the first plane in the morning," she said. "I hadn't planned to leave town. Smiling Jack told me he wasn't junketing this year, but I certainly don't want to miss this."

"This isn't a junket, Ms. Iris," Fowler protested. "This is real. All I want you to do is get out a press release."

"That, too," she said. "Where are we staying in London?"

"I'm afraid there's no time for us to wait for you," Fowler said. "As much, of course, as we would like to. Just the press release please, Ms. Iris."

"Leave a message where you are for me at the American Embassy," Ms. Iris said. "And don't worry about a thing. Just keep him away from the bottle." She hung up on Fowler, which was just as well; for at that moment, already into the fourth verse of an old folk-tune dealing with rolling over in the clover, the Secretary, the Deputy Assistant Secretary and the Farmer—Free Silver representative in the Congress of the Good People of the Eighth District of Arkansas, linked arm-in-arm reeled out of the Lobster Room of the Bide-a-While Pool Hall/Ladies Served Fresh Lobster & Clams Daily Restaurant and Saloon, Inc., and into the bed of Wrong Way Napolitano's pickup truck. Fowler had just barely managed to join them.

Ms. Iris Jackson made two telephone calls. She called the Swampy Meadows, Arkansas, stringer for the The Associated Press, who happened to be married to her sister Myrtle, and that journalistic luminary was rousted from his bed to flash the word to the world about the Congressman's Presidential assignment. Then Ms. Iris called the Swampy Meadows Travel Agency, rousting its proprietor out of bed, and ordered first-class passage on the first available flight to London. "That's in England, Janice," she said. "And damn the expense. The Government's paying."

The Associated Press's night editor in Memphis, Tennessee (the nearest A.P. central office), eyed the FLASH BULLETIN from the A.P.'s man in Swampy Meadows, Arkansas, with two questions in his mind: Who the hell was Congressman Edwards L. Jackson, and where was Swampy Meadows, Arkansas? He checked applicable reference works and ascertained that there was indeed a Congressman Jackson and a place called Swampy Meadows, Arkansas. Because there was nothing else to transmit at the time, he sent the story along, deleting only the most outrageously laudatory adjectives concerning Congressman Jackson and changing the priority-for-transmission from FLASH BULLETIN to FILLER-THREE, which meant that the story would be transmitted only after such world-shaking news items as "This Day's Reverent Thought" and "Stock-Market Closings in Lima, Peru".

Within a couple of hours, however (by the time Chief of Police Ernie Kelly of Spruce Harbor, Maine, had brought to a close the a cappella concert on the City Hall steps and installed the carollers in the Spruce Harbor slammer), the news item reached our nation's Capital and was duly distributed to A.P. teleprinters all over town, including the one in the Office of Data Analysis and Research (ODAR) in that magnificent $41-million edifice known as the House of Representatives Office Building.

Here it created quite a stir. It was the first inkling that any of the truly knowledgeable people in ODAR had that either the President or the Secretary of State even knew who Congressman Edwards L. Jackson was, much less thought enough of him to name him the President's personal representative to anything or anybody, even the funeral rites for some dead Limey.

Telephone calls were immediately made to the night public-information officers at the White House and the State Department, while another ODAR functionary checked his chart for the location of Congressman "Smiling Jack" Jackson. Both the State Department and the White House announced, "We'll check and get right back to you"; which was not the same thing as a flat denial. The location chart indicated that Congressman Jackson was either in England, or en route to England, aboard an Air Force V.I.P. flight, in order to investigate Anglo-American Cooperation on the High Seas. That certainly smelled like a cover story to mask his real purpose.

The White House night public-relations officer immediately contacted the President (who was playing gin rummy with the Rev. Billy Graham in the Blue Room) and asked him if he wished to make a public statement on Congressman Jackson's appointment. The President, who never really knew from one day to the next what the Secretary was up to, and would have been surprised at nothing, ordered that the question be put to the Secretary, wherever—the President had no idea—he might be found. For background information, the President informed his press agent that the Secretary had, earlier that day, telephoned him about some dead Englishman and some sort of a lease, but that—he was a busy man, after all—the details of the conversation escaped him.

The White House press agent telephoned his counterpart at the State Department and was advised that the State Department had just been in touch with Air Force Three, which had left Washington on a high-priority mission with the Secretary aboard. Air Force Three was in some place named Spruce Harbor, Maine, under orders to hold itself in readiness for an early-morning flight to London. The Secretary himself was in consultation at the moment with Congressman Edwards L. Jackson and could not be disturbed. Ms. Peggy-Lou Kastenmeyer, of Congressman Jackson's staff, was aboard Air Force Three. She was wakened and asked what she knew.

"No comment," Ms. Kastenmeyer replied, which was all the confirmation needed. ODAR went to work. The location chart was consulted. There were, in all, eleven Congressmen in Great Britain, investigating everything from Problems of Salmon Fishing in Scottish Rivers to the Condition of George Washington's Ancestors' Ancestral Mansion through Unfair Competition to the American Television Industry Brought About by the Export of British Television Programming of Intellectual Content. With their staffs and loved ones, there was a total of 107 Congressional junketeers.

The chief of each Congressional junket, through the worldwide facilities of the Armed Forces Communications System and the Communications Room of the United States Embassy, was sent the following message:

FROM ODAR
TOP PRIORITY

FOR YOUR INFORMATION: THIS OFFICE HAS LEARNED THAT ACTING UPON THE ADVICE OF THE SECRETARY OF STATE, THE PRESIDENT HAS NAMED THE HONORABLE EDWARDS L. JACKSON (FARMER—FREE SILVER, ARKANSAS) AS HIS PERSONAL REPRESENTATIVE AT THE FUNERAL SERVICES OF THE LATE VICE ADMIRAL THE DUKE OF FOLKESTONE SCHEDULED FOR THREE-THIRTY P.M. (LONDON TIME) THE DAY AFTER TOMORROW. SERVICES WILL BE HELD IN WESTMINSTER ABBEY AND INTERMENT WILL BE AT FOLKESTONE CASTLE. THE CONGRESSIONAL RELATIONS OFFICER, U.S. EMBASSY, LONDON, SHOULD BE CONTACTED FOR TICKETS. DUE TO THE LIMITED NUMBER OF SEATS NORMALLY AVAILABLE FOR A FUNCTION OF THIS KIND, IT IS SUGGESTED THAT REQUESTS FOR TICKETS SHOULD BE MADE AS QUICKLY AS POSSIBLE. A LISTING OF THOSE ATTENDING WILL BE FURNISHED THIS OFFICE, TOGETHER WITH PHOTOGRAPHS OF ATTENDEES, AND THIS OFFICE WILL HANDLE PUBLIC-RELATIONS NEWS RELEASES TO HOMETOWN NEWSPAPERS. FOR GENERAL INFORMATION, CEREMONIAL FUNERALS OF HIGH-RANKING NAVAL OFFICERS ALSO MEMBERS OF THE NOBILITY ARE INVARIABLY COLORFUL, INVOLVING THE HOUSEHOLD CAVALRY IN FULL DRESS, MASSED MILITARY BANDS, ETCETERA ETCETERA, AND OCCUR ONLY RARELY. THE BRITISH TAKE THEM QUITE SERIOUSLY, AND FOR THIS REASON, IT IS SUGGESTED THAT SOME THOUGHT BE GIVEN TO APPROPRIATE DRESS. THE WEARING OF WALKING SHORTS AND HOT PANTS IS APPARENTLY FROWNED UPON BY WESTMINSTER ABBEY AUTHORITIES.

Within minutes of receipt of the message in London, it was retransmitted by telephone, telegraph and messenger to the eleven Congressmen then in the British Isles. Within hours, through the cooperation of Her Majesty's Post & Telegraph, a telephone conference call was set up between ten of the eleven solons (the eleventh was investigating salmon fishing in a remote area and could not be immediately contacted).

After some discussion regarding the President's motives in naming Congressman Jackson as his personal representative, it was agreed among them that if they went singly, they were liable to be forced to sit with the common tourists. (There was one thing on which the Congressmen were agreed, no matter what their party affiliation or political philosophy: that all the lousy American tourists were ruining England. Running into one of one's dimwit constituents in a remote and quaint pub or the lobby of the London Hilton was enough to ruin the whole junket. As a matter of fact, it was mutually agreed, if it wasn't for the fact that the taxpayer was footing the bill, it would be hardly worth the trouble of coming over here.)

The dean of junketeering Congressmen was the Hon. Anthony J. Pasquale (Liberal-Republican, New Jersey), a diminutive gentleman whose stature and flowing silver locks had graced the halls of Congress for eight terms. By virtue of his seniority, than which there is nothing more sacred to a solon, "Tiny Tony" Pasquale was named over the telephone, during the conference call, Chairman of the U.S. Congress Ad Hoc Committee to Mourn the Duke of Folkestone. Congressman Pasquale was ordered to contact the U.S. Embassy and whomever else he felt it necessary to contact to make sure that the entire Ad Hoc Committee, plus hangers-on, could pay their last respects to the Duke. The way to do this, obviously, was from seats up front in Westminster Abbey during the services there, and from reserved seats in the bleachers at Folkestone Castle.

Congressman Pasquale was also ordered to have a

discreet word with Congressman "Smiling Jack" Jackson just as soon as that distinguished solon made his appearance in the British Isles. He was to point out to Smiling Jack that Smiling Jack wasn't playing the game according to the rules. Jackson was to be pointedly reminded that if he expected so much as a half-pound of fat back for his pork barrel as a result of legislation action by his fellows, he damned well better stop hogging all the glory and special privileges for himself and start spreading it out among his colleagues.

Tiny Tony anticipated no problems with Smiling Jack. He knew the distinguished gentleman from Arkansas, and they had a good deal in common. Both had been corporate attorneys before going into government. Both corporations had gone under, the Arkansas Mule Breeders Association, Inc., because of the growing popularity of the tractor and the Sicilian-American Fraternal Association, Inc., because of certain indictments returned by a Federal Grand Judy.

Both men had been faced with the choice of either returning to the private practice of law (which meant they would have to go back to sleeping lightly, so as not to miss the sound of ambulance sirens) or entering public service. They had opted for public service, and run for Congress. They had become, rather naturally, friends. Congressman Jackson could always be counted upon to vote for any legislation designed to keep the Immigration and Naturalization Service from deporting some stalwart, God-fearing, Church-going constituent of Tiny Tony's back to Sicily for some small misstep in his youth; while Congressman Pasquale could be counted upon to vote favorably upon legislation designed to improve the lot of the hard-working Arkansas farmers who kept returning Smiling Jack to the Congress.

Congressman Pasquale happened to be in London when the word from ODAR reached him. (He and his staff were investigating the British Casino System. Not only did Congressman Pasquale like a few friendly hands of poker from time to time, but investigating the British

Casino System gave him a chance to get together again with his old friends and associates of the Sicilian-American Fraternal Association, Inc.) It was no trouble at all for him to hop into a hired limousine and rush over to the American Embassy on Grosvenor Square and get things rolling.

Tiny Tony experienced some difficulty in gaining entrance to the Embassy Building itself. (The guards are British. The one on duty in the lobby was quite unable to believe that the silver-haired gentleman in the walking shorts and "Pizza Power" T-shirt could possibly have been elected to any office and denied him entrance until someone from the diplomatic staff verified his identity.) But from then on it was smooth sailing. He was given a copy of the TOP SECRET radiogram from the State Department, which announced the departure of Air Force Three from Spruce Harbor International Airport in Maine, and gave its estimated time of arrival as half-past eight that same evening. He was guaranteed seats up front in Westminster Abbey for the Ad Hoc Committee and its hangers-on; two cars on the private railroad train from London to Folkestone Castle and back; reserved seats in the bleachers at Folkestone Castle; and confirmed reservations in Folkestone Castle's Turret & Tower Motel for all hands (all of this to be paid for, of course, by the U.S. Government). Congressman Pasquale told the Congressional liaison officer he would "get back to him" about the other details. He really had no idea how many of his distinguished colleagues would be interested in the boat ride around the moat or the dungeon tour, and the Congressional liaison officer was not sure if the Folkestone Castle Passion play would be given during the official mourning period. Further liaison would be necessary.

Dinner, which is served to the hoi polloi in London at about eight P.M., was delayed for several different groups of diners that same night, as a result of several messages flashed across the Atlantic:

FROM CAPT. SIR BASIL V.P. SMYTHE
COMMANDING, H.M.S. INSUBMERGIBLE
TO HER MAJESTY'S ADMIRALTY, LONDON

FOLLOWING MESSAGE IN THREE PARTS

PART ONE. THE CONDOLENCES OF HER MAJESTY
WERE PASSED ON TO MIDSHIPMAN HIS GRACE THE
DUKE OF FOLKESTONE AT ZERO-SEVEN-THIRTY HOURS
THIS MORNING BY THE UNDERSIGNED.
PART TWO. MIDSHIPMAN HIS GRACE THE DUKE OF
FOLKESTONE DEPARTED SPRUCE HARBOR INTERNA-
TIONAL AIRPORT ABOARD U.S. AIR FORCE AIRCRAFT
AT ZERO-EIGHT-FIFTEEN HOURS THIS MORNING.
ESTIMATED TIME OF ARRIVAL HEATHROW AIRPORT,
LONDON, TWENTY HUNDRED HOURS, LONDON TIME.
PART THREE. PROPRIETOR OF JOLLY ROGER MARINA,
SPRUCE HARBOR, MAINE, HAS IN HIS POSSESSION SO
FAR UNPAID ROYAL NAVY PURCHASE ORDER EXE-
CUTED IN NAME OF KING GEORGE III BY REAR ADM.
J.D. MORGAN, R.N., COMMANDING, H.M.S. BARKEN-
TINE TRIUMPHANT ON 17 MAY, 1776, FOR SERVICES
RENDERED H.M.S. TRIUMPHANT BY HIS GREAT-GREAT-
GREAT-GRANDFATHER. IN VIEW OF FOREGOING, HE IS
NOT ONLY UNWILLING TO ACCEPT TELEPHONE AS-
SURANCES OF H.M. AMBASSADOR IN WASHINGTON
THAT ROYAL NAVY WILL PAY FOR NECESSARY RE-
PAIRS TO H.M.S. INSUBMERGIBLE, BUT HAS SEIZED
H.M.S. INSUBMERGIBLE FOR PAYMENT OF H.M.S.
TRIUMPHANT BILL. PLEASE ADVISE.

SMYTHE, CAPTAIN, R.N.
COMMANDING, H.M.S. INSUBMERGIBLE

That message took a four-man delegation of senior
Royal Navy officers from their scheduled dinners and
sent them through early-evening London traffic to meet
Midshipman His Grace the Duke of Folkestone on his
arrival, both to express the condolences of H.M.
Admiralty on his loss and to brief him on his role in the

official funeral services. A fifth senior naval officer was at the same time dispatched to the United States Embassy to have a word with the U.S. Naval attaché regarding the seizure of the H.M.S. *Insubmergible*.

FROM STATE DEPARTMENT, WASHINGTON, D.C.
TO U.S. EMBASSY, LONDON

HON. QUINCY WESTERBROOK, DEPUTY ASSISTANT SEC-
RETARY OF STATE FOR NORTHERN AND CENTRAL EU-
ROPEAN CULTURO-POLITICAL AFFAIRS WILL ARRIVE
HEATHROW AIRPORT, LONDON, AT 8 P.M., LONDON
TIME, ACCOMPANIED BY HON. EDWARDS L. JACK-
SON, PERSONAL REPRESENTATIVE OF THE PRESIDENT,
TO MEMORIAL SERVICES FOR HIS LATE GRACE THE
DUKE OF FOLKESTONE. THEY ARE ESCORTING MID-
SHIPMAN HIS GRACE THE DUKE OF FOLKESTONE, WHO
IS ACCOMPANIED BY DRS. BENJAMIN FRANKLIN
PIERCE AND JOHN FRANCIS XAVIER MC INTYRE, AT-
TENDING PHYSICIANS. IT IS BELIEVED ENTIRE PARTY,
WHICH ALSO INCLUDES TWO MEMBERS OF CONGRESS-
MAN JACKSON'S STAFF, WILL BE GUESTS OF HIS
GRACE, BUT PLEASE ARRANGE STANDBY ACCOMMODA-
TIONS, INCLUDING TRANSPORTATION, FOR SAME.
THIS MESSAGE CONSTITUTES AUTHORITY FOR YOU TO
ISSUE NECESSARY PRESS RELEASES POINTING OUT
ANGLO-AMERICAN COOPERATION ON HIGH SEAS.

CALDWELL EMMONS
PUBLIC AFFAIRS

This message put a lot of people to work in the U.S. Embassy Building. The Ambassador, of course, had to postpone his dinner so that he could be at the airport. He had never heard of Deputy Assistant Secretary Westerbrook, so the logical thing to conclude was that the Secretary himself was about to arrive under the nom de travel of Westerbrook. He had heard a great deal about Congressman Jackson in the last couple of hours, most of it unflattering, from Congressman Anthony J. Pasquale.

Congressman Pasquale, who had set up temporary headquarters of the Official U.S. Congress Ad Hoc Committee to Mourn the Duke of Folkestone in Claridge's Hotel, had been notified of the scheduled arrival of His Grace and Congressman Jackson, and an official Embassy car laid on to carry the Congressman to Heathrow.

The Secretary had, over the years, shown a definite preference for the Dorchester Hotel, so sufficient suites were arranged for at that hostelry. The Ambassador knew only that His Grace had been injured, but not the extent of the injury; and since he was being accompanied by two doctors, it seemed simply good sense to arrange for an ambulance to be at the airport, together with the two official Cadillac limousines.

The press was summoned, and word released of the Duke's arrival in the company of his stout American chums in an American airplane. It was released in time to make the regularly scheduled Home Service News of the British Broadcasting Corporation, which reported it in these terms:

Word has been received that Midshipman His Grace the Duke of Folkestone, who was injured while serving aboard the H.M.S. *Insubmergible* in American waters, is being flown to London by the American Government. His Grace is scheduled to arrive at eight this evening at Heathrow. His Grace, who acceded to the title upon the death of his Great-Uncle Vice Adm. Hugh Percival, the Duke of Folkestone, is being attended by two American physicians, but it is believed that his condition will permit his participation, at least to some degree, in the funeral services for the late Duke the day after tomorrow at Westminster Abbey.

In their temporary quarters at the Savoy Hotel, Hermione, the Duchess of Crimley and her daughter,

Lady Chastity Cheppingwhite-Browne, watched the broadcast on the telly.

"I have never really believed, darling," the Duchess said, "that the way to a man's heart is through his stomach."

"Neither have I," Lady Chastity agreed. "But even if he is physically up to it, how am I going to manage anything like that if he's on a stretcher and two doctors are hanging around?"

"You miss the point, precious," the Duchess said. "There will be time for that later. I don't suppose that dressing up in a nurse's uniform would be . . . credible . . . but we can certainly arrange for that darling boy to be met with an ambulance. The first thing he sees when he opens his eyes will be you, darling. Wear the dress with the low-cut neckline."

The Duchess picked up the telephone, asked for the concierge, and instructed him to have an ambulance (a first-class ambulance, not one of those dinky little Ford trucks) outside the hotel at 7:15, to follow the Crimley Rolls-Royce to Heathrow Airport.

There was a telly, too, set into the oak-paneled walls of the Directors' Room of the Yorkshire and Northumberland Life and Casualty Assurance Companies, Ltd., in the Northumberland Building in London, W.1.

The actuarial consultants to the firm had been gathered there to have the problem, and their role in solving the problem, explained to them. The reaction of the actuarial consultants (to a girl) had not been exactly what the senior executives of the firm had thought it would be. It quickly became apparent that each of them immediately realized it would be much more fun to be an actuarial consultant to an eighteen-year-old Young Gentleman who happened to own the company than it could possibly be (as experience had taught) being an actuarial consultant to a sixty-year-old executive of the firm.

There had been, in fact, a mad rush for the door by all six actuarial consultants when the time of His Grace's arrival had come over the tube. They were restrained only at the last minute. The general manager gave a little pep talk in which he emphasized that unless they all hung together to face this problem, they were all liable to hang separately. He made his point. The original plan (where His Grace would be given his option of the actuarial consultants) remained in force. The only change in the plans was made necessary by His Grace's physical condition, about which they had previously heard nothing. A telephone call was made arranging for an ambulance to come immediately to the Northumberland Building. It was to take its place in the line of Rolls-Royces immediately behind the lead Rolls, the one to be occupied by the general manager.

"I don't care if it will look like a hearse in a funeral procession!" the general manager flared. "Just do as you're told, or you'll never get to carry another Yorkshire and Northumberland casualty."

# Chapter Twelve

There was a rigid schedule of events at Folkestone Castle, Motel and Amusement Park, Ltd., beginning with "0700: Gates To Be Opened," running through eight closely typed pages and ending with "2100: Final Inspection of Grounds & Closing of Gates."

The final inspection of grounds was conducted with all the precision of a military operation and was, indeed, under the control of a retired Royal Army officer with long years of experience in the techniques developed by the army to keep the Irish from one another's throats in Northern Ireland.

Starting at one end of the castle grounds, two hundred security guards marched to the other, never out of sight of the next man, sweeping all the guests and their vehicles before them. Those guests who had arrived by car and were staying at the Turret & Tower Motel were required to park their cars in an assigned parking space, according to a little windshield sticker. All other cars were required to leave the grounds by 2100, or 9 P.M. There had been an unfortunate wave of deadbeats who had actually tried to get out of renting a room, and the price of another entry ticket the next day, by sleeping in their cars, and Florabelle Jenkins had been quick to stamp it out.

The security guards were not surprised to find an unauthorized Rolls-Royce parked in front of the castle itself (their experience, in fact, suggested that Rolls-Royce owners, as a class, rated high on the Deadbeat Scale) but they were shocked to the quick at the explanation of the chauffeur: "My employer, Mr. Angus MacKenzie, is in the Duchess's apartment with Miss Florabelle Jenkins," he said. "I personally watched him go in, and he's never come out. I'm not going to leave without him."

There was one absolutely off-limits area to everyone in Folkestone Castle and that was the Duchess's apartment—now the living quarters of the executive castlekeeper—and, at first, no one was willing to believe the chauffeur's story. Efforts to locate Miss Jenkins elsewhere on the grounds were to no avail however (she hadn't even shown up for the regularly scheduled Counting of the Cash in the Office of the Exchequer, itself reason for alarm), and, finally, one of the more courageous members of the security guard marched up the ancient, wide marble steps of the Main Hall to rap very politely at the door to the Duchess's apartment.

When there was no answer, and after a moment's thought, he tried the door. The handle turned easily, and the giant door swung smoothly open. The security guard barely managed to get it closed again in time to save himself from the vicious assault of the largest dog—a huge black monster—he had ever seen. He fled down the stairway and made his report to the chief of security, Brig. Montague Fyffe, Retired.

Brigadier Fyffe immediately put Plan M.C.O.P. (Major Crime on Premises) into effect, and organized his forces for an all-out assault up the wide steps of the Main Hall and then into the apartment. As he was about to put the whistle to his lips, and launch the operation, however, his Number One (Col. Desmond Collier, O.B.E., Retired) suggested that there just possibly might still be a functioning telephone line inside the Duchess's apartment; and that, if so, it might be possible to conduct a dialogue with the arch criminals holding Miss Florabelle Jenkins prisoner. Lives might thus be saved.

Miss Florabelle Jenkins answered the telephone on the fourth ring. She seemed to be in good health (indeed in high, good spirits).

Brigadier Fyffe laid the telephone back in its cradle. "Stand down from Plan M.C.O.P.," he ordered. "There is no crisis." He did not think that it was necessary to report the precise words of the conversation he had had with Miss Florabelle, which had been: "Bug off, Fyffe. If I need help, I'll ask for it."

Miss Florabelle had then returned to the drawing room of the Duchess's apartment and rejoined Mr. Angus MacKenzie.

"Who was that, sweetie?" Angus inquired. Angus was lying on the polar bear-skin before the fireplace, a large bottle of Scotch whisky beside him.

"Nothing important, Angus," Miss Florabelle said, settling onto the bearskin beside him. Both parties were dressed for the occasion, or dressed as well as they could be under the circumstances. Miss Florabelle was wearing an Indian sari and Mr. MacKenzie, the essential part (i.e., the kilt) of Highland dress.

The meeting, which both of them had truly dreaded, had not turned out at all the way either of them had thought it would.

First of all, Angus MacKenzie had not gone to see the Old Biddie in the Castle as the bearer of bad tidings, at least bad tidings beyond those regarding the passing of the Duke of Folkestone. He carried with him a small envelope, one of the two identical small envelopes which had been reposing in the safe of East Anglia Breweries, Ltd., for some years. Each was marked, beneath the

Ducal crest, "To Be Opened upon My Death". One was for Angus MacKenzie, and the other for Miss Florabelle Jenkins. Angus had opened and read his immediately upon learning that the Duke had sailed to join the Great Armada in the Sky. It had been brief and to the point:

> *Angus: Don't be a bloody fool when I kick off and give up your job. I have made sure that you will have an entirely pleasant relationship with the new owner of East Anglia Breweries. I will appreciate it if you keep your eye on the boy.*

> Faithfully,
> Folkestone.

He had jammed his note into his pocket and prepared to deliver the other one to the Old Biddie in the Castle, of whom he had never met a more convincing argument in favor of the old Indian custom of drowning females at birth but, for whom, for reasons which absolutely mystified him, the Duke felt some sense of responsibility.

Miss Florabelle Jenkins had met him by standing at the top of the wide stairway in the Great Hall of Folkestone Castle. Angus's wee black doggie, who was generally the epitome of canine wisdom, was suddenly bereft of his senses and ran up the stairs, tail wagging furiously.

"A gentleman, Mr. MacKenzie," Miss Florabelle Jenkins said, "would not bring a savage, foul-smelling beast into Folkestone Castle under the present, tragic circumstances."

"His Grace, Miss Jenkins," MacKenzie said, stony to the quick, "was fond of me wee black doggie. As a matter of fact, Miss Jenkins, 'twas His Grace what gave me second wee black doggie."

"Your second?" She was, after all, of the female persuasion and possessed of the curiosity common to that gender.

"Aye, me second. The first went down, God rest his

soul, with the H.M.S. *Indefatigable*. His Grace was then her Captain."

"I am quite aware of His Grace's distinguished naval record, Mr. MacKenzie. I was not previously aware that you had, so to speak, shared the rigors of the naval service with him."

"Aye, that I did, Miss Jenkins," MacKenzie replied.

"And may I inquire into the nature of your business here today, Mr. MacKenzie?"

"I come to tell you His Grace cashed in his chips," MacKenzie said.

"I beg your pardon, Mr. MacKenzie?"

"He kicked off," MacKenzie said.

"Are you attempting to inform me that His Grace has left this vale of tears, Mr. MacKenzie?"

"Aye, that I am. And I can't think of a better way to go."

"And how is that, Mr. MacKenzie?"

"I dinna think we need go into that, Miss Jenkins," MacKenzie said. "I have a message for ye from His Late Grace." He handed her the envelope.

"Thank you," she said, and tore it open, and read it.

A tear ran down her cheek. She stiffened her upper lip and looked at MacKenzie. He was standing there, examining her uncomfortably. A weeping woman was not his forte.

"And what are your plans now, Mr. MacKenzie?" Miss Florabelle asked. "Now that His Grace has gone to his reward?"

"Now that I done me duty and give you that note, Miss Jenkins," MacKenzie said, "I intend to hoist a wee cup in His Grace's memory."

"That was not my question," she said, and then went on without waiting for a reply. "Am I to understand that you delayed, as you so quaintly put it, hoisting a wee cup, in order that you could bring me that note?"

"Yes, ma'am, that I did. And now if you'll excuse me, ma'am, I'll be getting to it."

"Mr. MacKenzie, under these tragic circumstances,

I do think it appropriate that a glass be raised to his memory. I would be honored if you would join me."

"I was frankly thinking of something a wee bit stronger than sherry, Miss Jenkins," Angus said.

"As it happens, Mr. MacKenzie," she said, "while conducting a routine inventory of castle property, I happened upon several large wooden vessels . . . I believe the term is 200-gallon barrels . . . of some spirits apparently laid down by His Late Grace's father."

"Isn't that interesting?" MacKenzie said.

"I had one barrel brought here," she said, "to the Duchess's apartment. To keep it from evaporating."

"Naturally," MacKenzie said.

"And to test its quality from time to time, to make sure it wasn't deteriorating. I expect that you would really be a better judge than I."

"Happy to oblige, ma'am."

"If you will follow me, Mr. MacKenzie," she said. He followed her into the Duchess's apartment, the first male to enter those quarters in approximately sixty years.

Miss Florabelle filled a quart pitcher from the wooden spigot and set it on a table. She then poured three inches into each of two glasses and handed one to MacKenzie. As he sniffed it appreciatively, she put her own glass to her lips and tossed it down.

"It is apparently still good," she said, refilling her glass. "Wouldn't you say so?"

Angus tested the sample before him in precisely the same manner.

"Aye, that's decent," he said.

"Then I suggest we proceed with raising a glass to the memory of His Late Grace," Miss Florabelle said. They touched glasses and drank them down. Both smacked their lips.

"Ye have 200 gallons of this, ye say?" MacKenzie said.

"Perhaps more," she said. "There are at least eight barrels in the room. I think it reasonable to presume that at least some of them also contain this particular type of fermented spirits."

"In that case," Angus said, "I would suggest that another toast to His Grace would be in order."

"I quite agree," Miss Florabelle said. "And I do want an answer to my question, Mr. MacKenzie."

"What question is that, Miss Jenkins?" Angus asked, holding his glass out for a refill.

"I asked, if I may be so bold as to inquire, Mr. MacKenzie, what your plans are for the future, now that His Grace no longer walks among us?"

"Ye may be so bold as to inquire," Angus said. "Ye may also call me Angus. Any friend of me wee black doggie, so to speak."

The wee black doggie was sitting beside Miss Florabelle, nuzzling her. "He does seem to like me, doesn't he?" Miss Florabelle said. She scratched the wee black doggie's ears. His massive tail began to wag, encountering in its path a small cast-iron doorstop in the shape of a church, and weighing no less than twenty pounds. It went sailing across the room like a hockey puck.

"Why thank you, Angus," Miss Florabelle said. After a barely perceptible pause, she added, "And you may call me Florabelle."

"Thank *you,* Florabelle," Angus said. "Well, I got a note like yours from His Grace meself. Wait a mo'. Here it is." He handed it to her. "So, as you can see, Florabelle, I'll be doing the same thing. It won't be quite the same with His Grace gone, of course, but . . . "

Quite to her surprise, Miss Florabelle Jenkins rather liked the sound of her given name on MacKenzie's lips. His deep masculine voice, she decided, probably accented its femininity.

"You were fond of His Grace, weren't you?" Florabelle asked.

"Aye, that I was. He was the best friend I ever had, from India to Kenya."

"I hadn't known," Florabelle said, "that you had served the Crown in India, Angus."

"Aye, that I have," he said. "Do you suppose you could let me have another wee drop of that? I'd like to offer a toast, Florabelle, to my first wee black doggie, who went down with the H.M.S. *Indefatigable*." He paused. "I kin see him in me mind now, wagging his tail, as His Grace is piped aboard. They're together again, wherever they are."

"Under the circumstances, that seems only appropriate," Florabelle said, as she refilled the glasses. "And under the circumstances, Angus, it seems only fitting that I show you my last communication from His Grace." She handed him her note.

*Dear Florabelle:*
*I have made sure that you will never have to leave Folkestone Castle unless you want to. If you have any problems immediately following my death, contact Angus MacKenzie, who was my best friend, and whom I have asked to look out after the boy, and who would, I am sure, look out after you.*
*Folkestone.*

A tear ran down Angus MacKenzie's cheek.

"You are crying, Angus," Florabelle said, gently.

"Aye, that I am," he said. "And if you have any little problems, Miss Jenkins . . . "

"Florabelle, Angus, please," she said.

"Florabelle," Angus went on, "ye just bring 'em to me."

"That's very good of you, Angus," Florabelle said. "You're a fine man."

"Just an old Royal Marine doing his duty as he sees it," Angus said.

"I'll drink to that," Florabelle said. And did.

"I'm charged with keeping an eye on the boy," Angus said. "Could you find it in yer heart, Florabelle, if the occasion should arise, to gi' me a hand with that?"

"I would be honored, Angus," she said. "Oh, look at that," she said, in surprise. "That pitcher must have a hole in it. It's all gone."

"That's a bloody pity," Angus said, solemnly. "Just when we was getting to know each other and all."

"My late father, who also served the Crown in India," Florabelle said, "was fond of quoting the motto of the Royal New Delhi Bird Watchers' Society."

"And what was that?"

"You can't fly on one wing," Florabelle said, making her way somewhat unsteadily to the barrel and refilling the pitcher.

"I'll drink to that," Angus said. "Strange, the Royal Marines have the same motto. Wonder how that come to pass?"

"I loved India," Miss Florabelle said.

"Is that a fact?"

"Would you believe I still have my sari?" she said. "Would you like to see it?"

"It would be a pleasure and privilege to see you in a sari, Florabelle," Angus said.

"For auld lang syne," Florabelle said.

"Right," Angus said. "And I'll tell you what. If there's a MacKenzie tartan in the castle, I'll put it on, and you can put on your sari."

It seemed at the time, to be a splendid idea. It also seemed like a good idea, since the cushions of the couch on which they had been sitting had suddenly become quite slippery, to adjourn to the floor. They talked of many things, and finally the subject got around to food.

"If you could spare the time from your busy schedule," Florabelle said, "I could whip us up some chicken curry."

"I haven't had a good chicken curry since I left India," Angus said.

Miss Jenkins, at this point, moved to the kitchen, and carried on the conversation by slightly raising her voice. Angus didn't pay much attention to what she was saying, lost, so to speak, in his own memories of India, made more vivid by the MacKenzie tartan he was now wearing, the sari Florabelle was now wearing, the warm glow in his belly from the Scotch whisky and the smell of chicken curry in preparation.

It was at this point that the scout of the Castle Security Forces had made his way up the stairs, knocked, and then tried the door.

Florabelle stuck her head out of the kitchen.

"Oh, Angus," she said, "I don't want you to think me a nervous female, but I just heard a strange noise!"

"Put yer mind at rest, Florabelle," Angus said. "Yer under the protection of me wee black doggie. *Eat, Doggie!*" Angus barked in the firm tones of the Royal Marines Parade Ground. Wee Black Doggie jumped to his feet and raced, hair bristling, teeth bared, across the Duchess's apartment, to the door.

"Oh, Angus, you don't know what it's like to be a single woman alone!"

"I kin fix that," Angus said. Florabelle's heart started to beat faster. "I'll get ye a wee black doggie for yer own self."

"You are so kind, Angus," Florabelle said, although that wasn't exactly what she had in mind. "I'll stir the curry now."

A minute or two later, the telephone had rung, and Florabelle had had her little chat with Brigadier Fyffe.

"Who was that, sweetie?" Angus inquired.

"Nothing important, Angus," Florabelle replied, blushing at the term of endearment. "Here's the curry."

Angus ate three bowls of the chicken curry, washed down with some more of the ancient spirits Miss Florabelle had found in the bowels of Folkestone Castle, and then turned to look at her.

"I haven't been saying much," he said.

"You've been eating," she said.

"I've been thinking, that's what I've been doing," Angus said.

"Is that so?"

"I've been thinking what me life might have been, had I run into you when I was a younger man," Angus said. "There's damned few females who know how to make a real curried-chicken dish."

"Why, that's very kind of you, Angus," she said. "I'm

glad you liked it. Can I infer that you, too, have never been married?" She averted her eyes when asking the question. There was no answer. Eyes still averted, she went on: "Have you ever been married, Angus?" There was still no answer. Timidly, she raised her eyes to look at him. The reason there was no answer was that Angus MacKenzie, arms and legs spread, mouth open, was sound asleep. As she watched, his chest heaved, and a long, sonorous sound came out of his mouth.

He just, Florabelle thought, might not be very comfortable in that position. She crawled to the couch, took from it a petit-point pillow (bearing the likenesses of Queen Victoria and her Beloved Crown Consort, Prince Albert), crawled back to the polar bear-skin and, gently raising Angus's head, slipped the pillow under it.

Florabelle suddenly felt herself being wrapped in a massive male arm. Her heart beat furiously and, for a delicious moment, she thought that she was finally to live out all those horrible dreams of imaginative ravishment she'd had over the years. The moment passed. Angus was unmistakably still asleep, his snoring filling the room. She struggled to get free of his arm. She was faced with the realization that his massive arms were just as strong as they looked and that, frail creature that she was, she was helpless to escape. Her only hope was to stay where she was, to wait for him to shift his position, so that she could escape. She rested, just for a moment, her face on his chest. And a moment later, her eyes closed, and her mouth opened. A soprano whistling wheeze was added to the basso profundo rumbling. It made a duet unpleasing to Wee Black Doggie, who suddenly sat upright, raised his massive jowls, and began to howl.

Neither Miss Florabelle Jenkins nor Sgt. Maj. Angus MacKenzie, V.C., Royal Marines, Retired, heard him.

# Chapter Thirteen

"We have a small problem," Dr. John F.X. McIntyre said to Dr. Benjamin F. Pierce.

"I saw her crying," Hawkeye said.

"Tears at the cockles of me heart," Trapper said.

"But, of course, there's absolutely nothing that can be done," Hawkeye said.

"Nothing at all," Trapper replied. "A classic case of ships passing in the night, and that sort of thing."

"At his age, girls come along like buses," Hawkeye said.

"There are many fish in the sea," Trapper replied.

"Besides, taking her to England would be out of the question."

"A preposterous idea," Trapper agreed. "One without precedent."

"What would people thing?" Hawkeye asked.

"What would Esther Flanagan, better known as 'Old Iron Heart' think?"

"There's one way to find out," Hawkeye said. He picked up the telephone and told the operator to page Chief Nurse Flanagan and order her to report instantly to the office of the Chief of Surgery.

When she arrived, Old Iron Heart looked a lot more stern than usual. If the medical gentlemen were prone to think the worst of their fellowmen, which they were, they would have suspected that Chief Nurse Flanagan was hung over. Which might explain what happened to all the booze in the refrigerator.

"Good morning, Chief Nurse Flanagan," Dr. Pierce said. "You're looking bright and bushy-tailed this fine morning."

"A shining example to the younger nurses," Dr. McIntyre said.

"I am in no mood for sarcasm, subtle or otherwise," Chief Nurse Flanagan said.

"Farthest thing from my mind," Hawkeye said.

"I only give one warning," she said. "What's on your mind?"

"Far be it from me to interfere in the training program established under your wise leadership for our student nurses," Trapper John said.

"But we have been thinking," Hawkeye added.

"About what?" Iron Heart Flanagan demanded.

"Tell me, Chief Nurse Flanagan, do you consider travel broadening?" Hawkeye asked. "In a medical sense, of course?"

"Stop beating around the bush," she said. "I'm a busy woman."

"Can you think of a good reason for us to take Beverly Chambers with us to England?"

"There is no good reason for that girl to leave the hospital," Iron Heart said. "No reason at all. The whole idea of her going with Woody is insane."

"Then what excuse are we going to give?" Hawkeye said.

"I'll think of something, Hawkeye," Iron Heart said. She bent forward and kissed Dr. Pierce and Dr. McIntyre—chastely, of course—on the cheek. "How much time do we have to get her to the plane?"

"About five minutes," Hawkeye said.

"She'll be there," Iron Heart Flanagan said. "Hot Lips is helping her pack right now."

"What would you have done if we had been opposed to the idea?" Trapper John asked.

"Threatened to give Mrs. McIntyre a key to this office," Flanagan said, "for openers."

And so it came to pass that when Midshipman His Grace the Duke of Folkestone boarded Air Force Three at Spruce Harbor International Airport, he did so in the company of Miss Beverly Chambers, first-year student nurse. Her mother was informed that an unusual opportunity had suddenly come up for a student nurse to make a brief trip to England in the company of the chief of nursing training of the Ms. Prudence MacDonald Memorial School of Nursing, New Orleans, Louisiana, and that her daughter had been picked for that honor by a special committee consisting of the chief nurse of Spruce Harbor Medical Center and two of its senior physicians.

Air Force Three, carrying Woody, Beverly, Hawkeye, Trapper John, Smiling Jack, Chubby, Hot Lips, Quincy Westerbrook, L. Bryan Fowler, and Ms. Peggy-Lou Kastenmeyer, took off first, and then was immediately followed by Chevaux Petroleum's Number Seven, carrying Horsey de la Chevaux, His Royal Highness Prince Hassan ad Kayam, six members of his personal bodyguard and Boris Alexandrovich Korsky-Rimsakov.

Mr. Korsky-Rimsakov's peculiar medical complaint had posed some problems. He could not, as he pointed out, be expected to cross the Atlantic lying on his stomach. Neither would it be possible for him to stand up all the way. The problem was finally resolved by installing a blown-up inner tube in place of one of the seats, on which Boris perched in only mild discomfort.

As soon as they were airborne and the FASTEN SEAT BELTS sign went off, Horsey de la Chevaux walked back to Boris and extended a half-gallon bottle of Old White Stagg Blended Kentucky Bourbon to him.

"I never been to London, Boris," Horsey confided. "I got an office there, but I never been there. You think maybe I have trouble finding a hotel?"

"My dear, if somewhat backward Cajun crony, you are going to London with Boris Alexandrovich Korsky-Rimsakov, not by yourself. You will, of course, stay with me. Wherever our diminutive Arab friend has made the necessary arrangements."

"Not for me," Horsey explained. "For the Bayou Perdu Council, K. of C."

"What about the Bayou Perdu Council, K. of C.?" Boris asked, his eyes lighting up in anticipation.

"I call up, tell them we got a funeral parade, and to

come. They coming on one of the 707's." There were
three Douglas 707 Intercontinental jets in the Aviation
Department of Chevaux Petroleum Corporation International. They were normally used as aerial freighters
to carry supplies and equipment to various Chevaux
Petroleum Corporation operations around the globe. From
time to time, however, one was pressed into service to
ferry the Bayou Perdu Council, K. of C., around,
especially to locations where the New Orleans Saints were
playing what the Bayou Perdu Council, K. of C., referred
to as "footsball."

The council itself was something of a problem to the
Knights of Columbus generally, and to the New Orleans
Archdiocese, under whose spiritual domain it fell.

It had been founded by the New Orleans Consistory,
K. of C., about twenty-five years before, at the prodding
of the archbishop, who felt that the presence of the
Knights in Bayou Perdu—that which there was no lonelier,
more remote swampy bayou in all of Louisiana—would
have a beneficial, uplifting moral effect. The archbishop
was well aware that the inhabitants of Bayou Perdu
attended church regularly only when in the hands of the
law, when there was nothing else to do in the slammer
of a Sunday morning. When they were at liberty—when
they had not been caught and sentenced for distilling
whiskey, poaching deer or drunk and disorderly conduct—they attended church only for weddings, baptisms
and funerals.

The archbishop was a practical man, and he knew
that portion of his flock rather well. He hoped, when
he browbeat the consistory into subsidizing a council
of the K. of C. at Bayou Perdu, to accomplish only a
few things, primarily to keep up church attendance among
his Cajun flock by scheduling a greater number of K.
of C. affairs terminating in church services. He suspected
(correctly) that the Bayou Perdu Council, K. of C.,
would be fascinated with the uniforms of the Knights
and the rituals, and would welcome the opportunity to
wear the uniforms as often as possible, even if that meant
going to church.

For several years, his plot worked very well. To a man, the population of Bayou Perdu had flocked to the Knights, and they had indeed been willing, even eager, to participate in the various rituals prescribed for the group. During that period, the only problem the archbishop had was in handling the complaints of other K. of C. councils within the consistory whose fraternal feelings toward the Bayou Perdu Council were often severely strained by the behavior of Bayou Perdu Knights attending consistory functions.

The dignity of the consistory was weakened, the complainants said, by the Bayou Perdu Council's very appearance in parades. What people remembered, the complainants stressed, was not the dignified, decorous, uplifting participation of twenty-six other councils, marching with precision and even majesty along the parade route to the strains of appropriate martial music, but the appearance of the Bayou Perdu Council, gloriously drunk, lurching along in their ragged uniforms to the music of their own band—consisting of four trumpets, two ukuleles, a xylophone, a Jew's harp and a bass drum—playing the only song they knew, which happened to be "There'll Be a Hot Time in the Old Town Tonight."

All of this was before the discovery of natural gas under the 16,000 acres of land (officially described as "uninhabitable swamp") owned by Mr. Jean-Pierre de la Chevaux.*

The Bayou Perdu Council, K. of C., which had been meeting in an otherwise unused frame shack teetering on rotten pilings over the swamp, soon had a $500,000 Council Building with steam baths, cardrooms and the longest bar east of the Mississippi River. Their hand-me-down uniforms were soon replaced by the finest uniforms Brooks Brothers could supply. When negotiations for

* The story of Mr. de la Chevaux's rise to international prominence has been recorded for posterity in an attractive, superbly written, morally uplifting tome, suitable for gift purposes and on coffee tables, entitled *M*A*S*H Goes to New Orleans*, Pocket Books, New York, 1975.

the services of the Louisiana University Million-Dollar Marching Band broke down—after the exact nature of the services to be furnished was explained—the Bayou Perdu Council arranged for the services of Papa George's Original Dixieland Funeral Band.

Where previously they had journeyed to New Orleans for consistory functions jammed together in a rattletrap collection of whichever pickup trucks could be coaxed into life, they now made the journey in air-conditioned buses. They were identical to those used by the Greyhound Bus Company except that both the Bayou Perdu Council buses were painted bright yellow and had carefully tuned chrome-plated horns on the roof which blasted out a trumpet rendition of "Onward, Christian Soldiers" whenever the driver touched the horn button.

All of the money to pay for all of this had come, of course, from Jean-Pierre "Horsey" de la Chevaux. Soon after what His Eminence regarded as an ostentatious display of wealth came to his attention, His Eminence asked Mr. de la Chevaux to New Orleans for a little chat. During their meeting, His Eminence pointed out that the Knights of Columbus was a fraternal and *charitable* organization, and while the archbishop could find no fault with the fraternal activities of the Bayou Perdu Council, what about the charitable?

The result of that meeting was a small, discreet bronze plaque on The Gates of Heaven Hospital announcing that it was the gift from the Bayou Perdu Council, Knights of Columbus. And as the fortunes of Chevaux Petroleum Corporation had prospered, so had those activities dependent upon the charity of the Bayou Perdu Council K. of C.

The complaints about the behavior of the Bayou Perdu Council, K. of C., however, had continued until Horsey finally got the message. They were unwanted. He informed the archbishop that he was right: the Bayou Perdu Council was a disgrace to the K. of C. The obvious solution to that was to drop out of the Knights of Columbus and form the Knights of Bienville. The Sieur de Bienville was (a) French, as were Horsey and his cronies, and (b) had been the man who discovered New Orleans. (Columbus was, Horsey told the archbishop, nothing more than a confused Italian who had confused an obscure island in the Caribbean with India.)

After some thought, the archbishop decided that the Bayou Perdu Council, warts and all, still belonged in the Knights of Columbus; and from that day, he turned a deaf ear to the complaints of other councils within the consistory.

Boris Alexandrovich Korsky-Rimsakov had met the Bayou Perdu Council, K. of C., at the wedding, and subsequent funeral, of the late Rev. Buck Wilson and had found them all to be kindred souls. The admiration had been mutual, and he had been installed as their Only Honorary Knight Guardian of the Silver Fleece. Since Boris was of the Russian Orthodox persuasion, this had caused some consternation in the respective chancelleries, but it had all been worked out in the end.

Boris had last seen the Knights of the Bayou Perdu Council in convention assembled in Paris, a donnybrook involving them and the Garde Republicaine and the Gendarmerie Nationale which had provided Boris with more pleasure than anything he could remember.

"The Bayou Perdu Council is coming to London?" Boris asked.

"They be there about the same time we get there," Horsey said.

"Horsey, let's just keep this a secret between you and me," Boris said. "No sense spoiling the surprise, is there?"

"Well, what about a place for them to stay?" Horsey pursued.

"If all else fails," Boris said, "we can always send them over to Buckingham Palace. The rooms aren't much, but the kitchen is supposed to be pretty good."

"Just so they get to march in Woody's uncle's . . . God rest his soul . . . parade."

"I'm sure Woody wouldn't have it any other way," Boris said. Boris had not, frankly, been looking forward to the ceremonial planting of the late Duke, although

he was willing to go along with it for Woody's sake. But
now that the Bayou Perdu Council was coming, things
were looking up.

As soon as he could discreetly do so, he had a word
with Prince Hassan, who radioed ahead to the Royal
Hussid Embassy in London directing the Ambassador
to arrange for transportation for the Bayou Perdu
Council, and for a floor of the London Hilton to house
them.

The radio message was overheard by the radio operator
in Air Force Three, which was flying a half-mile ahead
of the Chevaux Petroleum aircraft. Having had some
previous experience with Mr. de la Chevaux, Maestro
Korsky-Rimsakov and His Highness, the Secretary of
State had ordered the radio operator to listen for any
transmissions from the other aircraft, and to bring them
immediately to his attention.

He quickly scribbled a message on a notepad, and
ordered that it be instantly transmitted to the London
Embassy of the United States Government in code. The
essence of the message was that unless the London
Metropolitan Police Force (the official name of the Bob-
bies) took extraordinary measures to keep the passengers
of a Chevaux Petroleum Corporation 707 due to arrive
at about the same time as Air Force Three far away from
Air Force Three, the solemn arrival of Midshipman His
Grace the Duke of Folkestone would be turned into a
riot.

When the Metropolitan Police Force received the
message, they immediately requested reinforcements
from elsewhere in Great Britain. They already had their
hands full with what they called Extraordinary Arrivals
and Departures.

A rock musical ensemble known as Porky Pig & The
Swine had chosen the arrival hour of His Grace the Duke
of Folkestone as their departure hour. Several hundred
fans of the group were already at Heathrow Airport and,
based on previous experience, there would be several
thousand howling, weeping, screaming teen-agers on
hand by departure time.

Furthermore, the Intelligence Unit of the Metropolitan Police Force had reported that the secret arrival of Boris Korsky-Rimsakov in England was no longer a secret. The first members of the Korsky-Rimsakov Fan Club had already arrived at Heathrow to greet their idol, and they were even harder to control than the Swine fanciers. With a few exceptions, they were adult females of respectable appearance, virtually impossible to identify until the moment Korsky-Rimsakov appeared, whereupon they instantly shed all resemblance to sane, middle-aged, middle-class females and fought like tigers to approach the singer. The problem was compounded further by weight. A Porky Pig fan could usually be carried off bodily by one—and never more than two—policemen. Korsky-Rimsakov fans required at least two policemen per fan, and often four, one grunting under the load at each extremity.

All this was, of course, in addition to the extraordinary security precautions already ordered. almost routinely, for the arrival of His Royal Highness Prince Hassan ad Kayam. Prince Hassan had no fan clubs What he had was the third-largest reserve in the world of Sweet Crude Oil beneath the sands of his homeland, and Sweet Crude was necessary to the well-being of the British economy. Word had come from Number Ten Downing Street that wheneve' His Highness chose to visit Great Britain, he was to be treated as an honored guest of the Crown.

And superimposed on top of this. of course were the arrangement for the arrival of the American Secretary of State accompanying Midshipman His Grace the Duke of Folkestone. This, too, was a state matter. on which the dignity of the British Empire hung. It simply had to be carried out with decorum, far from the screams of the howling mobs.

Normally. this would have been a matter of arranging for the aircraft to be parked at widely separated points. The problem was compounded by the number of Very Important People gathering at Heathrow to greet His Grace and the Secretary of State, His Highness Prince Hassan and Maestro Korsky-Rimsakov, and to bid fond farewell to Porky Pig & The Swine. There was only so much room in the official V.I.P. Waiting Room. It was very difficult, if not impossible, for example, to tell the president of the Yorkshire and Northumberland Life and Casualty Assurance Companies and his staff that he would have to leave the room to make room for Her Grace the Duchess of Crimley and Lady Chastity Cheppingwhite-Brown. Or to tell the Duchess and her daughter they would have to leave to make room for a delegation of American Congressmen; or to tell the Congressmen they had to get out in favor of a delegation of Admirals from H.M. Admiralty. Or to tell the Admirals to leave so that the American Ambassador could get in. On the other hand, you could hardly tell Her Majesty's Official Bearer of Mourning & Welcome that he couldn't get into the V.I.P. Room because it was already occupied by the Executive Council of the Porky Pig & The Swine Fan Club of Great Britain and Northern Ireland, or that the presence of the general manager of the East Anglia Breweries, Ltd., in the V.I.P. Waiting Room made it impossible to admit the general manager of the Covent Garden Opera House. Or to tell the Royal Hussid Ambassador that there was, so to speak, simply no room at the inn for him.

After some thought, the parking area normally assigned to Trans World Airlines, providing parking space for two 747 jumbo jets and three 707 Intercontinental jets, was temporarily appropriated in the name of the Crown. The aircraft were towed away. Police barriers were erected around the area, with a Bobby stationed each ten feet, facing outward. Portable toilets were rolled in. A first-aid station was erected. And, finally, a huge banner supported by poles was erected. It read: V.I.P. WAITING ROOM, PRIVATE.

The first plane to arrive was a 707 belonging to the Chevaux Petroleum Corporation. Immediately on landing, it and the bus sent to transport its passengers were dispatched to a remote corner of the airfield, together with the necessary customs officers and a portable passport-stamping booth. Debarking procedures were commenced. The passengers were off-loaded. A customs officer, armed with a portable megaphone, waited until the passengers were gathered in a group around him; and then, in clear, precise Oxfordian accents he detailed the procedure to follow. They were to find their luggage, and then carry it past a customs officer for inspection. They were next to step to the immigration officer, who would stamp their passports. Then they were to board the bus which would take them directly to their hotel.

He might as well have been speaking Aramaic. Not only were the members of the Bayou Perdu Council, K. of C., wholly unused to Oxfordian English but, to a man, they had passed the flight as they passed all flights, in merry song and by the comsumption of large quantities of Old White Stagg Blended Kentucky Bourbon. Those who were still awake when the plane landed were in no mood to be shoved around by a policeman; and those who had to be shaken awake to be informed they were in England were slightly grumpy.

Only one thing was clear to all of them. Horsey de la Chevaux had sent a message that they were to meet him at the airport in London, and that's what they intended to do. They weren't gettin' on no bus to go nowheres until Horsey said so.

As an attempt to translate this statement of policy was being made by H.M. customs and immigration officers, the parade of limousines bearing Porky Pig & The Swine entered the airfield. They had, naturally, entered the Heathrow complex by an obscure gate to avoid the crowds. Furthermore, they were traveling by chartered 707, rather than by a scheduled airline. There was a 707, and from the legend painted on its side (CHEVAUX PETROLEUM CORPORATON), it was a 707 customarily engaged in the business of transporting rock musical ensembles. While Mr. Porky Pig himself had never heard of the Chevaux Petroleum Corporation, he could judge by the ornate uniforms of its members that it was obviously a successful group. You can't afford uniforms like that, he thought, or a band that large, by playing one-night stands in Salinas, Kansas. They had obviously found their departure point.

"Elwood," Porky Pig said to his manager, "see if you can get our name painted on the plane at the first stop. I don't want us mistaken for the Chevaux Petroleum Corporation."

"Right, Porky," his manager said. "I'll get right on it."

Porky, dragging his bird by the hand behind him, got out of the limousine. His eye ran over his fellow musicians and finally came to rest on one who was certainly the leader. Not only was he six-foot-six and about 250, with his uniform tunic open to the waist, exposing a massive, hair-covered chest, but he had a half-gallon bottle of Old White Stagg Blended Kentucky Bourbon in each hand.

(It should be noted that Porky Pig & The Swine were truly an avant-garde ensemble. They were *way* beyond marijuana, LSD, the root of the peyote cactus, airplane glue and other such passé tickets to a trip, and into booze.)

"Hey, Brother," Porky Pig said to François Mulligan, Deputy Assistant Knight Commander of the Peace, "welcome to London!"

"Same to you," François Mulligan said. "Have a snort!"

"Don't mind if I do," Porky Pig said, taking the extended bottle. He took a healthy swallow, blanched, burped, batted his chest and expressed his appreciation. "Far out!"

"From New Orleans," François Mulligan said.

Other Swine emerged from other limousines, each accompanied by at least one scantily clad female. Even the grumpiest of the Bayou Perdu Council began to smile.

"Where did you get that booze, Brother?" Porky Pig inquired. He had to have some more of it.

"We brung it with us," François replied. He gestured toward the stairway of the airplane, down which several Knights were carrying cases of Old White Stagg.

"You want to make a swap?" Porky Pig asked. He had noticed the approval with which his fellow, if newly met, musicians were regarding the birds. There would be new female fans (the term was groupies) in Paris, their next stop.

"What you got in mind?" François asked, somewhat suspiciously.

"You're in England, man," Porky said. "You mean you never heard of a bird and bottle?"

François shook his head, admitting he had not.

"We'll swap you a bird for a bottle," Porky Pig said.

"Wait a minute, dearie," Porky's bird said, "I never even *heard* of these guys."

"Where you guys playing?" Porky asked.

François, thinking the word spoken was "staying," replied: "Some place called the Hilton."

"You're playing the Hilton?" the bird asked, in disbelief.

François now understood the word. "Nah," he said, smiling broadly at the bird. "We're *staying* at the Hilton. We're playing some place called Westminster Abbey."

The bird, who had been hanging onto Porky's arm, now turned him loose and took François's arm. "Are you the leader?" she asked, smiling up at him.

"I'm François," he said. He pointed up at the sky. Chevaux Petroleum's Sabreliner was about to land. "Horsey, he's the leader, he's coming in his own plane."

"Change groups, girls," the bird cried. "We got us a new group." She pointedly added: "A *two-plane* group, what's going to play at *Westminster Abbey*."

"I think I'm gonna like England," François said.

"You want a bottle a broad, right?"

"The word in England is 'bird'," Porky said. He himself was impressed. The Swine had not appeared in Westminster Abbey. His agent would hear about that.

"Bird, broad, what's the difference?" François asked. He shouted up at the pilot. "Hey, Homer, take these guys where they want to go, and then wait for us here, O.K.?"

The pilot, who had been dispatched to ferry the chorus line of Caesars Palace from Las Vegas to Bayou Perdu for a Columbus Birthday Party was not even surprised at the order. He made an "O.K." signal with his hand. François stood by the stacked cases of Old White Stagg and handed each Swine a half-gallon as he walked past. When the last Swine had entered the aircraft, the door closed and the huge machine began to taxi off.

"Everybody on the buses," François ordered. "Horsey's just landed. Wait till he finds out about England!"

# Chapter Fourteen

At ten fifteen that same morning, three hours and fifteen minutes after Miss Florabelle Jenkins had failed for the first time in her many long years as executive castlekeeper of Folkestone Castle to reign over the Executive Council Breakfast, Brig. Montague Fyffe bit the bullet. His duty required that he determine precisely what was going on in the Duchess's apartment of Folkestone Castle.

It was a combination of curiosity, and the necessity for Miss Florabelle to make certain decisions. The phones and Teletypewriters had been busy. The three American television networks had all submitted bids for the exclusive right to televise the final internment in the family crypt, and they needed an answer right now. The Turret & Tower Motel would be full, but the Foreign Office had called and made certain unpleasant threats regarding the absolute necessity to house something called The U.S. Congress Official Ad Hoc Committee to Mourn the Duke of Folkestone. That would require beds for 117 people, not all of whom could be tucked in two at a time. There was good news and bad news from the DeHavilland china people. They had been able to turn out the 15,000 souvenir funeral coasters on a crash basis, but the order had been telephoned in, not written, and there was an unfortunate misspelling—which might, by some people, be considered obscene—of the Ducal name. Only Miss Florabelle could make the decision to put them on sale anyway, or to order them destroyed, with the loss of revenue that would mean.

Brigadier Fyffe bit the bullet, to reiterate. The cherry picker, a truck-mounted device incorporating a small, man-carrying platform on a hydraulically extendable shaft was ordered up. Brigadier Fyffe climbed aboard, put his hands to the controls and skillfully guided the platform to a position outside the windows of the Duchess's apartment and, with his riding crop, gently pushed aside the heavy drapes. He instantly let the drapes fall back into position. He found it difficult to believe what his own eyes showed him.

Miss Florabelle Jenkins, wearing only a sari, the lower hem of which had in her sleep apparently worked its way upward over her hips, was lying sprawled before the Great Fireplace on a polar bear rug. Beside her, similarly sprawled, and similarly indecently exposed by the nocturnal movements of his kilt, was Mr. Angus MacKenzie, general manager of East Anglia Breweries, Ltd.

When the first shock had passed, Brigadier Fyffe put from his mind the incredible suggestion that Miss Florabelle Jenkins and the gentleman with her had been engaged in the sinful passions of the flesh. The most likely possibility was that they had both been murdered and then arranged in those obscene positions by a pathological sex murderer. Fyffe steeled himself for the ordeal and again pushed the heavy draperies aside with his riding crop. This time his mouth dropped open. As he watched, Miss Florabelle, still shockingly dishabille, rolled over in her sleep onto the body of Mr. MacKenzie, whose arm slowly but inexorably moved around her.

At that moment, there was a tug at Fyffe's riding crop. The draperies dropped back into position, and he looked in shock at his riding crop. There was no question about it: It had been neatly bitten in two.

Hastily, he pushed the DOWN button, and the cherry picker dropped away from the window. As it dropped away, Fyffe picked up the telephone with which the cherry picker was equipped. "Send someone to count the lions," he ordered. "I want a head count immediately."

On the polar bear rug before the Great Fireplace, Angus MacKenzie woke first. Wee Black Doggie was ferociously pawing the heavy drapes.

"Stop that, damnit!" he bellowed. The sound of his voice woke Miss Florabelle Jenkins. She raised her head and found herself looking at Angus MacKenzie, who was looking at her wide-eyed.

"Stop what?" she asked, quite naturally. There was a strange, not at all unpleasant, warmth in her body. And then, slowly (it was, after all, her first experience with the sensation), she realized what caused it. "Angus," she said, "you have taken my innocence!"

"Jesus Maxwell Christ!" Angus MacKenzie said.

"Please avert your eyes," Florabelle said, icily, "in the name of decency."

Angus closed his eyes. A groan passed his lips. He lay a moment that way, but then one eye flickered open to give him a brief but clear view of Miss Florabelle getting to her feet and rearranging her clothing. In the last second before modesty was restored, Angus got to see what no man had ever seen before. It was not an unpleasant sight.

Then he remembered his own condition. Looking not unlike a woman tugging at a foundation garment, his eyes again tightly closed, Angus tugged downward at his kilt until he, too, was modestly covered.

That accomplished, he sat up.

"Kin I open me eyes?" he asked.

"You may," Miss Florabelle said, "with the understanding that you are never to look at me again."

"Thank you," Angus said. He opened his eyes. "We seem to have dropped off for a moment," he said.

"That's one way of putting it," Miss Florabelle said.

"Well, it's getting on toward eleven," Angus said. "I expect that I'd better be getting on."

"Good evening, Mr. MacKenzie," Florabelle said. "I daresay this will be our final encounter on earth."

"I'm sorry you feel that way," Angus said. "For my part . . . "

"That will be quite enough, Mr. MacKenzie," Miss Florabelle said icily as she walked to the drapes. "I have not only lost my respect for you, but for myself . . . oh, my God!"

"Florabelle, what is it?"

"It's daylight!" she said, having perceived same through the drapes. "You have worked your wicked way on me all through the night. God alone knows how often you have . . . you have . . . you know what I mean."

"That's the first time that's ever happened," Angus said thoughtfully. "The first time I've ever done that."

"You aren't standing there expecting me to believe that I am the first woman you have ever known? In the Biblical sense, I mean."

"No," Angus said. "But yer the first one I ever spent the night with. Slam bam; thank you, ma'am, and out the door, as we say in the Royal Marines."

"You are disgusting!" she said.

"Florabelle," Angus said, "I have something to say to ye. I would be grateful if ye would hear me out."

"If you wish, Mr. MacKenzie," she said.

"The farthest thing from me mind was taking advantage of ye," Angus said. "As a matter of fact, the last thing I remember about last night was eatin' curry an' thinking how much me life would have been changed had I known someone like ye in me younger days."

"The last thing you remember was *eating curry?*" Florabelle accused. Before Angus had a chance to reply, she posed another question: "Why do you keep turning your head like that?"

"Ye tol' me never to look at ye again," Angus said. "And the way you keep looking at me, that's not easy."

That left her without much to say for the moment. There was an awkward silence, and then she announced: "You may continue."

"I need a wee drop afore that," he said. He picked up the previous evening's pitcher, which was now as dry as a bone, went to the barrel, filled it and poured two inches into a glass. He downed it, looked at it, refilled it and handed it to Florabelle.

"You don't actually expect me to drink an intoxicant at this time, do you?" Florabelle said. "Especially under these circumstances?"

He took it back from her, drank it himself, refilled it and handed it to her again.

"Drink it, Florabelle," he ordered. "I suspect that yer goin' to need it as much as I did."

There was something commanding and irresistible in his tone. Florabelle attributed this to both his naval service and to the fact that he had recently acquired her pearl of great price. She took it from him and tossed it down.

Angus sort of sank to the floor. In those ancient, historic surroundings, and dressed as he was, substituting a sword for the whiskey glass, the scene resembled a re-enactment of Mary of Scots about to knight one of her Highland warriors.

"What on earth are you doing?" Florabelle Jenkins asked.

"Ain't this the way yer supposed to do it? I damn well intend to do it right," Angus said.

"Do what?"

"What the hell else would I be doin' on me knees like this but asking ye to become me bride?"

Florabelle's mouth fell open and she stared at him wide-eyed. He misinterpreted her reaction.

"I realize I ain't much, Florabelle," he said. "But, on the other hand, you ain't hardly a spring lamb yerself."

"Oh, Angus," Florabelle said, and for the first time in her life used the term of endearment "darling" to address someone of the opposite gender. She dropped to her knees, pursed her lips, and leaned her head forward to be kissed. The kiss had all the passion one sees when a small boy is ordered to kiss a maiden aunt. Then, shyly, awkwardly, they broke apart and got somewhat unsteadily to their feet.

"Angus," she asked, "is it right for us to do this now? With His Grace so recently gone?"

"It's bigger than both of us," Angus said, after a moment. "And I think His Grace wouldn't mind a bit."

"You're right of course," she said. "You're a wise and profound man, Angus."

"I think I need another wee drop," Angus said. "Will ye join me, Florabelle?"

"It does seem to settle the stomach, doesn't it?" Florabelle said, reaching for the pitcher.

They touched glasses. "Here's to us, Florabelle," Angus MacKenzie said. A tear formed in Florabelle's eye and ran down her cheek. There was a slight tremble in her voice as she replied.

"To us, Angus."

He suddenly turned from her and strode purposefully to the telephone. He ordered the switchboard operator to connect him with East Anglia Breweries, Ltd., spoke briefly with someone there and turned to Florabelle.

"The Americans are flying His Grace to London," he said.

She looked at him in utter confusion.

"The *boy*, Florabelle," Angus explained. "I expect we should be there when he arrives." He looked at his watch. "Which means we should leave here in no more than an hour."

"That will give us time to have something to eat," Florabelle said. "Do you like kippers and eggs for breakfast, Angus?"

"Aye, I do," he said. "But that won't take a whole hour."

Florabelle Jenkins flushed. "Angus, what are you suggesting?"

"Hung for a sheep as a lamb, as we say in the Highlands," Angus said, and he flushed. There was a long, painful moment during which Angus came quickly to believe that, having come so close to finding a partner share his life, he had, in one moment's shameless, selfish lust, lost her.

And then Florabelle Jenkins slowly and timidly reached out her hand and took his.

An hour later, Miss Florabelle Jenkins appeared at the top of the staircase in the Great Hall, her hand on the arm of Mr. Angus MacKenzie. They marched slowly, even regally, down the stairs. Wee Black Doggie, tail wagging happily, marched behind them. Brig. Montague Fyffe and members of his staff, at the bottom of the stairs, came to attention.

"Good morning, Brigadier," Miss Florabelle said. "I don't believe you know my fiancé, Mr. MacKenzie?"

"How do you do?" Brigadier Fyffe said.

"Aways a pleasure to meet a fellow retired warrior of the Crown," MacKenzie said.

"Mr. MacKenzie and I are going to London to meet the new Duke of Folkestone," Miss Florabelle said. "I feel sure that you can handle things for me while I'm gone."

"Yes, ma'am," Brigadier Fyffe said.

"Carry on, Brigadier," MacKenzie said. "Come, Wee Black Doggie."

The three marched down the Great Hall, out the door, and got into MacKenzie's Rolls-Royce.

"Where to, sir?" the chauffeur asked.

"Head for London," MacKenzie said. "And as soon as you're off the castle grounds, stop at the first decent-looking place where Miss Jenkins and I can get some breakfast."

There had been time during the flight from Spruce Harbor to London for the subject of the lease of the village of Herstead-on-Heath to be discussed with Midshipman His Grace the Duke of Folkestone. Woody, Hawkeye, Quincy Westerbrook and Trapper John went to the compartment in which L. Bryan Fowler had planned to spend the trip in aerial dalliance with Ms. Peggy-Lou Kastenmeyer, and Quincy Westerbrook explained the situation.

Westerbrook was far more honest in the discussion than either Hawkeye or Trapper John had expected him to be. He told Woody quite frankly that the one pound per annum payment was recognized to be either outrageous or ludicrous and probably both; and that the United States Government, just as soon as Woody could arrange for someone to come up with a fair price, would be more than willing to pay it.

"Very frankly, Your Grace," Westerbrook said, "we regard the uninterrupted deployment of our nuclear-submarine force essential to world security. Herstead-on-Heath is essential to that deployment of our submarines. Moving from Herstead to someplace else would interfere with the deployment. What we would like from you now is simply your assurance that the Navy can stay there, at a price to be later determined by you. Your word will be quite sufficient."

Woody didn't say anything for a minute. That minute gave both Hawkeye and Trapper John plenty of time to reflect that at that very moment there were at several dozen scattered locations under the world's seas small groups of lonely, grossly overworked and grossly underpaid sailors manning the nuclear submarines, keeping the fangs of the Russian bear from biting off any more of the world than they already had.

"Mr. Westerbrook," Woody finally said, and at that moment he didn't look, or sound, like a nice eighteen-year-old English kid, but like, at the very least, a naval officer completely sure of himself and his role in the world, "there were those, I know, who thought my great uncle to be something of a buffoon. Perhaps his romantic escapades gave birth to that reputation. I prefer to remember him as the Captain of H.M.S. *Indefatigable*. She went down in the Pacific during World War II. My great uncle was the last man off her. To get him off his bridge, it was necessary for his marine orderly to render him unconscious by striking him in the jaw with his fist. He would otherwise have willingly gone down with her.

"I daresay that it is safe to presume that it was my great uncle's understanding of the role of your nuclear submarines in world strategy which caused him to make the lease in the first place. It is equally obvious to me that if he set a price of a pound per annum, then this was his way of showing his appreciation for the support your navy has given our navy over the years, and indeed, your country has given my country in two world wars. He was not the sort of man who was able to *say* something like that, but I believe he made his feelings clear.

"With that in mind, I see no reason to change the terms of the lease presently in force. I suggest, in the absence of a formal agreement, a handwritten agreement, signed by me with Drs. Pierce and McIntyre as witnesses, will suffice until such time as a formal lease can be drawn up."

Quincy Westerbrook was visibly embarrassed as he took a typewritten lease from his attaché case.

"Your Grace, this is a formal lease. It provides, as an interim figure, for the payment of one-million dollars per annum, subject to later adjustment."

"Thank you," Midshipman His Grace the Duke of Folkestone, Royal Navy, said. He took the lease, laid it on the table, held it down somewhat awkwardly with his cast, crossed off "one-million dollar" and "interim," wrote in "one pound sterling," and then turned to the last page. There was a signature block. *Hugh Percival, Duke of Folkestone, Viscount Wimberly, Baron Herstead.* With swift, sure strokes, he wrote the one word, "Folkestone".

He looked at Hawkeye as he handed the lease back to Quincy Westerbrook.

"That's the first time I've signed my name that way. It's rather an odd feeling."

"Thank you, Your Grace," Hawkeye said.

"My privilege, gentlemen," the Duke of Folkestone said, rather formally. "And now, if I am correct in presuming that this discussion is at an end, I will rejoin Miss Chambers."

When he had closed the door behind him, Trapper John spoke up.

"I think maybe we made a mistake, Hawkeye," he said.

"About him?" Hawkeye replied. "I don't know."

"I mean, about the Revolution. Maybe King George was no good, but if anyone was to ask me right now, I'd have to say that I'd rather have somebody like the Duke of Folkestone in Washington than most Congressmen I know."

Quincy Westerbrook's diplomatic savoir faire had been somewhat shattered, too, by the Duke's little speech. He said something he normally would not have said.

"I'm glad that's settled. We've gotten word that the Real Estate Department of the Yorkshire and Northumberland Life and Casualty Assurance Companies, Ltd., have been snooping around about the lease."

"So you would have had to pay the million dollars," Trapper said. "So what?"

"From what I understand of Yorkshire and Northumberland," Westerbrook said, "by the time the million had passed through the sticky hands of their executives, there wouldn't have been enough left for the Duke to pay taxes on."

They were not able to go into the subject further. The Duke of Folkestone, after first knocking politely, stuck his head in the door. "Dr. Hawkeye," he asked, pleadingly, "the Reverend Mother says I can't have a beer unless you say so. May I?"

"Hot Lips," Hawkeye bellowed, "give Woody a can of suds!"

Hot Lips did as she was ordered, but came to the compartment a moment later.

"I hope you know what you're doing, giving that boy intoxicants," she said.

"In case you haven't noticed, Hot Lips," Trapper John replied, "there are boys, and then there are *boys*."

"How is Beverly Chambers?" Hawkeye asked. "Feminine heart all aflutter about going to Old Blimey?"

"A little gloomy," Hot Lips said. "She won't be staying in England. Woody will."

"All we can do about that," Hawkeye said, "is see that she has a good time while she's there."

"By all means," Trapper said, "let's make it a Fun Funeral."

# Chapter Fifteen

There are parallel runways at London's Heathrow Airport, permitting the near-simultaneous landing of aircraft. Air Force Three and Chevaux Petroleum Corporation Number Seven landed within seconds of each other, and because it landed on the runway nearest the terminal building, Chevaux Number Seven taxied up there about thirty seconds before Air Force Three.

Immediately, knowing that His Highness Prince Hassan was aboard, the Golden Shadow* Rolls-Royce of the Royal Hussid Embassy glided out of the V.I.P. Vehicle Motor Park toward the aircraft, whose doorway was now opening.

The drivers of the three ambulances—sent by the American Embassy, the Yorkshire and Northumberland

---

* The Golden Shadow is the deluxe version of the common Silver Shadow; it is two feet longer, $17,500 more costly, and has golden—rather than the standard sterling-silver—fittings.

Life and Casualty Assurance Companies and Her Grace
the Duchess of Crimley—naturally presumed that their
patient, His Grace the Duke of Folkestone, would be
given the honor of first arriving and was on the Chevaux
plane. Whoopers whooping, they raced around Air Force
Three and toward the door of Chevaux Seven.

In the wake of the ambulances came the executives
of the Yorkshire and Northumberland Life and Casualty
Assurance Companies, Ltd.; Her Grace the Duchess of
Crimley; the delegation of Admirals from the Admiralty;
the representatives of the U.S. Congress Ad Hoc Committee to Mourn the Duke of Folkestone; the U.S.
Ambassador; and the representatives of the H.M.S. *Indefagitable* Association. All that was left within the
temporary V.I.P. Waiting Area was managing director
of the Covent Garden Opera House and his staff; the
Boris Alexandrovich Korsky-Rimsakov Fan Club; and
the twenty-member-strong executive council of the Porky
Pig & The Swine Fan Club of Great Britain and Northern
Ireland who were, of course, unaware that the Swine
were already on their way to Paris.

There is a spirit, an élan, if you will, common to
ambulance drivers, born of the wholly satisfying experience of scattering traffic and jaywalkers alike in your
path with flashing lights and frightening noises.
Accustomed as they were to having the right of way
granted to them by all comers, the three ambulances
converged at the stairway to Chevaux Seven as Boris
Korsky-Rimsakov appeared in the door.

The right front fender of the Daimler ambulance
crashed into the left front fender of the Rolls-Royce
ambulance; and the two, now more or less permanently
joined together until welding torch could cut them
asunder, were joined seconds later by the Rover ambulance. Clouds of steam came from ruptured radiators, and
there was the not entirely unpleasant, if rather monoto-
nous, sound of their horns merged together and forming
what Boris recognized as G-flat.

Moments later, the buses carrying the Bayou Perdu

Council, K. of C., from the other side of the airfield, pulled up, and the Knights off-loaded, a bottle and a bird per man.

The managing director of the Yorkshire and Northumberland Life and Casualty Assurance Companies, Ltd., reached the bottom of the stairs, precisely at the moment the Hon. Anthony J. Pasquale attempted to be first aboard. As they were trying to elbow each other out of the way, Lady Chastity Cheppingwhite-Browne, who had been riding in the Rolls-Royce ambulance, nimbly jumped from the hood of the Rolls over them, crying, "Make way for the nurse!" and gained the top of the stairway first.

The first person she encountered was Boris Alexandrovich Korsky-Rimsakov.

"God knows, you magnificent animal, that normally you would be all I would dare ask for," she said. "But these are trying times, financially speaking. Where is His Grace the Duke of Folkestone?"

"On the other plane," Boris said. "Would you be interested in an Arab Prince?"

Lady Chastity turned and went down the stairway. "The other plane, Mommy!" she cried. "Run interference for me!"

The members of the Boris Alexandrovich Korsky-Rimsakov Fan Club had by then recognized their idol; and about two hundred middle-aged ladies of ample dimension now headed for the Chevaux aircraft as the horde, which had first approached it, now reversed course.

"There was a general melee," as *The Times* put it in the evening edition, "during which several arrests were made." It was watched by the passengers of Air Force Three, including His Grace and Miss Beverly Chambers. Beverly, whose only experience with riots had been at football games, was slightly unnerved by the sight, and slipped her hand into that of His Grace as they looked out the window.

Although he had never laid eyes on the boy, Angus

MacKenzie, who had been watching the arrival from the rear seat of his Rolls (Miss Florabelle had not felt up to standing in the V.I.P. Waiting Area), recognized him immediately, even through the hazy plexiglass window of Air Force Three.

"Come, Wee Black Doggie," he said, "we'll gae after His Grace, and save him from these maniacs." Wee Black Doggie disliked crowds. When faced with one, the hair on his neck and back stood up, his bright-red gums curved backward, exposing long, white teeth, and a heart-chilling snarl came from his massive chest.

Angus marched toward Air Force Three, as the crowd parted before him and Wee Black Doggie like the Dead Sea in a Cecil B. DeMille Biblical epic. He marched up the stairs and inside the aircraft. Wee Black Doggie gave the steward the impression that he didn't like stewards individually any more than he liked crowds generally. The steward fainted. Wee Black Doggie and Angus stepped over him. His eyes fell upon His Grace and a young woman.

"What a *darling* dog!" Beverly Chambers cooed. She let go of Woody, and wrapped her arms around Wee Black Doggie. Wee Black Doggie started wagging his tail. His tongue lapped Miss Chambers wetly.

"Me name is MacKenzie, laddie," Angus said. "I've come to take ye from these crazy people."

"You were my great uncle's friend?" Woody asked. "Mr. Angus MacKenzie?"

"Aye, that I was," Angus said. "God rest his soul!"

"This young woman is with me, Mr. MacKenzie," Woody said.

"Ah," Angus said, approvingly. "Yer a chip off the old block, Your Grace! Bring her along. I can see from the way Wee Black Doggie likes her what a splendid lass she is."

The trio, preceded by Wee Black Doggie, marched off the airplane. The rioting crowd parted miraculously again. They got into the Rolls and drove off: Woody was between Angus and Florabelle in the back seat;

Beverly, nearly invisible under Wee Black Doggie, who elected to sit on her lap, sat in the front.

As they left the Heathrow Airfield Complex, they were waved (with the polite deference the police always pay to Rolls-Royces) to a stop. A sergeant approached the car, saluted politely and said: "Very sorry to trouble you, sir, but would you mind telling me who you are?"

"I'm Angus MacKenzie, general manager of East Anglia Breweries," Angus replied. "What's going on here?"

"We have just received word that an attempt has been made, or may be made, to kidnap the Duke of Folkestone."

"My God, Whaley!" Angus shouted at the chauffeur. "The Irish are after His Grace! Will they stop at nothing? Get moving!"

The police sergeant saluted again as the Rolls raced off.

"Don't ye worry about a thing, laddie," Angus said. "Ye're safe as can be with Angus MacKenzie. I know a place to take you."

"The castle, Angus?" Florabelle asked.

"If they'd tried to grab the boy at the airport, they'd try to grab him at the castle," Angus said. "Take us to the Sword, Crown & Anchor, Whaley. Let them crazy Irishmen try something funny there!"

"But why would anyone want to kidnap me?" Woody asked.

"I can only tell ye, laddie, what your great uncle used to say to me all the time: 'They're daft, drunk or sober, they're daft'."

When they reached the Sword, Crown & Anchor, Angus got out of the car first to have a word with the proprietor, Sgt. Amos Davis, Royal Marines, Retired.

"What are you doin' dressed up like a damned banker, Angus?" Amos greeted him.

"There'll be time later for explanations, Amos," MacKenzie said. "In the meantime, you got to trust me."

"Whatever you say, Angus," Amos said.

"I'm going to bring a young lad in here," Angus said. "And his girl. And a . . . uh . . . a lady acquaintance of mine."

"Yer gonna bring the Old Biddie in the Castle in here, Angus?"

"Under other circumstances, Amos Davis, I'd make ye eat yer dentures for a comment like that about the lady I am to marry," Angus said. "But right now I need you."

"What do you want me to do?"

"Nothing."

"Nothing?"

"If anybody . . . anybody at all . . . asks, the bridal suite is vacant. Ye can say yer fixing the plumbing. Ye've seen nothing and heard nothing."

"Sounds like ye're running from the cops."

"And keep a watch out for suspicious looking Irishmen," Angus said, ignoring him.

"Which side?"

"Don't know," Angus said. "They're daft on both sides."

"Aye, that they are," Amos Davis said.

"I wouldn't want them to know why ye suddenly got generous," Angus said, thrusting a thick wad of pound notes at Amos. "But maybe if the house was treatin', some of the boys might stick around—in case they was needed, if you follow me."

"I follow ye, Angus," Amos said. "Put your mind at rest."

"Won't be for more than a couple of hours, just until I find out what's going on," Angus said.

After His Grace and Miss Beverly Chambers and Miss Florabelle Jenkins were installed in the bridal suite, and Angus had arranged for food and drink to be sent up from the Sword, Crown & Anchor's kitchen, he began to make a telephone call.

What he heard was baffling. According to his friend on the police force, His Grace had actually been kidnapped, by a wild-eyed Irish madman who traveled around with an enormous, man-eating black bear. According to one somewhat hysterical witness, the bear had been seen jumping over the Heathrow Airport fence with His Grace in his mouth.

The dirty Irish blackguards had also, his informant told him, made off with an American nurse. Maybe more than one nurse. The head count of assorted Americans was still in progress. There were some Arabs also involved, but just how was not yet clear.

Angus thanked him and hung up. He stopped at the bar for a quick one to clear his head. It took three nips before he came to the conclusion that the story about His Grace being kidnapped had been put out to lull black-hearted Irishmen on kidnap duty elsewhere, say at Folkestone Castle or the Dorchester Hotel, into a false sense of security.

Scotland Yard, probably assisted by the Royal Marines, was more than likely at this very minute rounding the blackguards up. All he had to do . . . the obvious thing to do . . . was stay where he was until Scotland Yard had done their duty. His Grace was as safe in the Sword, Crown & Anchor as he would be in the Tower of London with the whole damned Household Cavalry riding around it on their horses.

He climbed the stairs to the bridal suite, fixed the story he would tell in his mind, and entered.

"It will, I'm afraid, be necessary for us to stay here a bit until things can settle down," he said. "The moon's full again, and the Irish have gone daft. But not to worry. We kin have a nice little supper, and it'll soon be over."

"Mr. MacKenzie," Miss Florabelle said, "has extensive experience with the Royal Marines dealing with rebellious natives in India."

Beverly Chambers sought the comfort of His Grace's arm around her.

"Beverly," Woody said, "we're in good hands. Mr. MacKenzie has been taking care of my family for years. He saved the life of my great uncle, you know."

She did not know, of course, and it was necessary to tell the story. Both females were suitably impressed. It was not, all things considered, for any of them, a very unpleasant way to pass the several hours they spent together in the bridal suite of the Sword, Crown & Anchor.

Back at Heathrow Airport, however, and later at the American Embassy, the Dorchester Hotel, Number Ten Downing Street and at New Scotland Yard, it was, as it says in The Good Book, a time of travail and heavy labor.

The following is an extract from The First After Action Report submitted by Deputy Assistant Chief Inspector Reginald J.K. Wormsworth, O.B.E., Metropolitan Police Force, to the Home Secretary:

What had been the V.I.P. Waiting Area was converted into a Temporary Holding Facility of the Metropolitan Police Force until such time as buses could be obtained from the London Transport Organization to ferry those arrested to places of arraignment and detainment.

Bruce J. Ludwell, chairman of the board of the Yorkshire and Northumberland Life and Casualty Assurance Companies, Ltd., had, after warning, been arrested and charged with disturbing the peace. So had the Hon. Anthony J. Pasquale, chairman of the U.S. Congress Ad Hoc Committee to Mourn the Duke of Folkestone. Both prisoners had been arrested as they had attempted to force their way onto Air Force Three and had, as a matter of course, been handcuffed together. It had then been necessary to separate them, in their own interests, after Congressman Pasquale had referred to Mr. Ludwell as a "lisping Limey" and Mr. Ludwell had referred to the Congressman as a "bloody Wop". Before they were separated and handcuffed at separated locations, and using, of course, one hand only, they had managed to give each other a bloody nose and a black eye, respectively.

The major source of trouble, however, which had required most of the First and Second Flying

Phalanx of the Metropolitan Police Force to quell, had been Mr. Boris Alexandrovich Korsky-Rimsakov, the opera singer. Mr. Korsky-Rimsakov, seeing the crowd surge toward the aircraft on which he believed His Grace the Duke of Folkestone was a passenger, had seen it as his duty to come to his aid. He had thereupon exited the aircraft on which he had arrived and attempted to make his way to Air Force Three.

The bodyguard of His Royal Highness Prince Hassan ad Kayam, having standing orders to come to the assistance of Mr. Korsky-Rimsakov in crowd situations, had attempted to protect him. They had naturally misunderstood the intentions of the Boris Alexandrovich Korsky-Rimsakov Fan Club, who began to scream and otherwise demonstrate when they saw their idol, so to speak, in their midst.

At this point, mistaking the intentions of both the fan club and of the bodyguard with regard to Mr. Korsky-Rimsakov, the Bayou Perdu Council, K. of C., had attempted to come to Mr. Korsky-Rimsakov's assistance. They probably would have been successful in this effort had not the members of the Survivors of the H.M.S. *Indefagitable* Association mistaken the efforts of the Bayou Perdu Council, K. of C., to come to the aid of Mr. Korsky-Rimsakov for an unlawful assault upon the duly constituted law-enforcement officials of the Crown. They rose, naturally, as one man, to come to the aid of the Crown.

And, finally, at this point, the executive council of the Porky Pig & The Swine Fan Club of Great Britain and Northern Ireland somehow got the idea that the source of the disturbance was the awaited appearance of Mr. Pig & The Swine. They then apparently came to the conclusion that the Metropolitan Police Force was (as indeed they had in the past) attempting to keep the Swine separated from their fans.

It was first necessary for the police to separate

the various groups from one another and from their leaders. (It took the efforts of six officers of the Metropolitan Police Force to restrain Mr. Korsky-Rimsakov alone, to give some idea of the magnitude of the problem.) This took approximately thirty minutes, and would have taken longer had it not been for the fortuitous presence at Heathrow of the Upper Warwickshire Constabulary Singing Society. The Society was returning home following an appearance at the Anglo-German *Singerbund* Competition in Hamburg, at which they had taken third place in category C (fifty men or more). The Upper Warwickshire Constabulary rushed to the aid of the Metropolitan Police, and their help was of great value; and it would have been of even greater value had all of them been in uniform.

It was not until peace had been restored that it became known for sure that His Grace the Duke of Folkestone was missing, together with his nurse, from Air Force Three, although that alarm had been given earlier. The first report had been discounted because of the somewhat hysterical condition of the alarm giver. The major thrust of this complaint was that he had been attacked by a man-eating black bear and only after a time (following his medical tranquilization by two physicians who happened to be aboard Air Force Three) did it come out that the man-eating bear was in the company of the man now being sought in connection with His Grace's disappearance.

Insofar as it is possible under the circumstances, the participants in the melee were incarcerated with other members of their organization, or affinity group, in various detention facilities in the London area. Because of the load placed upon available cell resources, this posed some problems, and the division by group was not always possible. Those detainees of special status (the bodyguard of H.R.H. Prince Hassan, for example) all carried diplomatic passports. And among those detained were: the Duchess of Crimley; Lady Chastity Cheppingwhite-Browne; six United States Congressmen; several senior officials of the Yorkshire and Northumberland Life and Casualty Assurance Companies, Ltd.; and thirteen members of the Boris Alexandrovich Korsky-Rimsakov Fan Club who represented themselves to be wives of Members of Parliament. They were transported to the Tower of London in commandeered taxicabs, rather than in police vans or buses.

An hour and fifteen minutes after Air Force Three touched down, a London taxicab pulled into Downing Street and stopped before Number Ten. Dr. Benjamin Franklin Pierce and Dr. John F.X. McIntyre emerged. The entrance to Number Ten was ringed with a circle of policemen.

"This must be the place," Hawkeye said.

"You can tell by the number on the door," Trapper John agreed.

They marched toward the door, Hawkeye's hand raised to grab the highly polished brass knocker. Their way was blocked by a very large Bobby.

"Have you an appointment, gentlemen?" he asked, very politely.

"Actually, no," Hawkeye admitted. "What we are, you see, are two American taxpayers who wish to speak with a couple of our public servants who we understand are in here."

"The only Americans in there, sir, are the American Secretary of State and the American Ambassador and certain members of their staffs."

"Those are the ones," Trapper John said.

"They are in conference, sir, with the Prime Minister and the Foreign and Home Secretaries."

"I'm glad to see they're earning their pay," Hawkeye said.

"And cannot be disturbed," the Bobby concluded firmly.

"But we wish to participate in the conference," Hawkeye said.

"We have, in fact, something to contribute to the conference," Trapper John added.

"Perhaps, gentlemen, if you would telephone for an appointment, one could be arranged." He was, of course, an experienced security officer, and had long ago learned that the best way to deal with Kooks & Nuts was to reason with them if possible.

"I'll tell you what," Hawkeye said, "could we get a message inside?"

"To whom, sir?"

"To the Hon. Quincy Westerbrook," Hawkeye said. For the first time, the Bobby looked at them with interest. The ordinary run-of-the-mill Kook & Nut did not know the names of junior staff members.

"I think that could be arranged, sir. What is the message?"

"Would you be good enough to tell Mr. Westerbrook to tell Chubby that unless Chubby lets us in to tell us what he knows, we're going to tell what we know to Howard K. Smith? That we've already placed the call?"

The Bobby, scribbling furiously, wrote this all down, read it back to make sure he'd caught it all, and then banged the brass knocker and gave the message to the liveried butler who answered, with instructions to deliver it to the American Diplomatic Gentleman, Mr. Westerbrook.

Five minutes later—after Drs. McIntyre and Pierce had passed the time inquiring of the security officer whether or not he liked his work, his marital status and the number and type of his children, and his opinion of the Common Market—the door to Number Ten Downing Street opened.

"Admit these gentlemen," the butler told the Bobby. He stepped back as if to avoid contamination as Hawkeye and Trapper John, after a friendly wave at the Bobby, stepped through the door.

# Chapter Sixteen

The Resistance-to-Arrest-Rating of the Bayou Perdu Council, K. of C. (9.5 on a scale of 10) was as high, generally speaking, as any ever awarded to any group, including the Royal Marines, by the Metropolitan Police Force. They were logically detained in the detention facility (the Canningtown Municipal Gaol) in which, as a long and honored tradition, members of the Royal Marines were, when necessary, housed.

They had been installed in the damp and dismal dungeons just over an hour when the ancient barred door creaked open and Boris Alexandrovich Korsky-Rimsakov was added to their number, carried inside by six sturdy stalwarts of the law.

Mr. Korsky-Rimsakov, who had been originally detained at the Tower of London with the other Special-Status prisoners, had caused a disturbance there, and had also been responsible for another. The Lord Warden of the Tower of London was an experienced penologist and quite prepared to turn a deaf ear to the prisoner's bellowing complaint that being "jugged with a pansy and a politician (he had been placed with Mr. Bruce Ludwell and Congressman "Tiny Tony" Pasquale) constituted cruel and unusual punishment forbidden by the Magna Carta," but he was not equipped to deal with the fifteen ladies whose mates sat in the House of Parliament.

Once they had learned that their idol was in the Tower, they had become quite uncontrollable. About half of them were enraged by the idea that he was jailed at all, and the other half by the Lord Warden's announcement that he could not arrange for Mr. Korsky-Rimsakov to be jailed with them.

Some of the Special-Status ladies vented their displeasure by banging on the cell doors with their metal food trays. Others set fire to their mattresses. Several attempted to bribe guards with diamond rings and other valuables. The decision to move Mr. Korsky-Rimsakov came when word reached the Lord Warden that several ladies in cells facing the moat (which was now dry, turned into a garden and filled with tourists) were calling attention to the Lord Warden's cruelty by dancing before the barred windows in their birthday suits, which tactic seemed to be affecting ticket sales.

An hour after the creaking dungeon gate opened screechingly to admit Mr. Korsky-Rimsakov, however— barely time for he and the Knights to compare notes, and fortunately before the Escape Plans had gotten beyond the Initial-Planning Phase—the dungeon gates screeched open again, this time to admit the Royal Jailer, with word that on direct orders of the Home Secretary, after representations by their government, they were to be released on their own recognizance pending further investigation and resolution of the matter.

"Boris," François Mulligan said, "I finally got it figgered how come you can get a broad here for a bottle of booze. The men are all sopranos. What's that pansy saying?"

"We're sprung," Boris said. "And it's about time. I have a terrible thirst."

Having had some previous experience with the bureaucratic requirements for exiting a site of durance vile, the Knights and Boris went through the process at Canningtown Municipal Gaol smoothly, and in record time. They were long gone from the slammer, in other words, when the Daimler bearing the managing director of the Covent Garden Opera House (himself sprung only minutes before from the Tower of London) and the Deputy Home Secretary pulled up at the gates to greet Maestro Korsky-Rimsakov with the most profound regrets of Her Majesty's Government for the lamentable misunderstanding.

They were, in fact, following François Mulligan's infallible nose for intoxicants, already several blocks away from the Municipal Gaol and approaching a quaint English hostelry, identified by an ancient sign hanging out over the street as the Sword, Crown & Anchor.

"That's a dumb name for a saloon," François Mulligan said. "But I'm too thirsty to be fussy."

"We must all make sacrifices from time to time," Boris agreed.

As the Knights (who were in what was left, post-Heathrow, of their uniforms) approached the Sword, Crown & Anchor, they were spotted by several former members of the Royal Marine Corps. These luminaries had been promised a steady supply of Half-and-Half by the proprietor in exchange for keeping a sharp lookout for some daft Irishmen who were acting up in the full of the moon. He had kept his word, and they were now given the opportunity of keeping theirs.

"Amos," one of them called, "here come the crazy Irishmen. There's a whole bunch of them."

"Who you calling a crazy Irishman, you turnip-nosed tea-drinker?" François inquired. "Out of our way, or we'll do to you here what we done to yer damned tea in Boston Harbor!"

And so, in the quaint parlance and patois of the military, "the battle was joined".

Amos Davis, who had been led to believe that there would be no more than a dozen or so crazy Irishmen, stuck his head out the door of the Sword, Crown & Anchor and saw the 90-odd members of the Bayou Perdu Council, led by two giants, marching up the street.

He was an old marine, and he quickly saw that the valor of his men would not be enough to overcome overwhelming odds. His defensive military position was untenable. The best he could hope for was a successful withholding action, while Angus, the boy and the ladies made their escape as best they could.

Purely as a routine matter, the Metropolitan Police Force had detailed two of its best plainclothes operators to be waiting outside Canningtown Municipal Gaol when the American barbarians were released. They bore watching.

When François Mulligan had turned onto Crown Street, site of the Sword, Crown & Anchor, the plain-clothesman had instituted, as a precautionary measure, Potential Riot Condition III (likely, but not inevitable). At the first exchange of greetings between the two groups, they had quickly radioed Riot in Progress, correctly suspecting that Riot Condition II (imminent, probably unavoidable) would simply be a waste of time, procedure-wise.

The first faint far-off whoop-whoop-whoop of the Riot Squad could be heard at about the same moment the first punch was thrown.

At that exact moment, Amos Davis somewhat shamefully confessed to Angus MacKenzie that for the first time in his life, his fellow Royal Marines had failed him.

"We're outnumbered, Angus. It's every man for himself! Take your friends and run for your lives!"

The Duke of Folkestone rose to his feet. "Mr. MacKenzie," he said, "I would remind you of the ancient motto, *Illegitumi Non Carborundum,* which it is now my proud duty to carry on."

Tears formed in Angus MacKenzie's eyes. "I'm proud of ye, laddie," he said. "And the Duke, wherever he is, is looking down, or up, at ye, with pride!" He handed the Duke of Folkestone a stout, knurled Scottish walking stick (known to museum curators as a "bludgeon") and, pausing just long enough to kiss their loved ones good-bye, the Duke of Folkestone and Mr. Angus MacKenzie descended from the bridal suite to do battle.

The Duke and Boris Alexandrovich Korsky-Rimsakov spotted each other at the same moment, as Boris returned his attention to the fray after having thrown Gunnery Sgt. Joseph Highden, Royal Marine Corps, Retired, through the window of the Canningtown Ironmongery (whatever the hell that was!), across the street.

In a voice which could, and indeed, *had,* rattled false

teeth in the farthest back row of the old and new Metropolitan Opera Houses, Boris gave the alarm.

"Woody, Your Friend Boris is here to save you," he called first, to put the boy's mind at rest, and then, to urge on his fellows: "Massacre all of them but the lad with the arm in the cast! These are the scoundrels who have stolen him from the bosom of his friends!"

The Duke of Folkestone opened his mouth. "I say," he said, "there appears to be some sort of frightful misunderstand . . . " He never got to finish the word or the sentence, for he was struck on the head at that moment by a large paving stone and crumpled to the ground.

And shortly thereafter, as Boris charged through the Royal Marines' final defensive line (they had formed the traditional square of last-ditch defense), the first of the eight riot vans responding to the call turned onto Crown Street and began disgorging the first elements of the First and Second Flying Phalanx of the Riot Division.

Eight men of this force, in full battle dress, immediately jumped on Angus MacKenzie and François Mulligan. They were standing facing one another, their hands around the other's neck, the mighty muscles of their arms quivering with fruitless exertion as the irresistible force met the immovable object. The first eight men were not enough. It took ultimately a dozen officers to knock them to the ground and separate them.

Miss Florabelle Jenkins, her arm draped maternally over Miss Beverly Chambers's shoulders, watched the affray from the window of the bridal suite. (Fortunately, they could not see, because of the angle, where the Duke of Folkestone lay unconscious on the street.) Miss Florabelle said nothing, nothing at all, until the battle was over, and the last of the participants had been carried off. And then, finally, she spoke.

"I don't want you to be alarmed, my dear," she said. "I have every confidence that the Prime Minister, once he hears about this, will put things in good order straightaway."

"But how's the Prime Minister going to hear about it?"

"I'm going to tell him about it," Miss Florabelle said, "just as quickly as we can find a taxi to take us to Number Ten Downing Street."

At Number Ten Downing Street, the Bobby who had been able to reason with Hawkeye and Trapper John was having no such luck with Miss Florabelle Jenkins.

"What do you *mean,* I can't see the Prime Minister?" she asked. "I'll have you know that I am a British citizen and *demand* to see him!"

The Bobby was about to push the discreetly hidden little button which summons the Metropolitan Police Force's Kook & Nut Squad when the door to Number Ten opened and a small parade of Americans, led by the Secretary of State, began to troop out.

"You mean to tell me," Miss Florabelle exploded, recognizing the Secretary of State, "that the Prime Minister was wasting his time with this Colonial Disraeli while a British citizen has been waiting outside to tell him that revolution is rampant in the streets?"

"If you'll just stand to one side, madame," the Bobby said, laying a very gentle hand on her arm. He suddenly found himself flying into the air and landed in the street.

"Take your foul hands from me," Miss Florabelle said. "Haven't you heard of the Magna Carta?"

And then Miss Beverly Chambers spotted familiar faces from the Spruce Harbor Medical Center. In her moment of excitement, she simply forgot that student nurses are not supposed to address doctors out loud by the names by which they are known behind their backs.

"Hawkeye!" she cried. "Trapper John!"

"Why, hello there, Beverly," Trapper John said. "Fancy meeting you here."

"Beverly, where have you been?" Hawkeye asked. "If you don't mind my asking, in which case, where the hell have you been?"

"There's been a riot," Beverly said.

"I wondered what that was," Hawkeye said.

"Not that one, another one," Beverly went on.

"Revolution in the streets is what it is," Miss Florabelle Jenkins said. "You there: Prime Minister! Have you the slightest idea what's going on in the very streets of London while you chatter on meaninglessly with these Americans?"

"Madame," said the Prime Minister, "I have just found out how little I do know. Since you are apparently known to these gentlemen, may I ask who you are?"

"I have never seen any of these people before," Miss Florabelle said, and then, pointing, "except that short, fat one, and anyone who has a telly can't avoid that."

"I don't suppose, Beverly," Hawkeye said, "that you have any idea where Woody might be found?"

"I suppose he's with Boris and Angus," Beverly said. "That's what we came here about."

"Boris, I know. Who's Angus?" Hawkeye asked.

"Mr. Angus MacKenzie, V.C.," Miss Florabelle Jenkins informed him, "general manager of East Anglia Breweries, Ltd."

"And where is Boris?" Hawkeye pursued.

"I don't know about any Russians," Miss Florabelle said. "But the last time Mr. MacKenzie was seen, he was locked in mortal combat with a crazy Irishman."

"Crazy Irishman?" John Francis Xavier McIntyre, M.D., said indignantly. "There are eccentric Irishmen. There are angry Irishmen. A few of us are even a little weird. But crazy? Never."

"It was Boris," Beverly said. "There was some sort of misunderstanding."

"Misunderstandings," the Secretary of State announced solemnly, "presuming goodwill, a sense of fair play on both sides, can often, with luck, be resolved."

"May I ask who this young woman is?" the Prime Minister asked.

"One of the kidnapees," Trapper John said. "How did you get away, sweetie?"

"I wasn't kidnapped, and I didn't get away," Beverly said. "Woody and I and Miss Florabelle were at the

Sword, Crown & Anchor when the others showed up."

"Young woman," the Prime Minister, who had been in his youth a Lieutenant of the Royal Marines, asked, "did I understand you to say that you had been at the Sword, Crown & Anchor?"

"Yes, sir," Beverly said. "A *darling* little old hotel."

"We can't be talking about the same place," the Prime Minister said. "It didn't, by any chance, have a proprietor named Davis?"

"Yes, sir," Beverly said. "Sgt. Amos Davis, Retired. A darling little old man, sweet and kind. While we were waiting, he played the bagpipes for us."

"My God!" the Prime Minister said. His face was ashen. "Do you have any idea why the Royal Marines would wish to kidnap the Duke of Folkestone?"

"Can't you get anything straight, Prime Minister?" Miss Florabelle asked, angrily. "His Grace was not kidnapped by the Royal Marines. The Royal Marines came nobly to his aid when the crazy Irish showed up. They were hopelessly outnumbered, but they went down fighting."

"Then the Irish have His Grace?" the Prime Minister asked. Before Miss Florabelle could reply, he went on. "Madame, I still do not know who you are."

"I am Miss Florabelle Jenkins, executive castlekeeper of Folkestone Castle," Miss Jenkins said, with pride and dignity. "It seems to me that you should know that."

"Where, Beverly," Hawkeye demanded, "are Boris and Woody?"

"The police came and hauled everybody away," Beverly said.

"I'll get to the bottom of this," the Prime Minister said. He turned to the civil servant behind him. "Get me the Home Secretary on the phone right away," he ordered.

"Prime Minister," the civil servant said, "I *am* the Home Secretary."

"Good," the Prime Minister said. "Explain this all to me, and be quick about it."

Immediately on being released from the Tower of London, Mr. Bruce J. Ludwell, chairman of the board of the Yorkshire and Northumberland Life and Casualty Assurance Companies, Ltd., sought medical attention for his nose. Because of the hour (it was four A.M.), it was necessary for him to seek such attention at Saint Alphonse's Hospital. It was the opinion of his attorney, who had arranged for bail, that a disinterested medical opinion of his condition should be obtained as quickly as possible, so that Mr. Ludwell's legal suits could be prosecuted properly. Mr. Ludwell was going to sue Heathrow Airport, the Metropolitan Police, Her Majesty's Government and, first and foremost, the Hon. Anthony J. Pasquale, chairman of the Ad Hoc Committee to Mourn the Duke of Folkestone.

Mr. Ludwell was at first rather frustrated by the medical personnel at Saint Alphonse's. They were unwilling to sign duly notarized statements testifying that Mr. Ludwell had suffered grievous and permanent damage to the proboscis, resulting in great pain and suffering.

"What you have, old boy," the doctor had said, "is a rather common belt in the shnozzle. Put some ice cubes on it, if you will. You'll have forgotten about it by morning."

As Mr. Ludwell and his attorney stood at the emergency entrance of Saint Alphonse's mentally going over a list of those doctors who owed something to the Yorkshire and Northumberland Life and Casualty Assurance Companies, Ltd., and thus could be counted upon to recognize a grievous, painful and irreparable physical trauma when they saw one, the First-Aid Section of the First Flying Phalanx of the Metropolitan Police Force arrived with sirens screaming and off-loaded a young man, his head wrapped in a bandage, and lying on a stretcher.

Mr. Ludwell looked at him with distaste. He loathed common brawlers. And then his eyes widened.

"My God! That's His Grace!" he said. He was firmly, and none too politely, barred from accompanying His Grace into the treatment room, but he was able, from the Metropolitan Police who accompanied the prisoner, to patch together the story.

Bruce J. Ludwell had risen to be chairman of the board by recognizing opportunities when he saw them. For the first time that day, and it had been a long day, a smile crossed his face. A perfectly glorious opportunity had just been dumped into his lap, an opportunity which solved all his problems.

"How well are you acquainted with the Orphans' Court?" he asked his attorney.

"Not too well, I'm afraid," his attorney admitted. "After that unfortunate newspaper exposé, we have rather kept our distance. Bad public relations, you know, for us to go back there and try to get out of paying. After *The Times* said our behavior was 'shamelessly criminal and unconscionable.' "

"I thought we sued them about that? Two million pounds for libel?"

"We did," the lawyer said. "The Libel Court found for *The Times*. We even had to pay their legal expenses."

"Well," Bruce J. Ludwell said, "we're going to be in Orphans' Court at eight tomorrow morning."

Bruce J. Ludwell strode purposefully out to his limousine with his lawyer in his wake. He did not see as his Rolls rolled out of the parking lot, the official Rolls of Her Majesty's Home Secretary roll in. (His vision was blocked at the time by his actuarial consultant who was making Brucey-Wucey's nosey-wosey feel better by kissing same.)

Dr. Benjamin Franklin Pierce and Dr. John Francis Xavier McIntyre were out of the Rolls even before it stopped rolling.

"Where's the boy who was hit on the head?" Hawkeye demanded of the policeman outside the emergency-treatment room.

"In there, sir," the policeman said. "But you are not permitted to go in there."

A phrase Hawkeye had recently heard came suddenly to his mind.

"I come on the Queen's business," Hawkeye announced, grandly.

"God save the Queen!" Trapper John said, solemnly.

"God save the Queen!" the policeman parroted. He came to attention, and Hawkeye and Trapper John marched past him into the emergency room.

"I assure you, sir," Woody was saying as they entered, "I am perfectly all right." A doctor in a white coat was flashing a light into his eyes.

"Shut up, Woody," Hawkeye said, "and let the man work."

"Dr. Hawkeye!" Woody said. "Dr. Trapper!"

The doctor turned to look at Hawkeye and Trapper John.

"Are you gentlemen, physicians?"

"Finest kind," Hawkeye said.

"Sir, you are addressing the senior physician, surgeon and social-disease consultant of the Finest-Kind Fish Market and Medical Clinic," Trapper said. "How bad is our little buddy broke?"

"Doctor," Woody said, suspecting that his American friends had not quite taken the correct approach to establish their medical credentials with the British physician, "these gentlemen are my friends Dr. Benjamin Franklin Pierce, Chief of Surgery of the Spruce Harbor Medical Center and his associate, Dr. John Francis Xavier McIntyre, Fellow of the American College of Surgeons."

"A couple of Yankee cutters, huh?" the doctor replied. "He looks all right. Took a nasty crack on the head, but there's no fracture and no sign of concussion."

"But, of course, you can never tell about concussion, can you?" Hawkeye said.

"I don't know where I'll find one," the doctor said, "but I'll have a nurse watch him during the night . . . or what's left of it."

"Doctor," Hawkeye said, "by a strange coincidence, I happen to have with me at the hotel one hell of a fine nurse, who I suspect would like nothing better than watching our little pal to make sure he doesn't have a concussion. Under those circumstances, would you be willing to release him to us?"

"Normally, no," the doctor said. "But every bed in this place is full. They had a frightful riot early this evening at the airport."

"You don't say?" Hawkeye said. "What's the world coming to?"

# Chapter Seventeen

By noon the next day it was apparent that Woody had not suffered a concussion. Or, as Trapper John put it, there was additional proof that the head of an English nobleman was harder than a paving stone.

Boris Alexandrovich Korsky-Rimsakov and Mr. Angus MacKenzie had been released from their widely separated prisons and reunited under somewhat different circumstances in the bar of the Dorchester Hotel. They had, not too surprisingly, become instant fast friends, once their mutual friendship for Woody had been explained, and their new friendship might have blossomed even further if Miss Florabelle Jenkins had not come into the bar, stolen their bottle from them, and pointed out that they both had roles in the funeral service, and that solemnity and sobriety was called for.

Mr. Korsky-Rimsakov was to sing during the memorial service at Westminster Abbey, and Mr. MacKenzie was to attend His Grace as his official equerry.

Miss Florabelle reported, too, that at the recommendation of the Rev. Mother Emeritus Wilson, R.N., and with the approval of Drs. McIntyre and Pierce, His Grace would be accompanied during the memorial services, for medical purposes, of course, by Nurse Beverly Chambers.

The Bayou Perdu Council, K. of C., as a result of

their fine showing on Crown Street, had been designated
Honorary Official Royal Retired Marines for the duration
of their stay in Great Britain, and been invited to make
what use they desired of the Sword, Crown & Anchor.
As a token of both their gratitude for the honor and of
the fighting ability of the Marines, the Bayou Perdu
Council's social secretary, Mr. Jean-Pierre de la Chevaux,
announced that all bar bills would be on the K. of C.,
stipulating only that nothing stronger than beer would
be served until the late Duke had been put to his final
rest.

After a little chat with Mr. de la Chevaux, furthermore,
Miss Florabelle Jenkins had announced that the
Amusement Park at Folkestone Castle, Motel and
Amusement Park, Ltd., which had been closed, would
be opened immediately after the burial for the exclusive
use, at no charge, of the Bayou Perdu Council, K. of
C., the Royal Retired Marines Association and the
Survivors of the H.M.S. *Indefatigable* Association, at
least until such time as travel arrangements for the return
of the Bayou Perdu Council to America could be
finalized. Their aircraft was missing. Initial reports indicated that when the pilot had radioed Paris's Orly Field
for permission to land ("Orly, this is Chevaux Petroleum
Number Seven, request landing instructions"), a flight
of Mirage III fighter planes had been launched. These
aircraft, after firing a warning burst of cannon fire across
the nose of the Chevaux plane, had indicated the plane
would be shot down if it attempted to land, and then
indicated they were going to escort the plane out of
France.

It had last been seen near Rabat, Morocco. The
Secretary of State had already been in touch with the
French Foreign Ministry about the incident, and a
mutually satisfactory resolution of the misunderstanding
was believed to be forthcoming. In the meantime, it was
believed that the amusement park would keep the Knights
occupied.

The only real problem then, until the little man in
the blue uniform showed up at the Dorchester at five

minutes after twelve, was what to do about Woody and Beverly. Hot Lips and Miss Florabelle were agreed that, because of their ages, marriage was obviously out of the question. Both were also, tearfully, agreed that separating the two young people would be exquisite cruelty. Neither female could see any solution. Beverly obviously couldn't stay in England, and Woody, obviously, could not come to the United States.

Hawkeye and Trapper John, aware of the situation, had gone off to see the Secretary and the Prime Minister, but neither Miss Florabelle nor the Reverend Mother felt that any good would come of their efforts.

And then, to reiterate, the little man in the blue uniform showed up at five minutes past twelve in the Dorchester, and was, a few minutes later, ushered into the suite occupied by the Duke of Folkestone.

It was the suite occupied previously by the previous Duke of Folkestone, and the décor reflected the late Duke's artistic tastes. When Miss Florabelle Jenkins had first seen the décor, she had firmly insisted that His Grace wait in the corridor until the housekeeping staff could rush up a supply of sheets to modestly drape the oil paintings and statuary filling the suite. "It might be perfectly proper in a restricted area of a museum for study by scholars," Miss Florabelle had announced, "but that sweet and darling boy will enter this place in its present indecent condition only over my dead body."

The Duke of Folkestone and Miss Beverly Chambers were playing Monopoly in the sitting room when the man was ushered in. Miss Chambers was, in fact, blushing prettily, a gust of wind having just then blown off the sheet covering the little-known Van Gogh painting (oil on wood, 44 by 66 inches), *Home Is The Sailor*.

It had been painted, coincidentally, from life, in the ancient sailors' rendezvous, *La Maison des Toutes les Nations*, in which the late Duke had seen the American Admiral and negotiated the first lease on Herstead-on-Heath, although the current Duke, of course, had no way of knowing this.

"Excuse me, Your Grace," the butler said, "this . . . person . . . wishes to see you."

"Are you," the little man said, stepping into the room and reading from a legal form, "the orphan child known as Hugh Percival Woodburn-Haverstraw?"

"I am the Duke of Folkestone," Woody said

"According to this," the little man said, "you haven't been officially decreed by Her Majesty's Lord Chamberlain as the rightful heir to the late Duke."

"That's right," Woody said. "We are to meet him at half-past one today."

"In that case, then," the little man said, "you are the orphan child known as Hugh Percival Woodburn-Haverstraw."

"Who are you?"

"I am Fernwicke T. Pfister," the little man said, "orphan custodial officer for H.M. Orphans' Court. You may consider yourself in my custody."

"I beg your pardon?"

"I'll be with you, you poor orphan boy, until a suitable guardian can be appointed for you and your property by the judge. I 'spect that will be Mr. Bruce J. Ludwell."

"Who?" Woody asked.

"Mr. Bruce J. Ludwell," the little man said. "He had petitioned the court to be appointed your guardian, so as to save you from the corrupting influence of . . . uh . . . here it is, a lady known as Miss Florabelle Jenkins and a gentleman known as Angus MacKenzie, who have been exposing you to corrupting influences—riots, fights, brawls, houses of ill repute and the like. If you're Miss Jenkins, little lady, I'll have to ask you to run along."

"I am not Miss Jenkins," Beverly Chambers said.

"In that case, then, you can stay."

"This whole thing is preposterous," Woody said. "I am eighteen years of age and a midshipman in Her Majesty's Navy."

"If you was an *ensign,* what is a real officer, you'd be all right," Fernwicke T. Pfister said. "But a midshipman ain't really an officer. Sort of a naval cadet, so to speak. And by yer own admission, yer eighteen. That makes you, since you ain't got no living kin, a poor orphan boy. That's the law."

"I'll be right back, Woody," Beverly said.

"Where are you going?"

"To get Hawkeye," she said. "He'll fix this up."

"You'd better hurry," Fernwicke Pfister said. "Me and this poor orphan boy is due in Orphans' Court in an hour."

Beverly could not find Hawkeye or Trapper John, but she did find Miss Florabelle Jenkins, Mr. Angus MacKenzie and Mr. Boris Alexandrovich Korsky-Rimsakov. It took all of Miss Jenkins's newfound influence over Mr. MacKenzie to keep him from assisting Mr. Korsky-Rimsakov in what they were agreed was the easiest way to settle the problem: drowning Mr. Pfister in Hyde Park Pond.

"We'll stay with Woody," Florabelle said. "You go get us a lawyer, Angus."

"You might as well go with him," Beverly said. "When that little creep thought I was you, he was going to throw me out."

"That brings us back to the original idea," Boris said. "Let's drown him."

"No," Florabelle said. "You and Beverly stay with him, and Angus and I will get legal counsel. We'll meet you in Orphan's Court."

Mr. Bruce J. Ludwell had, of course, anticipated that both Miss Jenkins and Mr. MacKenzie would seek legal counsel. He was prepared for them. He was, in fact, prepared for them to the point that his bulging briefcase, as he entered Orphans' Court, already contained notices of dismissal for the both of them, from Folkestone Castle and East Anglia Breweries, Ltd., signed by him "as guardian of the estate of His Grace the Duke of Folkestone." They would be presented before they got out of the courtroom.

"My Lord," the Honorable Counsel for Mr. Bruce

J. Ludwell, in his opening remarks to the bench in
Orphans' Court, said, "my client in this matter is Mr.
Bruce J. Ludwell, chairman of the board of Yorkshire
and Northumberland Life and Casualty Assurance Companies, Ltd. That property was among the most valuable
of His Grace the Duke of Folkestone, whom we are to
put to final rest this afternoon."

"Your client," Angus MacKenzie said, "is a liar, a
cheat and a blackguard, who's been stealing the company
blind for years."

"One more outburst like that, sir," My Lord Judge
said, "and I will have you gagged."

"As we all know," the Honorable Counsel went on,
"after a long and distinguished naval career, His Late
Grace began to act . . . shall we say . . . rather oddly
in recent years. I trust Mr. MacKenzie will have the
decency to stipulate that the very circumstances of his
death, proving this point, need not be brought out on
the day of his burial."

"I should say," Woody said, "that quite the contrary
is true. That anyone able, at the age of my great uncle,
to both appreciate the ladies and to avoid an angry
husband armed with a shotgun, was in full possession of
his faculties."

"My Lord," the Counsel said, "I trust the Court will
judge for itself the depth of corruption a remark like that
by an innocent youth implies."

"Go on, sir," the Judge said.

"My Lord," the Counsel said, "that evil woman and
that evil man, Miss Florabelle Jenkins and Mr. Angus
MacKenzie, themselves provide the best proof that they
are a corrupting influence on this poor child. The instant
that orphan child arrived on English soil, MacKenzie
and that woman spirited him away to a 'hotel' . . . I use
the word loosely . . . known as the Sword, Crown &
Anchor."

"I cannot allow you, sir," the Judge said, "to make
an accusation of such magnitude without challenge. The
Sword, Crown & Anchor is, of course, well-known to

me, for my previous experience on the Criminal Bench. I would find it hard to conceive that anyone would subject an innocent youth to its corrupting influence. Mr. MacKenzie, is what Counsel for Mr. Ludwell states true in any form?'

"My Lord," MacKenzie said, and then because whatever else he was, he was not a liar, he finished: "We was at the Sword, Crown & Anchor."

"Until four in the morning," the Counsel went on, "at which time you were involved in a street riot, which resulted in your arrest and the hospitalization of the boy, is that not so?"

"They thought I was going to be kidnapped," Woody protested.

"But in fact, My Lord," the Counsel said, "it was that terrible woman and that terrible man who in fact kidnapped this boy from an airplane at Heathrow, as the Metropolitan Police are prepared to document."

"And what say you to that charge, Mr. MacKenzie?" the Judge asked.

"I never thought I'd meet a worse liar than Ludwell, My Lord," Angus said, "but one stands before you." Miss Florabelle began to weep.

"Under these circumstances, My Lord," the Counsel went on, "my client submits that he should be appointed guardian for the child. His Late Grace's faith and confidence in him is quite clear. He was in charge of His Grace's largest single holding . . ."

At that moment, there was a disturbance at the rear of the courtroom. Ludwell had carefully seen to it that the COURT IN SESSION, NO ADMISSION sign had been posted, and the doors locked. The doors were suddenly sprung from their hinges.

"What is going on?" the Judge asked angrily.

"Hold on, Woody," Boris Alexandrovich Korsky-Rimsakov called out, "here comes the cavalry!" A half-dozen properly wigged-and-gowned attorneys-at-the-bar trooped into the room, followed by His Royal Highness Prince Hassan ad Kayam, Drs. Benjamin Franklin Pierce and John F.X. McIntyre, and two other civilians, one of whom stood five-feet-tall, had flowing silver locks and a glorious shiner.

My Lord Judge recognized Mr. Korsky-Rimsakov, of course. A photograph of him was on his wife's dressing table. It had been because of Mr. Korsky-Rimsakov that My Lord Judge had been summoned at two-thirty that very morning to take his wife from the Tower of London.

His immediate reaction was to order the singer carted off to the Tower again, but the Judge restrained the impulse. He did have to go home that night, after all, and he did not want to go home publicly identified as the man who had jailed Boris Alexandrovich Korsky-Rimsakov.

"My Lord," the senior of the newly arrived barristers said, "I trust the Court will forgive our unseemly entrance. But the door was locked, obviously by mistake, for locking a court of law is illegal."

"You may proceed," My Lord Judge said.

"My Lord," the barrister said, "we have just come from Buckingham Palace. The last will and testament of the late Duke of Folkestone was, as the law requires, opened and read on the morning of the day of his burial."

"Counsel," My Lord Judge said, "I am about to appoint a guardian for His Grace's sole heir. The exact extent of the estate has no bearing in this matter."

"My Lord," the barrister said, "the orphan child before you is neither the sole heir of the late Duke of Folkestone nor, per se and de facto, an orphan."

"I think you had better explain yourself," My Lord Judge said.

"My Lord, I will try," the barrister said, giving the impression he wasn't sure he would succeed. "My Lord will understand that we have only recently entered this matter, at the request of His Royal Highness Prince Hassan who was, in turn, acting at the request of these gentlemen, Drs. McIntyre and Pierce."

"What's their interest?" My Lord Judge inquired.

"Woody's our pal," Trapper and Hawkeye said, together.

"And these gentlemen, My Lord, are members of the United States House of Representatives. May I present to the Court the Hon. Edwards L. Jackson and the Hon. Anthony J. Pasquale?"

"And what's their connection?" the Judge asked.

"Mr. Jackson is the President's personal representative to the funeral of the Duke of Folkestone, My Lord, and Mr. Pasquale is chairman of the U.S. Congress Ad Hoc Committee to Mourn His Late Grace."

"I'm touched by the interest of the American Congress," the Judge said, not sounding especially sincere, "but I fear I don't quite understand."

"Under certain circumstances, My Lord, British nationals are admitted to the United States Naval Academy at Annapolis, Maryland. It takes nomination by two members of the Congress and approval of Her Majesty. At the suggestion of Drs. Pierce and McIntyre, Congressmen Jackson and Pasquale were happy to nominate His Grace to Annapolis."

That wasn't quite the truth, the whole truth, and nothing but the truth. Both Smiling Jack and Tiny Tony had at first flatly refused. They had changed their minds, however (in fact, had become positively enthusiastic about the whole idea), after Dr. McIntyre showed Tiny Tony a splendid, clear photograph of the solon handcuffed to the Heathrow fence and already wearing a shiner, and of Smiling Jack with Ms. Peggy-Lou Kastenmeyer sitting on his lap, feeding him martini olives aboard Air Force Three and announced his intention to make them available to the press.

"I see," My Lord Judge said, "or do I? Go on."

"Dr. Pierce believed that a fully completed appointment of His Grace to Annapolis, one that is approved by Her Majesty, would be of interest to this Court."

"You're not going to tell me you all burst into Buckingham Palace the way you burst into my courtroom?"

"No, My Lord. Her Majesty's Minister of Oil and Petroleum was able to arrange an audience for His Royal Highness Prince Hassan on rather short notice. As a matter of fact, Her Majesty was gracious enough to meet our car in the courtyard. An unfortunate rumor that Prince Hassan had decided to suspend oil sales to Great Britain had somehow reached her ears, and she wanted to discount it as quickly as possible."

"I see." My Lord Judge said.

"And in conversation, as Her Majesty approved His Grace's appointment to Annapolis, it came out that the last will of the late Duke was about to be read. There was something of a problem."

"Which was?"

"Neither Miss Florabelle Jenkins nor Mr. Angus MacKenzie who were, according to the instructions left by the late Duke, to be present at the reading, could be found. They were, of course, dealing with this matter. We felt we should hear the will read, and we did."

"My Lord," Counsel for Mr. Bruce Ludwell said, "what has all this to do with the matter at hand?"

"I frankly don't know," My Lord Judge said. "Get to the point, Counselor!"

"My Lord," the barrister said, "here is the last will and testament of the Late Duke of Folkestone. It is self-explanatory." He handed the document up to the bench. My Lord Judge began to read it. His snow-white eyebrows rose an inch up his forehead.

"I think," he said, "I should read the pertinent paragraph. skipping over, in interest of saving time and maintaining the decorum of this court, the late Duke's somewhat unflattering opinions of the British legal system and of Mr. Bruce J. Ludwell." He cleared his throat and began to read:

"There have been many women in my life, but only one love," he read. "On March 11, 1925, Mrs. Ernestine Jenkins, widow of the late Maj. Homer P. Jenkins, Eighteenth Bengal Lancers, was delivered of a female child which was named Florabelle. Major

Jenkins was not only impotent and sterile, poor chap, but had gone on to his reward following a fall from his horse some eleven months before his widow was delivered of her child. In deference to her rather peculiar middle-class concept of morality, I gave my beloved Ernestine my word as a gentleman that I would not reveal the circumstances of the conception of that child during her lifetime and mine. My beloved Ernestine went on to her reward in 1934, and since you are now reading my last will and testament, ergo, I have gone on to mine.

"The child was conceived sometime during the first three weeks of June 1925, during which period Mrs. Jenkins and I occupied the Maharaja Suite of the Royal Nepal Hotel, New Delhi, under the *nom d'amour* of Mr. and Mrs. John Smith. Any doubt that the child is mine should be removed by the fact that Miss Florabelle Jenkins bears on her lower abdomen, in the vicinity of the junction of her legs, the small red birthmark—in the shape of a clover—with which all Folkestones are marked."

"I wondered what that was," Angus MacKenzie said. "I didn't think it could be a tattoo."

He got a foul look from My Lord Judge who then resumed reading:

"I declare then, and proudly acknowledge, the woman now known as Miss Florabelle Jenkins to be my issue. To my beloved daughter, who becomes with the reading of this document the Dowager Duchess Folkestone, I give and bequeath all of that property known as the Folkestone Castle, asking of her only that she keep a protective eye on my great-nephew, Hugh Percival, who now assumes my title, and asking her forgiveness for my keeping my word to her mother."

The Judge stopped reading. Miss Florabelle Jenkins was sobbing softly into her handkerchief.

"The document," My Lord Judge said, his voice breaking just a little, "is signed 'Folkestone.'"

"Stop yer whimperin'," Angus MacKenzie said, a tear running down his cheek. "One thing I can't abide is a whimperin' woman." Florabelle threw herself in his arms, and he held her.

"Your Grace," My Lord Judge said. Woody started to get to his feet. The Judge motioned with his hand for him to stay seated. "Your Grace," the Judge repeated, and then, "madame, I am addressing you!"

"Yes, My Lord?" Florabelle Jenkins asked.

"Your Grace, these proceedings are ended. You may take your nephew and leave."

# Chapter Eighteen

It was not hard for Woody to begin to think of Miss Florabelle Jenkins as "Aunt Florabelle." They had liked each other from the moment they had met at Heathrow, and had become friends in the bridal suite of the Sword, Crown & Anchor.

Angus MacKenzie, however, was a proud man, and he simply could not accept his little Florabelle as the Dowager Duchess Folkestone. What would a Dowager Duchess, with blue blood running through her veins, want to have to do with a Retired Royal Marine Sergeant Major?

He brooded on this all through the memorial service at Westminister Abbey, and confided his thoughts to Boris Alexandrovich Korsky-Rimsakov in the bar car of the private train taking the official mourning party from London to Folkestone Castle.

Boris had a little difficulty understanding the precise nature of Angus's worry. His own experience had been limited—since the first whisker had appeared on his chin the day after his thirteenth birthday—to getting rid of unwanted female attention, and he had never once worried that his attentions, once offered, would be rejected, or be in any way undesired.

But he could see that his pal was down in the dumps and he was sympathetic; so he went to his one friend of the opposite gender, the Rev. Mother Wilson, and explained, as well as he could, Angus's problem.

The Reverend Mother understood the problem, as stated, and knew that it wasn't simply a matter of telling Florabelle that her new Ducal status bothered Angus. Throwing herself at Angus would chase him away. The Reverend Mother, in turn, went to find Hawkeye and Trapper John.

She found them on the observation platform of the last car wearing robes and crowns borrowed from two Peers of the Realm who had passed out soon after boarding the train, and graciously acknowledging the cheers of the people on the platforms of the stations as the train passed through.

"You say he's hitting the bottle?" Hawkeye asked.

"Plural," Hot Lips replied.

"Keep him at it," Hawkeye said. "I'm going to have a word with the Dowager Duchess and Woody."

It was not difficult to ply Angus, in his present frame of mind, with spirits. By the time the train reached Folkestone Castle, he was, in fact, as stiff as a board. He was shaken awake and provided with another quart, and consequently did not participate in all of the final rites for the Duke, although he did witness the final interment.

Propped up between Hawkeye and Trapper, he was half-carried into the Folkestone crypt. Long years of training sustained him, however, if only for a moment. As the casket was slipped into the wall, Angus MacKenzie shook loose of Hawkeye and Trapper, snapped to attention and rendered a perfect, quivering, British-style Royal Marine salute.

"If yer where I think ye are, Hugh, old buddy," he said, "I'll be down there with ye in a bit." Having said that, he collapsed onto the floor.

As he was being carried (Boris at his feet, Hawkeye and Trapper each at an arm) through the Great Hall in the direction of the Great Staircase, a gentleman spoke to them.

"Oh, damn," he said, "I had hoped to have a word with Mr. MacKenzie."

Hawkeye recognized him after a minute (he was no longer wearing a white-powdered wig and a robe as he had been in the courtroom) as the lawyer Hassan had hired.

"What about?"

"Well, things have happened so suddenly," the lawyer said, "that I didn't have a chance to tell him that the Duke had a bequest for him, too. He is now the sole owner of the East Anglia Breweries, Ltd."

"So much the better," Hawkeye said.

"How long is he going to be like that?" the lawyer asked.

"Why don't you come again at, say, nine-thirty tomorrow morning?" Trapper said.

"Splendid. We need someone to take over the Yorkshire and Northumberland Companies. The chairman of the board has suddenly resigned and gone to Brazil."

"Angus is your man," Hawkeye said. "We'll see you tomorrow."

They resumed their journey down the Great Hall and up the Great Stairway and into the Duchess's apartment.

At six fifteen the next morning, since all other means had failed, Mr. Angus MacKenzie was wakened by a pitcher of ice water thrown into his face. He sat up suddenly to find himself in the Ducal bed in the Duchess's apartment.

"Aunt Florabelle!" the Duke of Folkestone said in shocked, horrified tones. "What are you doing in bed with Mr. MacKenzie!"

"Jesus Maxwell Christ!" MacKenzie said. "What are you doing in here?"

"Miss Chambers and I came to ask Aunt Florabelle to have breakfast with us," the Duke of Folkestone said, piously. "And this is what we find!"

"Now, just a minute, laddie," Angus MacKenzie said. "It's like this . . . "

"Like what?" the Duke asked.

"Mr. MacKenzie," said the Dowager Duchess suddenly, "and I have been married secretly for some time."

"That's what it is," Angus said, grateful for any straw.

"In that case," the Duke said, "would the both of you like to have breakfast with us?"

"Perhaps later, dear," the Dowager Duchess said. "But your Uncle Angus and I rise somewhat later than you young people."

"Well, then, we'll see you later," the Duke said. "I'm glad that my foul suspicions about your conduct were unfounded and that the truth of your marriage has finally come out."

"We would be heartbroken if you weren't married," Miss Chambers said. "Our very set of moral standards would have been crushed."

They left the room.

"For God's sake, Florabelle," Angus said, "what did you say we was 'secretly married' for?"

"Have you any better idea what I should have done?" she replied. "You're the one came charging in here saying he couldn't live without me."

"I said that, did I?" Angus said. "Well, you know what they say, 'In Wine, Truth'." He got out of bed. "But how the hell are we going to arrange it?"

"Arrange what?"

"Arrange to get married without anybody finding out when. We can hardly go anywhere in England, now that you're a damned Duchess, without everybody and his bloody brother finding out."

"Why don't you have a word with your friend Mr. Korsky-Rimsakov? Perhaps he is experienced in these matters. Whatever else he is, he's certainly a man of the world."

"Aye, that he is," Angus said. "Now if I can find me pants, I'll go look him up."

Five minutes later, he was back in the bedroom.

"Boris says he can fix it, but it has to be right now. Get your clothes on, Florabelle."

"How is he going to arrange it?"

"Damned if I know," Angus said. "I don't see we have any choice but to trust him."

They left Folkestone Castle by the servants' bridge across the moat and made their way in U-Drive-It golf carts (which had been taken out of For Hire service for the duration) to the airport. Air Force Three was sitting there, the door open.

"Where the hell are we goin'?" Angus demanded.

"Trust me, Angus," Boris said.

They climbed aboard and the door immediately closed after them. The engines were started and, two minutes later, they were airborne.

The Secretary of State stepped out of the one private compartment.

"You know," he said, "a lotta people got the wrong idea that a ship captain can marry people. He can't. And neither can an airplane pilot." He waited until this had sunk in. "But I'll tell you what," he said. "The minute an American airplane leaves the ground, it becomes American soil. All that you need then is an American minister."

He extended his hand to the door of the private compartment. Hot Lips, in full vestments, stepped out with a Bible in her hand, and began a ritual that opened with "Dearly beloved," and ended, "By the power vested in me by the God Is Love in All Forms Christian Church, Inc., and the state of Louisiana, I pronounce you man and wife."

Boris Alexandrovich Korsky-Rimsakov sang "I Love You Truly" and was joined in the chorus by Drs. McIntyre and Pierce.

Following the ceremony, a small reception was held in the Great Hall, and immediately after that, the American guests left for their homeland. With them in the plane were the Duke of Folkestone and Wee Black

Doggie, whom Mr. MacKenzie (with the blessing of the
Dowager Duchess of Folkestone) had given to Miss
Beverly Chambers to keep her company while Woody
was down in Annapolis at the Naval Academy.